MW01392842

The Parts We Play

Honi Olmedo

Copyright © 2024 by Honi Olmedo

All rights reserved. No part of this publication may be reproduced, stored or transmitted in any form or by any means, electronic, mechanical, photocopying, recording, scanning, or otherwise without written permission from the publisher. It is illegal to copy this book, post it to a website, or distribute it by any other means without permission.

This novel is entirely a work of fiction. The names, characters and incidents portrayed in it are the work of the author's imagination. Any resemblance to actual persons, living or dead, events or localities is entirely coincidental.

Honi Olmedo asserts the moral right to be identified as the author of this work.

Honi Olmedo has no responsibility for the persistence or accuracy of URLs for external or third-party Internet Websites referred to in this publication and does not guarantee that any content on such Websites is, or will remain, accurate or appropriate.

Designations used by companies to distinguish their products are often claimed as trademarks. All brand names and product names used in this book and on its cover are trade names, service marks, trademarks and registered trademarks of their respective owners. The publishers and the book are not associated with any product or vendor mentioned in this book. None of the companies referenced within the book have endorsed the book.

For Ruben and Esme. Everything I write will always be for you.

One

He is my favorite place to be.

My cheek is pressed against his heartbeat, and our legs are entwined like vines. His breath moves us up and down, forward and back, like an incoming tide flowing in as steady as it retreats. Slowly, his eyes dance from sleep to awake, back to sleep. His hands twist mindlessly, scratching, circling, then resting around the small of my back. Time is passing outside our sanctuary. Light filters in through dusty window shades. Another morning greets us. We do this for years, and I never take a moment for granted. Waking to him is my favorite moment, even when I am no longer his. The look of a lover can be devastating, namely when you come to know their look is no longer one of love.

The shift happens fast. Suddenly, he's looking for a way out of the room. I'm running, shouting, begging to understand exactly when he met this conclusion. He's yelling. He's packing a bag. He's angry. *Just come back to bed.* He's telling me he doesn't love me. *But you do, you must.* I tell him I'll do anything. There isn't anything left for me to do. I don't know this yet.

The next time I see him, he tells me he is sorry. And that he's with her. I don't see them again after that. I wish I could say I'm growing used to goodbye, but time passes, and I still think of only him.

They say time heals all wounds. So far, they are all liars, and the wounds have left me beaten and stranded—metaphorically speaking—in my childhood home.

Though give it enough time, and I may come to blows with my parents.

***

I can tell it's early from the moment I open my eyes. The faint sounds of birds confirm my suspicions. What a disappointment. Lately, my only hope is that time is passing as quickly as possible.

When I must have a morning, it all begins the same. I debate the color of the wallpaper. Today I can say, in my expert opinion, it is a color slightly more yellow than white, untouched but still colored by time. Yellowish, with exceptions. I took down all signs of my life in this room before I left for college. The places that once held my drawings and notes from friends are barren and painted over in a brighter, whiter square.

I admit the room still looks nice from the outside, but from in here, knowing what it once was, it feels forgotten. It reminds me of TV shows when kids come home from college and their parents have taken over their rooms with exercise equipment and wrapping paper, except my parents didn't put anything inside this forgotten room. Instead, they've taken from it. Outside of my old twin bed, the only things remaining are a dresser my grandpa pieced together in 1971, and a lamp from my parents' living room placed on top. It is a room of misfit things that don't belong, laughing at a girl who shouldn't be here.

I can smell they are making breakfast downstairs, and I know within the hour, my mother or father will climb up the steps and offer me a dish. They will ask how I'm doing, and then begin their interrogation.

Why haven't you showered? You really need to learn how to take care of yourself.

Then they'll ask, in a not-so-roundabout way, if I've started to look for a job.

You need to put in the effort. A job isn't going to just find you.

Next, it will be about him.

I haven't seen Oliver in a while. Is everything okay?

And for the grand finale?

Why did you move so quickly out of your pleasant, two-bedroom apartment? You were so looking forward to living with Jocelyn.

And I will not tell them why, when, how, or where exactly in my lovely two-bedroom apartment my ex-best friend slept with my ex-boyfriend. Though I'd love to see the look on their faces.

I check my phone. It's 7:56 a.m. Another day, just beginning, and I still haven't heard from him. I've given him eighty-eight days of passing time. Eighty-eight days to explain, and to beg for me back. I've thought about what I'd do if I heard from him. I wouldn't make it easy. I couldn't, after all he had done, but I would learn to forgive.

I notice the quiet in my room and the noise in my head, so I put on a Spotify playlist titled Heartbreak City, before tossing my phone to the end of the bed. I convince myself to move and place my feet heavily on the floor. Stretching my arms over my head, I pull at the muscles along my rib cage until I think they might snap. Releasing my arms down to my sides, I decide it's time to meet my makers before they walk upstairs. I reach for a sweatshirt and pull it over my unbrushed hair. I grab headphones, placing one into an ear, and toss my phone into my sweatshirt pocket. Music may be playing, but I can still hear them from the moment I step onto the top stair.

"Tom? Really? She's not a lunatic. She's not depressed. She's probably just exhausted. You know how hard she works, and when she works, she burns the candle at both ends. She's just finished school and she's looking for what's next, okay? Please have some empathy," my mother breathes out loudly.

How dare he question the fabric of my mental state. To her, such a thought would signal her failure as a parent. Any deviation from perfection was an insult. I did appreciate her faith in me, or herself. I pause the playlist and lean in to hear his response.

"Charlene, please. She isn't okay. You don't just hole up in a room for weeks, let alone months, not speaking to anyone because you're tired—"

"Tom—"

"No. Charlene, you always have to have the last word an—"

"Thomas. *Now.*" Her lips contract tightly together, and she gives him a look as if to say, *Shut up, Tom. Your depressed, crazy, to-be-discussed-later daughter is standing right behind you.*

He quickly throws his head around to meet my eyes. "Reagan. Good morning. How's it going?" He says with a furrowed brow and a high-pitched enthusiasm in his voice.

"Super. I'm going for a walk," I mutter as I inspect a plate of muffins on the kitchen counter. Breathing in the warm scent of cinnamon, I paw at the muffins. I know they aren't for me. Mrs. Blair down the street just lost her husband and my mother made them for her. I heard her on the phone the other day with another one of the neighbors.

"Fifty-five years. Can you believe that? They were married for fifty-five years. I can't even imagine what she's going through... God bless Tom. Even on his bad days, I don't know what I'd do without him. Yeah, yeah, you're right. I'm making her something sweet. Sugar always helps."

As a fellow member of the heartbreak hotel, I had little faith in the curative power of muffins, but hey, I've been wrong before. I feel some remorse grabbing a full muffin, but Mom and Dad stay quiet, and I need to let my parents know I'm not above being a dick to a widow. I'm sad and I mean business. Circling around on my heel, I open the back door and let it hit me on the way out.

"What was that, Tom?" I hear Mom hiss as I slide out the back gate.

I don't stick around to hear his response. Stepping outside, I can tell today will be an all-around gray day, which is not much different from any other day in the Pacific Northwest from late September to April. My parents live at the bottom of a hill that peeks into the Puget Sound. From down here, you can see a glimmer of city lights, but I prefer the full city view, so I start my climb to the top. When I finally reach it, I find myself breathless. I cross the street to collapse in the grass of a pocket park. The city lights are flickering off as the light of the day takes over. I feel the muffin settle inside of me and decide to rest for a while. I'm still listening to the Heartbreak playlist, but scramble to turn it off as a pop song turns on. I'm nowhere near that stage of a breakup where I'm ready to listen to anything that identifies as happy music.

On day eighteen, I curated a playlist of songs that I enjoyed crying to, aptly titled Sad Girl Songs. I may not have a job, but I certainly know how to curate a playlist. Now, if only I could make that lucrative.

The first song on the playlist is from a band I used to listen to in high school, Right Away, Great Captain. Jocelyn and I argued about this band once. She thought they were boring. I thought she had no authority to have an opinion in the realm of talented musicians because she knew nothing about music. But for better or worse, she managed to have an opinion on everything. Her opinions annoyed me at first, but then I realized she was just insecure. Because of that, Jocelyn was like an opinion tornado, constantly tossing out each thought no matter who it hit. But inside, she was made of glass. She also had a magic inside her. If she cared about you, well then you were like magic too. It hurts not hearing from Oliver, but each day, I hope to hear from her too. Months ago, I was a promising college graduate with a boyfriend to start a new life with and she was my wild and free best friend. I had it all figured out, and she was an artist of life. We both played our parts very well, until she took my parts from me.

My thoughts, as always, turn to him.

Was he with her? Someone new? Was he thinking of me? I needed some part of him to be missing me.

I skip the song and remove it from the playlist. I hate how they are everywhere, especially in my head. They are unwanted, unwelcome visitors. I turn the next sad song up as loud as my headphones can go. Closing my eyes, I try to focus on the present but really, I'm focused on holding back tears. The songs keep playing, one after another, and I'm hoping that means hours are passing. Eventually, I feel a raindrop fall on my head, first hitting my ears, then more on my face, neck, and legs. I can't hold it back anymore. The sky and I cry in unison.

When I can breathe again without tears, I decide to move, and head somewhere that isn't home. Call it emotional procrastination or an afternoon walk, I turn the next corner and start down the hill.

I turn down a street lined with shops, restaurants, and dozens of fancy houses. I poke my head into one shop after another, wishing I had money to spend on fabulous and expensive clothes. I settle for an Americano and take a seat inside the café to watch people pass by the window. When the rain lets up, I head back out again.

Eventually, I get to the neighborhood library. It is a decorative building about the size of two houses. I check my watch and notice there are still hours left in the day, so I wander inside. A white-haired man in a brown blazer greets me. His hair flies in a few different directions as the wind from the door meets his face.

"Well, hello there. How can I help you?" As he smiles, the edges of his mustache touch the inside of his mouth.

I am not prepared for help, so I panic and ask him to help me find a book I've already read. "*The Great Gatsby*, please?"

He tells me that is a very good choice, and his validation warms me up. He asks about my week, and we exchange a few sentences to express how excited we are for fall. He seems like the kind of person who doesn't know heartbreak. I wonder what he thinks of me. He only knows this single moment of Reagan Wilde and would probably tell a stranger I'm a voracious reader, with great taste in books. Or that I'm new to the library system but will certainly be back.

I ask him to help me checkout because I've never done it before. He agrees, and when we proceed to the checkout, he sticks out his hand and says, "Be my guest" in his deep, welcoming voice, signaling me to walk ahead. He seems happy, and that seems easy.

I wave to him as I exit, grateful to have met him, like now I can breathe easier. But the relief of the library fades quickly as I get farther away. I take the book to the nearest bar and ask the time to pass.

***

By the time I get home, all the lights are off, and the dinner leftovers are packed away. The only light left on to say hello is a faint glimmer from underneath my parents' bedroom door. The flickering of late-night television reminds me to find my way to bed because there isn't anything better to do. For a moment, I feel relief that I don't have to explain where I've been. But then I realize I don't want to be alone.

I spent the evening at the neighborhood dive bar where the average age of patrons is a worn fifty-five. No one tried to speak to me, outside of a few words from the bartender who wasn't thrilled when he had to remake my drink. I had ordered a martini and opened my book, wondering if this was the type of person I was meant to become: a book reader, classy drink haver, lingering in bars while people wondered who I was. I felt sophisticated until I realized I didn't really like my martini. I traded it in for a fruity house-made cocktail. Nevertheless, it was a successful attempt at emotional procrastination. Being surrounded by people I didn't have to talk to helped me feel less lonely.

But now, returning home, I feel lonelier than ever. It doesn't take long for me to start thinking about them again. I'm picturing the moment I *found* them together. I swear I could see Jocelyn smile. The look on Oliver's face wasn't one saying, *I'm sorry*, but rather, *oh shit, I've been caught.* If I go to bed now, I know I'll spend the evening replaying this moment over and over. So instead, I head towards our family study.

Entering the room again, I also start my playlist over. I plop down on the large, leathery desk chair and trade in my library book for a stack of photographs that Mom set aside on the desk with some unknown intention. I inspect the first photo. It's from a high school cake walk fundraiser where we wore powder blue shirts printed with the saying, *Life is a Cake Walk*, along the back. I look happy, almost unstoppable, with long blonde hair and a grin that says the best is yet to come. My arm is around Jocelyn.

My high school was split into two: the promising, and the hopeless. We were labeled by the teachers, so the promising were the nerds, and the hopeless were the people having all the fun. I was a promising student. My grades were competitive, I ran the book club, played the piano, and was a part of the improv team for a brief, embarrassing moment. Jocelyn was on the side of the hopeless, always having fun, but never in school. She was blessed with parents who wouldn't let her fail financially or socially, so she had nothing to fear. They always found a way to get her into the best organizations and clubs. Over time, I would claw my way into those same groups, and then we worked well together. She'd give direction, and I'd manage the execution while she flirted with the cutest boy in the room.

I flip through a few more photos before stopping on another one of a high school-aged Jocelyn and Reagan. We're posed in front Union Station in downtown Denver. We had gone to visit a friend of hers who had just moved there. I sold it to my parents as a potential college visit. We drove right past the University of Denver and partied at Boulder, so I think it counted. It was a dumb picture, and I looked dumb doing it. Not Joce, though, she was always confident. In high school, Jocelyn was already the tallest, coolest, most beautiful girl in the room. Her hair was a dark shade of auburn. She was slender, had an air of ease about her, and was, not so coincidentally, easy to sleep with. Not much has changed.

When it came time to choose a college, I chose Gonzaga. Jocelyn decided she wanted to take a gap year and started to work at a small art gallery in downtown Seattle. Four months later, she got bored and tried to convince me to move to Denver. "Just think of the adventure. The boys. We could hike every day and party every night."

I crumple up the photo and toss it into the garbage. Jocelyn will not be missed. I repeat it to myself, begging for it to become true. Spinning around in the chair, I jump to my feet to shut off the light. But then, I see *him* just sitting on the bookshelf. The textbook title is *Introductory Finance*, but what it says to me is, *remember how we first met?*

It was in a general finance class during my last semester of freshman year. He had dark brown hair, a warm smile, and was more attractive than I felt I deserved. I noticed him the first day I walked into class, but never thought he'd notice me. One day, I thought I caught him smiling at me, but brushed it off. I came back the next week, and there was that smile again. This happened for weeks. I'd walk into class, my eyes would meet his, and his whole face would light up. No one had ever noticed me this way before. I loved him instantly.

Three weeks and four days after the initial smile, we spoke. It was before the first exam of the semester, and I had more than adequately prepared for the test. I felt untouchable, until I realized I'd forgotten a pencil and immediately retreated into a panic. Pointing at each student, I began shouting, "Do you have a pencil? Do you have a pencil? Does *anyone* have a pencil?"

In my blurry state of horror, I had hardly taken notice of Oliver falling over himself to hand me a pencil. My dizzying panic paused for a moment, and I saw only his fantastic smile. He launched the utensil in my direction, and I caught it with the ease of a practiced catcher.

"Oh shit. Does it have an eraser?" The sweet moment of observation had passed.

"Oh, um, no..."

He appeared to regret his offer. The awkwardness was shattered when a girl in the front row called up to me, offering one of her three spares. God bless the other A-types of the world. I had written off our first real interaction as awkward and made no effort to change the course of our non-existent relationship. I relaxed into the rest of the year, wearing sweatpants to every class, and taking the occasional shower. Appearance alone was counting me out on any dates.

Our next interaction came after midterms. Standing up to turn in my test, I noticed him watching me. Moments later, he was behind me in line, smiling the kind of smile that begged you to start a conversation. I obsessed over the smile for a week. This was the first time Jocelyn learned about Oliver. She reminded me I should let him make the first move. I hadn't planned on doing anything more than adoring the guy from across the classroom.

Class finished early on a particular Thursday, and I was set on getting home to nap away the rest of the day. Sprinting out of the class, I let the lecture door drop behind me. It slammed on a "*Hey*." I spun around to issue a half-assed apology to the victim of my door drop, but then I saw it was him. He was wearing a red flannel, accessorized with a five o'clock shadow. I found him wildly attractive.

"Oh, hi, sorry," I nervously answered back. "I didn't realize anyone was behind me." I was confident that would be the end of our conversation.

"How did you do on the test?" he responded, ignoring my apology.

"Oh, yeah, pretty okay. What about you?"

"Got a C," he chuckled. "You got to tell me how you did. I'm convinced no one can pass this class."

"Oh, yeah, it's tough. I got a B."

"Oh shit. You're smart."

"Well, I mean, I don't feel very smart. I heard someone got an A+. Whoever they are, they're the smart one."

"Do you think we could study together?" he asked.

He didn't wait for a response as he coolly passed along his phone number. It made me wonder if he hadn't noticed the growing tension between every denied pencil and shared smile. I, too, played it cool, but on the walk home, I called Jocelyn, nearly shouting out of excitement. A boy had gone out of his way to talk to me. To give *me* his number. Jocelyn reminded me it was because I was a study buddy, not a *wink, wink* buddy. She droned on and on with reasons why he wasn't interested in me like that. That brought the high down a little, but just a little.

On Friday afternoon, I texted him to let him know he could text me over the weekend and we could get together to study. Jocelyn scoffed when I told her what I'd done.

"Are you serious?"

She took my silence as a response.

"The message just seems a little sad. Essentially, you're saying, 'Hey, I'm totally free to study with you, a random stranger over the weekend, because I won't be at any cool parties or dating any cute boys. Pick me. Pick me.'"

To my surprise—and Jocelyn's—he responded and invited me to a party for his intramural soccer team that weekend. When Jocelyn heard that, she went from doubting me to quickly planning my outfit for the party. She hopped in the car and drove to my dorm so she could lend me one of her many low-cut tops, and piece together a look that said I was cool and did this sort of thing all the time.

And then there was the first date with Oliver. I wish I could say I remembered every detail of that night, but I don't. Perhaps I was too involved in the moment, or perhaps it wasn't worth remembering at all.

Two

Before all my dreams were reserved for Oliver, I used to have a recurring one where I am a princess awakened in the morning with staff shuffling in, throwing open my curtains and calling me down for a full breakfast, during which I will only eat one strawberry. But as I'm learning, dreams are just fantasies. In real life, I wake up with my face pressed against the carpet of the study floor and drool dripping from the corner of my mouth. Straining my neck to move, I feel more tin man than human.

Pushing myself up, I stumble over to the desk and grab my phone. The screen lights up, illuminating three truths: it is just past seven a.m., I have a killer hangover, and I have no new messages. I sneak out of the study and slip into the kitchen, startling my mom. "Good morning, mother."

I slide to the coffee pot just behind her as she jumps up on her toes, almost as if controlled by a startled puppeteer. "What are you doing up?"

"Trying to get an early start on the day. Got a lot to do today."

"Oh, wow. Really?" She leans heavily on the word *wow*, articulating extra o's that don't belong. Too bad I'm lying.

"Nope, absolutely not. I fell asleep on the study floor. Today's plans include drinking so much coffee I can hear light, and maybe standing in the rain until I can't feel my toes." I take a long swig of my coffee, letting it burn the insides of my mouth.

"What? Are you trying to break some type of world record?"

"Mother, is that any way to speak to your heartbroken daughter?" I give her a sassy wink.

She counters with a serious look as if to say. *Is that what this has all been about?* But thankfully, she doesn't say that. "Well, a heartbroken daughter can still do nice things for her mother. In fact, I like to think she can do them better than a daughter with a full heart who may get distracted by her happiness."

She lets a small smile escape, and I meet her with a long, loud groan.

"I'm not asking much. Please take these muffins over to Mrs. Blair. I've been meaning to get these over to her since yesterday. If she's not home, will you just put them inside? The key is in the front yard underneath the bunny."

The bunny statue was originally a gift my dad and I gave my mom for Mother's Day when I was eight. We bought a purple hanging plant and the statue. She said she liked it at the time, but clearly not enough because it was soon regifted to Mrs. Blair, who openly admitted to loving it over the years.

"Alright, let's return some karma into my life because clearly, I fucked up somewhere along the way." I let the word *fucked* drip out of my mouth, hoping to shock her, but she doesn't give anything away. I chug the remainder of the coffee while Mom turns to grab the muffins and places them delicately on top of a decorative plate. I grab a coat, and the plate, slip-on shoes, and storm out.

Once outside, the cloud cover feels repressive, and the grayness only lets a blinding brightness squeak through the clouds. I won't see blue skies for months, and I remind myself not to take the grayness personally. Large rain drops begin to hit the pavement, so I move quickly across the lawn. Knocking gently on the door, I realize this is the first time I'll see someone I know outside of my home in weeks. It's different from the librarian or a stranger at the neighborhood bar because Mrs. Blair knows me from my life before the breakup. I knock once more, praying she isn't home, but if she is, I'm praying she won't ask any personal questions. After a few minutes pass, I thank the universe and head to the bunny.

"Hello, old friend," I whisper while staring eye-to-eye with the bunny before flipping him right-side down and slipping out the key. I slid the key into her lock, and step inside with nothing to fear.

"Mrs. Blair, hello?"

She may not have answered the door, but I'm realizing it's still early morning. I plan to scold my mother when I get home. Isn't there some sort of rule about not calling or visiting a guest before nine in the morning? But when I still don't hear anything, I'm confident she isn't home. I decide to leave her a note, so when she returns, she doesn't think she's had an intruder who leaves muffins as some sick sort of sign of what is to come.

I shuffle into the kitchen and open one drawer after another in search of a sticky note. Each drawer is organized; she has silverware in one, kitchen utensils in the other, and finally a junk drawer with paper scraps. I dig through the drawer, tossing aside postcards from loved ones, a receipt from the market, and stamps before finally finding sticky notes. With a pen I find left on the counter, I scribble a note as kind as I can muster up:

Hope you enjoy these. Please remember, we're there whenever you need us. Love, the Wildes

I move the muffins and the note to her center island so she can't miss them when she walks in. After setting aside the tray, I realize that's all I've planned for the day, and up until twenty minutes ago, I didn't even have that planned. My stomach growls, but I don't want to go home. There's a chance Mom will start in on her questions, and I'm too tired to fend her off.

When I was a kid, Mrs. Blair used to feed the neighborhood children lunch. I was lucky because I was an only child, but the cul-de-sac was full of kids my age, so every weekend, we'd get together and play basketball, football, night games, tag, or whatever idea one of us came up with. On summer Saturdays, Mrs. Blair would make peanut butter and jellies or grilled cheese with apple slices for the cul-de-sac kids. We'd sit out on her long driveway and gobble up the snacks before she'd let us play with chalk and decorate the driveway.

She really is a kind woman, and I decide she would want me to be happy and full, so I open her fridge to see if she has any snacks. I find pickles, mustard, a loaf of bread, four apples, nearly spoiled milk, and some cheese. I don't want to put her out, so I decide I'll just grab an apple.

I rinse it off in the kitchen sink while my eyes wander into her family room again. Mrs. Blair's decorating style can be described as decidedly old woman, and I mean that in the nicest way. Her family room color scheme is exclusively varying shades of maroon with only a few exceptions. She has deep, maroon-colored curtains which are closed, though I'm not sure what they're keeping out. Her worn velvet couch is also maroon with decorative floral patterns. Her wooden side tables almost break the trend and are topped with lamps adorned with green shades and red wine-colored tassels. Still within the color palette, as far as I'm concerned.

She has a beautiful fireplace mantel topped with photos. I take a bite of the apple and stroll over to the frames. I know if she were here, she would want to show me photos of her family, so I doubt she'll be upset if I examine them closer.

In one frame, she's with her husband, Gregory, and they must be in their twenties. They are dressed up far nicer than anyone in their twenties today. His hand is resting on her cheek, and she's pursed her lips like she plans to kiss him. They are in love. There's another of her and Gregory settled into middle age. He's holding a puppy who I knew as an old black lab named Twister. They have a few family photos with all the children and grandchildren. The final frame is just of the grandchildren. I pick this one up and bring it closer to my face.

I once knew a few of her grandchildren—three brothers who belonged to Mrs. Blair's son, Marvin, and his wife Mary. Two of Mrs. Blair's children lived on the East Coast, so they rarely came to visit and never brought their children. But Marvin and Mary lived in Idaho and came to visit every few years. One year, they were in town the whole summer, and our cul-de-sac of kids loved adding in the three boys, who were eager to play with us. It was the best summer as far as I can remember, but mostly that's because I had a crush on the brother who was the same age as me. At the time, that was twelve. In this photo, he's probably sixteen, and I think it would be weird if I thought he was cute, but he's certainly cute for a sixteen-year-old.

He has dark brown, almost black, hair, and deep brown eyes. I take another bite of my apple and wonder where in the world he is today.

When he came to visit, the moms of the neighborhood dreaded it. As he got older, he had a bit of a rebellious streak and graffitied a few too many mailboxes for the moms. But when he spent a few minutes with me, I felt like the coolest girl in Seattle. He taught me how to use his skateboard, and once shared his Oreos with me, and only me. I hadn't thought of him much since he stopped coming to visit, but I'm sure he was off doing something amazing. Maybe he was a photographer for *National Geographic* or a model living in New York.

I stop short thinking about this boy I once knew when I was younger because suddenly, I hear a thud.

"Uh, hey, um, hello? Mrs. Blair?"

There's another thud.

I pull the frame close to my body and drop to the ground, waiting to hear a response. These houses are old, and it could be nothing. But what if it isn't?

"Ms. Blair? I'm sorry if I startled you... I just came to drop off a treat from my mom. Well, from all of us," I squeak out.

I'm not sure how I'll explain the apple core and the frame, but I've yet to hear a response from Mrs. Blair, so I'll worry about that later. Maybe Mrs. Blair has bad hearing, but she also hasn't confirmed nor denied she's the creator of the thud. The footsteps are growing louder, and closer, and don't sound as if they could be made by an old lady.

This is how I go. Unloved, and murdered in my neighbor's house. I can imagine the murder mystery specials they'll spin up. *Why was she alone in the house? Why was she holding an apple core? Was it poison?* Jocelyn will come out of hiding to remind everyone she was my best friend and will inevitably steal my spotlight. The thought crosses my mind that I don't have to get murdered. There's still time to hide. I start crawling toward the old velvet couch and slide my body between it and the floor. Maybe I'll have the element of surprise on the intruder. As the steps grew closer, I begin to doubt my ability to attack.

Buzz, buzz, buzz.

I hear the steps stop and evaluate.

No, no, no, no, no. How could I literally go days without human contact and get a phone call right *now*? I slide my hand to the side of my phone and ignore the call. Maybe the steps didn't hear the buzz. Or maybe they did, and then decided they were more flight than fight themselves.

Buzz, buzz, buzz, buzz.

You have got to be *kidding* me.

The steps move closer, and I try to silence the buzz again. This time, I see the name on the screen: Mom. *Seriously, now? Oh, and a news update. Thanks, CNN.* When the steps murder me, at least I will be remembered for my multitude of friends and political awareness.

The steps close in. They shuffle over to the curtain and fling it open. They move toward the mantel.

"Fight time," I mumble to my frame.

I wait until the steps stop, and I can see the back of their feet in front of the fireplace. I quickly slide my body out from under the couch and prepare to attack. Eyes closed; my hands are swinging. I throw the frame, but it lands above the killer's head and crashes glass side down against the fireplace. The murderer moves closer. My eyes flash between closed and open, giving me only a brief glance at their face.

Open: They have dark hair.

Close: Their hands push me back onto the couch.

Open: The intruder has the figure of a man.

Close: They shout out, "I really don't want to hit a girl."

Open: I shout back, "Then don't."

Close: I kick him hard in the chest.

Open: He falls to the ground gasping, "Mother of God."

Mary, herself. I know that face.

"Asher Blair?"

Three

He runs his hands swiftly through his hair, revealing a tattoo on the backside of his forearm. It has mixed colors of red, green, blue, and orange, but I don't have time to make out the design. I feel myself melting and forget that I was just trying to fend off an attacker—this too-hot-to-handle attacker. As he leans back, his foot lands against the glass from the picture frame.

"I'm so sorry about that. I can pay for it."

"Pay for it? How? That's a priceless antique." he shouts.

"That— The... the picture of your family is a priceless antique?" I point in the direction of shattered glass, but I'm confident the actual photo is intact, and the frame has a Fred Meyer sticker on the back.

"How do you know it's my family, huh?"

Maybe he isn't who I thought he was. I feel my heart drop into my stomach like a grenade that sends nervous needles prickling throughout my arms and legs.

"Okay fine, it's my family, but now you need to tell me who you are. And what's with the MMA skills?"

"MMA? I'm honored," I joke, desperately trying to change the mood of the room.

He can't tell I'm joking, or at least he doesn't think I'm funny enough to laugh.

"I know this is weird, but I can explain. I'm Reagan Wilde, the next-door neighbor. We knew each other when we were kids which is why I was walking down memory lane." I can't deny that I'm hoping his face will light up like he's been waiting to meet me again, but this attempt, like my previous one, doesn't yield any response. "I was stopping by to give Mrs. Blair some muffins. If she didn't answer the door, I was instructed to grab the spare key and drop them off. I wanted to write a note so that she didn't think she had an intruder. Then I was just taking a moment..."

He breathes out heavily in response, and I can feel my shoulders relax with the hope that he's remembering me, and we can finally move on from this embarrassing moment to a casual discussion on whatever we've been doing for the last ten years.

"Hard day, huh?" he says, letting the words slip out in an annoyed whisper. I can't tell if the annoyance stems from having to deal with me or the fact that he clearly doesn't believe me.

"Why would you say that?"

"Taking a minute alone... in someone else's house... then attacking the person living inside the house."

"I promise I wasn't trying to attack you. I just was trying to protect myself."

"Tell that to the cops," he says, while reaching for something in his pocket that I fear could be a cell phone.

"Come on we don't need to do that," I say breathlessly like I'm a balloon losing air. "My mom told me to just let myself in. She didn't know anyone was here. Her name is Charlene Wilde. She will explain all of this. We can give her a call right now."

I shove my hand inside my pocket, pulling out my cell phone, ready to dial her in to explain the whole scene. I can't go to jail. I would never get Oliver back; Jocelyn would mock me endlessly. My career would be crushed before it even got started. Luckily, my panic attack is interrupted by his laughter.

"Okay, I think we're even now. Shake on it?" He extends his hand, and when ours touch, there is an undeniable moment of electricity.

"Even?" I can barely get the word out. Not sure if it's because of him or because I'm afraid about what happens next.

"Yup, we're even. Clearly, you are having a panic attack, so I think the kick to my chest can be forgiven. And the frame was ugly, so no real loss."

He brushes the glass off the rest of the picture and puts the photo up on the mantel. He looks at me straight on, and I feel myself slip into the warm brown of his eyes. "Plus, apparently, we're friends from a long time ago. What'd you say your name was?"

"Reagan, Reagan Wilde." I expect a look of acknowledgment to register on his face, but he stares at me blankly. "We used to play games in the cul-de-sac. There was a whole group of us. Some people called us the cul-de-sac kids. There was Asia with the extra curly brown hair and Georgie who was two years younger than us but always a foot taller. And then there was Tanner, the competitive one." I'm hoping this helps him remember, but I don't wait for his response before launching into an update he doesn't ask for. "And now Asia is in med school and Georgie moved to Wyoming with some girl he met at a bar, which is pretty on-brand for him. He was always a hopeless romantic. And Tanner, well, I guess he still lives here. Works for a tech company or something."

I realize he has no memory of these people or me. The look on his face tells me he also doesn't care that he can't remember. I suddenly feel small, and incredibly awkward but I try not to take it personally.

"Well, we aren't kids anymore. Who needs a drink?"

He shuffles back to the kitchen, and I feel my brows furrow with confusion. For someone who doesn't care about me, it sure is strange that he'd invite me to stick around, but I try not to flatter myself. I pick up the apple core from the floor, hiding it behind my back. As he opens the kitchen drawers looking for something, I tiptoe over to the trash can, opening and closing it before he has a chance to see me dump the evidence.

He puts two large, Costco-sized bottles of liquor on the counter. "I have whiskey or gin. What'll you have, kid?"

I guess we really are having a drink. I stall so I can decide which evil I'd rather have for breakfast. "Kid? Wow. Didn't you just say we aren't kids anymore?"

He looks at me impatiently.

"Oh wait, you're joking. Well, that's good because we *are* the same age you know."

"Right, which is?"

"Twenty-two. I think you were born a few months before me, so you're like, what? Practically twenty-three?"

"I have a serious question."

My stomach drops.

"Are you sure you are not a stalker?"

"*Ha*. Listen, the summer before seventh grade, you were here like every week. I have a great memory. Maybe you need to find out what's wrong with yours."

"Ah, yes, the summer of 2007. How could I forget?"

He doesn't wait for me to respond before pouring whiskey into a glass. He opens the fridge, grabs a few cherries with his bare hands, and tosses them and some of the cherry juice, into the glass. He spins over to the sink and lets a little tap water run into the drink. I can't imagine this is how real bartenders make a drink, but I cheers with him when he passes me my glass.

We talk about nothing until we've drained our drinks and then he finally warms up to me. I ask about his brothers; he tells me about them and asks why I care. I tell him I'm polite and give examples of helping old ladies at the grocery store. He tells me he hates the grocery store and is glad he can order all his groceries online. I ask if he's been to the fancy market around the corner. He asks me why the hell he'd go there? I tell him they have the best bread. He explains he's on a carb detox. I stare at him with disgust. He chuckles and says we're *definitely* even, and maybe I should find out why I'm so gullible. He gets up to make another drink. I feel like spending time with him is the first time that has been worth spending in eighty-nine days. He floats over to the living room, turns on a Bluetooth speaker, and asks me if I like music.

"Lately, music has been the only thing as sad as me. It's the only thing that can really empathize with me because whoever wrote those songs went through it too. So yes, I love music. Before recently, I liked it even when it wasn't sad."

I surprise myself with my honesty. I expect he'll mock me, but he doesn't. I wonder if one day I'll tell him about the heartbreak playlists.

"I get that," he says. "Music talks to me. Like, lyrics talk to everyone I guess, but I listen to what they're saying. When the music starts talking, say a new song or just one I really love, I focus all my energy on it. It's like when you're eating something amazing, and you know you're about to take the best bite so you close your eyes and stop talking just so you can take in all the flavors. Of course, I listen to the beat, but I tune in to the lyrics. That's what makes the difference for me—that's the meaning."

It feels nice to agree on something, but the whiskey is starting to get to me, so I lay down on the floor and don't say anything else. I put the glass down on the side table and pull out my phone to text Mom, *I'm A-OKAY* and will be home later. The clock says 11:47. He notices me checking the time.

"So is it safe to assume you're staying for lunch?"

"Only if I can get whatever I want." I try to sound playful.

"And what does the distinguished guest want?"

"To go from stalker to distinguished guest in an afternoon. No idea the heights I could climb."

He chuckles and my insides light up.

"I think I'd like pizza. Mm, Garfield's." I pick up my drink to take a sip.

"Seriously?" His thick eyebrows raise, and I realize he has thick eyebrows. They look like handsome caterpillars, and I'm laughing and spinning and laughing. I realize I should take a break from my drink for a while.

"Yes, and maybe some water? The room is spinning."

"Well, water's out of the question." He jumps up and fetches me a glass. It feels like opposite day when he speaks.

"I want pineapple and banana peppers; you won't live to regret it. *Ooh* and a peanut butter lava cake."

"And to think, I once thought of you as classy." He orders the pizza on his phone.

We fall quiet and let the music play. I wonder what the words are saying to him. I run my hands over the rug in Mrs. Blair's living room. It feels cozy, and I want to stay in this moment forever.

"How often do you get to come back here?" The words slip from my mouth before I know what I'm saying.

He takes a moment to respond, and I sit up quickly to make sure he's still here. He is, but it looks like he's thinking very hard. Maybe he's lost in the song. Or maybe this was the wrong thing to ask. He did just lose his grandfather; he may regret the time away. The seconds between his response and my question grow. I fidget with my hands, hoping I can twist them in the right direction and elicit a faster response.

"Not enough." He says sternly staring off into space before turning abruptly to look me in the eyes. "Do you have somewhere to be?"

"What? No... I mean, we just got pizza. I'm sticking around for at least that." I hope we can go back to joking. "Plus, I don't really have anything else planned today. Not that being drunk at noon is a plan." My voice trails off and I cover the quiet with a nervous laugh.

"Well, if you don't you have anywhere to be..." He winks. "I think it's time for another."

"Isn't Mrs. Blair going to be pissed we had all her whiskey?"

"No way. Personally, I think she'll be relieved. Imagine knowing you have all this liquor lying around and you could die never having finished a bottle."

"Wow, you stunned me into silence. Except for this speaking part right here."

"Let me rephrase, we could all die at any moment. More reason to drink up."

"You are wild."

He passes me another drink and a cup of water. "I thought you were the wild one?"

"Oh wow, I haven't heard that one before." I tease before taking the drink to my mouth and taking a small sip. His pours are getting heavier. "Where is she, anyway? Your grandma?"

"A lovesick cruise. She and Grandpa—sorry, Mr. Blair to you—had a trip planned, and without him here, she decided she still needed to get away. But she didn't want to leave the house alone. Voila, enter grandson of the year."

"Oh, is that supposed to be you?"

"I don't see any other Blair grandsons in the house now, do you?"

"Well, to be fair, I didn't see you at first either."

"Oh touché, Ms. Wilde. Well, rest assured, it is just me. I was the only one with any time." He chuckles but it sounds more like sadness than laughter.

"And why is that?"

"Nothing going on." He gestures to himself. "Hence why I'm drinking with a delinquent like you."

"You *do* remember me?"

"You were my first crush after all." A smile spreads across his face, but I'm sure mine is bigger.

I knew he hated that summer. It was the year his parents divorced. They gave him a skateboard as a consolation prize. He'd skate every Saturday and Sunday he stayed at his grandparents' house while blasting music the other neighbors referred to as "racket." The neighborhood moms called him a delinquent. I never thought of him as anything other than competition in neighborhood games until that summer. He'd skateboard down to the end of the street to harass me while I listened to music or choreographed dances with the other neighborhood kids. Eventually, I'd find a reason to get them off my driveway and then Asher and I would talk for ten glorious minutes before Mom would find us alone at the end of the driveway and usher me inside.

"Wait, how did you know the neighborhood used to call you a delinquent? You were like twelve."

"Ah yeah, well, my grandma tried to get me to clean up my look, which was a sign. Then one day, Mrs. Lohaus literally yelled it to me across the street, so I kind of put two together. And then one day, you were with the pale neighbor with the bright orange hair... what's her name? Did you already tell me her life story?"

"Gretchen, no. How could I forget her? No freaking idea what happened to her."

"Yeah, pale girl Gretchen. I think you waved at me, and she shouted something like you weren't allowed to speak with me because I was a delinquent. And then you dropped that hand and we never waved again."

"Oh my gosh, Asher, I'm so sorry."

"No hard feelings. I've been waved at since. Plus, I was probably on my way to go smoke pot."

The doorbell rings and we change the subject.

"Let's see what terrible misfortune you've gotten me into now." He rushes to the door, and I wave to the pizza woman before quickly throwing down my hand. I'm not sure if waving is still a sore subject. As he puts the pizza down on the counter, I can't help myself.

"Listen, this is going to be a spicy *and* sweet explosion. You won't regret it. Now come to mama."

"I'm sorry *what*?" He looks genuinely entertained. I'm almost not embarrassed. "Mama? Is that what we are to call you now?"

"Please don't. Anyway... intentionally changing the subject now, how long are you here for?"

"I guess a few weeks, not sure." The uncertainty in his voice makes me sad.

"Well, we shouldn't waste any time then. Tell me more about what you've been up to since seventh grade."

He tells me he spent middle school between his parents' houses, and then his dad moved to Vancouver. All three Blair brothers went to high school in northern Washington, and his brothers still live there. One's a therapist, and the other's a farmer. Asher went to college at the University of British Columbia and studied communications, but the highlight of college—and the last ten years—was his band. He tells me they were good. Really good. They almost made it big, but it all fell apart, as things sometimes do. When that didn't work out, he tried working in PR at a few small companies. That also didn't work out.

"Now, it's my turn to ask you something. You've caught me up on all the neighborhood drama, so it can't be about that. Hm, let's see... What's your biggest fear?" He pauses, looks at his phone, and changes the music. I stop to listen to the lyrics, but it sounds like the song is foreign. Maybe French?

He jumps up and starts making another drink. He gestures as if to ask if I want another, and I point to my half-full glass. I study him while he pours.

He catches my eyes and misunderstands studying for stalling. "Hey now, I deserve honest answers. Get to talking."

But now that I am about to share, I wonder how much I should say. I can't talk about Oliver. Just his name sends my stomach spinning. Plus, no one wants to hear about your ex. I plop down against the carpet again and wave my hands above my head like I'm making snow angels. He's walking back this way. He stops and lays down next to me. His hand rests on my knee. I word vomit the next best truth.

"I guess not having direction. Or figuring out what I should do with my life."

And there it was, just in front of me—a fear I didn't know was living inside of me until I said it out loud.

He doesn't say anything right away, and I notice the room is spinning faster now. I try to make a few more snow angels and feel electricity spark in my body each time my hand slightly grazes against his. I keep waiting for him to respond, and while I wait, I close my eyes.

Then I pass out.

When I wake up, I'm confused. I check my phone and see a response from Mom from hours ago—*OK, thanks*. That was at 12:30, it's now 4:15. I look for Asher, and his hand is no longer near mine. He's moved to the other side of the carpet, sprawled out on his stomach. His plate of pizza is a few feet from him on the floor. Mine is on one of the two side tables. The peanut butter lava cake is untouched on the counter. I want to crawl in closer to him but decide against it.

What would a cool girl do? I think to myself. I decide she'd sneak out undetected. On my way to the door, I grab my shoes, which are still a little damp from the rain. I close Mrs. Blair's front door as quietly as I can and slide the shoes on once on the porch. As I make my way down his driveway, my head is swimming with warm feelings. So warm in fact, that I'm starting to think it may be the alcohol's fault. I pray Mom is out so I can have a few minutes to freshen up and stop smelling like whisky. It hits me then that I had not showered nor brushed my teeth when I saw Asher. I check myself out in the front entryway mirror and wince. My hair is sticking in every direction. I hope he didn't notice.

I walk quietly into the kitchen and see Mom has left a note on the counter.

Out getting groceries, be home around 5:30. Dad's bringing home dinner.

I drag my body up a flight of stairs and into my room, where I collapse on the floor. I start to undress, arching my back against the carpet to wiggle my leggings off. The carpet is far less comfortable than the rug at Mrs. Blair's.

I think about that boy again. My head is so fuzzy, I'm not sure which one.

Four

"Reag? Reagan? Is anyone home?" She is shouting and I have no idea how long she's been looking for me. "I need your help."

Suddenly, I'm wide awake. I roll over to my side and laugh at the thought that I find myself waking up on the floor of this house again today. It feels good to smile, but I won't keep smiling if Mom catches me here. Jumping to my feet, I rush to the door and swing it open. She's starting up the stairs.

"Just a second, I'll be right there."

I keep the door open until I hear her exhale an annoyed sigh. She mutters, "Okay," and heads back down the stairs. "Come help me when you... can." She says, reluctantly. It seems like we're both adapting to me being home.

"Will do," I sing back.

I smile victoriously but close my mouth quickly to catch vomit before it spills out. I rush to the bathroom, turn on the faucet, and let out Mrs. Blair's whiskey. My breathing steadies, and I think I can keep the rest down. I'm glad I didn't get into the lava cake. I splash lukewarm water onto my face and cup some into my mouth. Looking up at the mirror, I can't stop myself from smiling so I don't. The smile and I head downstairs together.

"Okay, how can I help?" I say as I dance into the kitchen.

"Doesn't that smile look good on your face?" She lights up, and I remember that all she wants is for me to be happy. "Well, tell me about your day. How was it?" She hangs an eager smile on her face like it's there to stay.

"Well, it was very fun. I hung out with Mrs. Blair's grandson, Asher."

Her smile starts to dim, but I may also be imagining it.

"It's a funny story. I didn't expect him to be there, I don't know if you did. But he was, and we both scared each other, because I used the bunny key, and he was upstairs when I came in, so he didn't hear me come in. Imagine our surprise," I chuckle and wait for her to join me. Instead, I see the smile disappear. "Anyway, he was housesitting, so we just caught up for a while."

"Caught up? What in the world could you have to catch up on? And you were there the whole day?"

"Well, believe it or not, a lot has happened since the seventh grade. Like eighth grade, high school, and we even went to college."

I'm not sure what she expected I did today, but I'm realizing this wasn't it.

"Mom, are you upset?" I ask.

"No, I'm not upset. I just don't like it."

"That sounds like you're upset."

Her lips contract together tightly, and she looks like she can't hold in her politeness anymore. "He was a little shit," she says, confirming her politeness has walked out the door.

I can't stop myself from laughing. She joins in, and suddenly we can't stop.

"Mom. He was a child; you can't say that."

"I know. Gosh, I know. But I've said that about a lot of kids. I think you were the only kid I ever really liked."

"I didn't even know you liked me."

"Stop that. You know I love you. You are the hardest thing I've ever loved and the thing I love most in my life." She takes my hand in her own. "I had no idea that boy would be in that house, or I wouldn't have told you to just march inside."

"It kind of felt like a setup, Mom. If you wanted to help me move on, you could've just sent in an application to *The Bachelor* or forced me onto a blind date."

"Ha. If I'm doing the setup, we're bringing in doctors, lawyers, and businessmen. Not bad influences."

"Really, Mom, how could *he* be the bad influence on me? Like is there much farther for me to fall?" I pull my hand away from hers and take a seat at the kitchen counter.

"My love," she moves closer to me again, and puts both of her hands to my cheeks, cupping them like she's holding a prized possession. "Don't be so hard on yourself. You're doing a good job. I'm proud of you. I just want you to take care of yourself."

I don't know how to respond so I shift uncomfortably in my seat as silence spreads throughout the room like an invisible gas.

She drops her hands from my face. "Do you want to talk about what happened, dear?"

She adds "dear" to the end like I won't notice what she's doing. I shift again in my seat, trying to decide if I'm ready to talk. If I do, there's no way she'll ever forgive him, and then there's no hope of getting back to the Reagan and Oliver we were before this. And even if I do tell her, there's no way she'd be able to fix this.

There was one night after the breakup before I moved home when I thought there was still time to fix things with him before they were really broken. That night, at the bottom of my closet, I found a sweatshirt he loved. I sent him a photo of me wearing the sweatshirt, reminding him of when we went on a trip to Portland earlier that year. It was windy, and he gave it to me because I was freezing. He responded to the text, saying I always looked better in it than him.

The response made me realize I could forgive him. I understood where Oliver was coming from with Jocelyn. I'd seen what he'd done with her happen to dozens of men before him. Jocelyn was fun, beautiful, and daring. Of course, he was tempted to try his time with her, but after trying, he'd see what he was missing. Beautiful, fun, and daring would become tired, superficial, and a one-time mistake. At this time, I had no idea they had decided to try and make it work.

So, after getting that text from him, I felt better and decided to meet a few friends at a bar in town. I was drinking and dancing, filled with hope when Jocelyn walked in and immediately danced over to us like she hadn't ruined my life.

"Reag. Do you have a second?"

She reached for my hand, and I let her hold it for a moment. I wanted to know what she had to say. We hadn't spoken since I stopped taking her calls, at which point she quickly stopped trying to call me.

She started with a confidence that told me she expected this conversation to happen.

"I am sorry things went the way they did. I didn't know that I felt that way. Or that he did. And I didn't know it would mean something."

"Mean something?" I asked.

She tightened her grip on my hand. "We're trying—Oliver and I—to make it work."

There was no way my mom could fix this for me, and the truth would only hurt us both.

"I'm not ready yet, Mom, but soon."

She smiles, knowing the "but soon" is something closer to a conversation.

"So, anyway, while catching up with Asher, I learned that he went to school in Canada, and he started a band. Apparently, they were *almost* famous."

Mom groans. "Oh honey, let's not even go there. He's bad news; I just know it. When he was little, he used to spray paint the sidewalks. Why do you think he stopped coming around as often after that summer? The HOA couldn't handle any more of his mischief."

"HOA? Mom, that is so dumb. They don't have any real power... do they?"

"Outside of what color you paint your house, not really. But they complained a lot to his grandma, which was obviously embarrassing. For everyone."

"Mom, that is so stupid. You are probably the only person who ever talked about him like that, and the only person talking about him now. Plus, what he's doing for Mrs. Blair is so kind. No one else would come to watch her house or help her, but he is doing that. So don't act like you know him."

"Oh darling, I'm not judging him. I'm sure he's a nice man now. I just, honestly, I don't want you to focus all your energy on him. After everything that's happened, I don't think he's going to solve your problems."

"You're right, you don't know him, so you shouldn't act like you do. And you don't even know my intentions. People change from when they were children. People change when they stop dating their boyfriend, but it doesn't mean they are desperate for another boyfriend."

"People?"

"Yeah, Mom, *people*."

"Okay, well, all I'm saying is I want you to focus on you, and not on other people trying to figure out their own lives."

Maybe she has a point. I don't know what I mean to Asher. I don't know why I need to mean anything, anyway. I think about my biggest fear conversation with Asher, and I decide that is much more a problem than Asher Blair.

"Mom, I am taking a break right now so I can figure out what I want to do for myself. So that when I make the choice, it is 100% what I want. It isn't about another boy."

"Good, that's great. That's what you *should* be doing." She checks the time and tells me she's needs to get a few things done for work before Dad gets home. In reality, she needs a break from me, and I need one from her.

I decide to take my break in the front yard. The sky is sprinkled with clouds, but rays of sunshine are fighting through before the close of the day. I look at Mrs. Blair's house and wonder what Asher is doing. I want to see him again, but I don't want him to be the only thing getting me through this breakup. I don't want to care more about him than he cares about me.

Before I can give it much more thought I see Dad's car turn down our street. I turn to head inside, but then I hear my name.

"*Reagan. Reagan Wilde.*"

I whip my head around and there's that boy. He's shouting from a window in the back of the house.

"Asher Blair," I shout back, in an eager tone. Catching myself, I adjust the tone down to a neighborly voice. "Did I leave something at your house?"

"Just all your best secrets," he shouts back. I swear I can hear him wink when he talks. He continues, "I didn't expect for you to be gone when I woke up." I feel myself getting hot, and I wonder if the neighbors can hear us. I don't get a word out before he says, "So, what're you up to tonight?"

"Uh," I swallow hard trying to find the words to speak, "Just planning to have dinner with my parents." I gesture awkwardly toward my dad's car growing closer and closer before he pulls into the driveway. He hops out of the car and gives me a wave but doesn't stick around to see what I'm doing. Maybe he's just happy to see I'm outside.

"Did he have a pizza box?" Asher blurts out, "Very robust diet over at the Wildes'."

"You've got great eyes. Are you looking for dinner?" I quickly offer but hope he doesn't want to join.

"Oh no, I've got a peanut butter lava cake that is supposedly going to blow my mind. I'm looking for a friend. So no plans tonight?"

"Well aside from dinner, not really."

"I guess you do now."

"What're we doing? I hear myself shout back in that eager tone.

"Going to confront my biggest fear."

Five

In the weeks since our breakup, I've thought about Oliver every single day. I picture his life with Jocelyn. Did they brush their teeth together? Eat dessert after dinner? Had they said I love you? Would they tell their children how they met? I would allow myself to dream about their life together until it hurt, and then I forced my brain to think about something new. But now, with this invitation from Asher, all I could think about was what it would mean to Oliver. Would it hurt Oliver to see me spending time with someone new? What if it didn't? What if it brought him back? What if it drove him further away?

Asher's voice gets higher like an insecure teenager taking his first steps toward confidence as he asks me what I think.

"Sorry, say again?"

"Uh, well." He coughs, adjusting his voice an octave deeper. I realize this time he's the eager, awkward one. "I got invited to play a gig, and since you're such a fan of local music..."

That was another lie I told him after drinking too much. I loved music, and it wasn't that I didn't like local bands, it's just that I didn't know anything about them.

"I thought maybe you'd be willing to come to see me play in person. It's been a while since I played, so it'd be nice to have a friend with me."

My heart flutters when he says the word *friend*. Even if it isn't romantic, it feels nice to be asked to go somewhere with someone, I know I can't say no. Plus, there's a chance Oliver wouldn't want me to go, and that is almost reason enough to do it.

"Okay, let's go."

"Really? Oh man, if there wasn't a full window between us right now, I'd give you a big hug. I'll grab my things and come by to get you in like fifteen minutes?"

His voice gets high-pitched once again. It is nice to know he isn't always as cool as he seems.

I skip across the lawn, back towards my parents' house. Telling Mom and Dad I'm bailing on our plans for tonight will not be a big deal. I think every passing evening I spend holed up in the house is making them more uncomfortable. But I know Mom will be disappointed to learn that I'm spending my evening with Asher. I can't be mad at her. I know she wants me to protect my heart, and she's right—I can't just go falling for Asher. I can't assume this invitation means more than it is.

I reach the front porch of the house and rehearse what I'll say to them both. I love music, I want to get back to living my life, and this will be a fun way to meet some new people. There's nothing between Asher and I, other than he's reminded me of how fun live music can be. I repeat the talking points over and over in different ways until I believe them, and then I walk inside.

My parents are sitting on the couch with their eyes glued to the TV screen. They're shoveling pizza into their mouths and I'm glad they didn't wait for me.

"There's some warm pizza in the oven," Dad spits out in between bites.

"Thanks. I think I'll take it to go if that's okay."

Dad starts to say yes, but Mom snaps her head in my direction.

"To go? To go where?"

Dad turns down the sound on the TV. It looks like they were watching a cooking competition show. I always find it funny when people eat while watching cooking shows because it seems like a recipe for dissatisfaction. You're rarely eating what you're watching, and how can you stop your eyes from wandering, and your stomach from asking if what they're having on TV is better than what's on your plate?

"Well," I take a deep breath before beginning the rest of the sentence, "Asher Blair invited me to go to a concert with him tonight. As a friend." I add the last part specifically for my mother.

The first name, and last name clues Dad in quickly, and his eyes get huge. I wonder if they've talked about Asher.

"He's performing tonight, and as you may remember, I love live music, so it would be good for me to go out and do something I like."

I speak slowly and deliberately, trying to demonstrate to Mom that going to see Asher play is as much for me as it is for him. It's not a sacrifice I'm making to spend time with a boy. Dad's attention is fully on the words left unsaid between my mother and me. None of us expect what she says next.

"Don't forget your coat. Have fun."

She turns her head back to the TV, and I almost think I see her smile. Dad starts to choke but manages to clear his throat and get out something about having a good time. He turns up the TV, and I don't question it. I grab my leather jacket, two slices of pizza, and my wallet, and run out the door.

As I step outside, the streetlights flicker on while dusk exits for the day. I scarf down my pizza, so Asher won't have to see me eat. I keep the other piece for him. When Asher pulls up to the curb, he's smiling, and it feels so good to have someone smile at me like that. Climbing into the car, I notice there's no spare room in the back seat. A guitar, an amp, some clothes, and takeout napkins sprawl across the three back seats with no intention of moving aside for a new passenger. He's watching me examine this part of his life, and his face twists into a look of shame, like a dog who got into the trash.

"Good thing I pack light," I say, as I open the door and climb inside.

The smile returns to his face. I pass him the piece of pizza and he bites into it without a word.

"So, where are we headed? I haven't been to a show in... awhile." I'm not really lying. I haven't been in a while, or maybe ever.

With his eyes locked on the road, he turns on some music, before coolly exhaling. "The place is called the Barrel Wheel."

I nod like that means something to me. He's very quiet. Maybe he's nervous or regrets the invitation. I don't want him to think I'm thinking too much about it, so I'm quiet too. As I stare out the window, I feel like the world is alive. I wish Oliver and Jocelyn could see me now. They're missing out on the person I'm becoming. I'm off with a musician who is talented (presumably), handsome (undisputed), interesting (great conversationist), and wants to be around me (I mean, he did invite me).

"Wait, why are we getting on I-5? Seattle is south of here?" It quickly crosses my mind that he could also be a kidnapper.

"Yeah, Seattle is. The show is a little outside Seattle."

"Oh, I never really go out of Seattle for shows. Are we going to Edmonds? Or Everett? Do they have good venues there?"

"Well, I mean, I'm sure they do. But we're going to Bellingham. It's a good scene, and I know a lot of the people out there from high school, and my brothers live there now. So, it was easier to get booked."

Panic hits me, and I feel it slide down my insides like a big gulp of water. Bellingham is almost two hours away, and I don't know if we have two hours of conversation in us. I want to be too cool to care, or confident enough to know that he'll like spending time with me, but I'm afraid I can't be either version of that person. We're already barreling up the highway, and I can't just ask him to turn around. That would be a far worse fate.

Instead, I turn up the song that's playing and try to buy some time. "Woah, I like this song. Who is this?"

"Oh sorry, I don't know how this album came up." He checks his phone quickly. "It's Umbrella."

"Dumb name, great song." I chuckle to myself and turn the volume up.

"Thanks, named them myself." He goes to change the song, but I intercept his hand like a safety overlord of Musicland. His fingers rest in mine for a moment, and I'm glad he doesn't pull away.

"Oh, no, no. We're staying here."

"You sure?" He smirks.

"Uh, yes. Why are you being weird? I like them."

The song switches over to a second, then a third, then a fourth Umbrella song. We sit in silence, and I listen to the lyrics, wondering if he's doing the same. When the songs stop, I grab his phone again and start the album over. He protests while turning a deep shade of red. I almost miss it, but then I see it again—the tattoo on the back of his arm.

"Wait. Your tattoo...is it an umbrella?"

He doesn't have to say anything because I've put it together.

"You really *did* name them yourself. That's your band and your album? I loved it."

He shivers in his seat like a chill has run down his spine. Asher's face turns a bright shade of pink, and then the blush disappears. "Did you already say you loved me?"

I silently curse his confidence but decide to try on a little confidence myself.

"I believe I said I loved *it,* meaning the album, not you." I smirk.

"Hilarious. Don't expect anything like that tonight, okay?" The excitement on his face dims and I can tell he may be confident, but he's also nervous.

"Asher, Umbrella is *good*. Really good. I'm sure you'll be amazing too." I curse myself as I let the compliment slip out of my mouth, but he seems to miss it.

"I told you we were good." He sounds a little more confident than he looks. "I don't sound like that without them though. I'm still trying to figure out how to do my own thing. So tonight, it won't be like that," he says staring straight ahead in a tone that makes me think he's already decided he won't be good tonight.

"I'm sure it'll still be good. You're very talented. You wrote those songs, didn't you? I mean, the lyrics alone are amazing."

"Yeah, I wrote some of them. But I won't play those tonight. I haven't written in a while, and it's not right to play that stuff by myself. So tonight, I'll play mostly covers, but hopefully it'll be fun."

"It *will* be fun," I'm happy to reassure him—and myself. "And good to get back out there."

He doesn't respond and I want to be able to do more. I reach across and rest my hand on his shoulder, trying to comfort him, but my hand feels different resting there, and that different feeling turns into something dark that quickly spreads throughout my body. He must feel it too because he jerks away. He utters something about stopping for gas, and before I can say anything, he's off the highway. He jumps out of the car, and I'm alone.

It's then that I realize I'm holding my breath. The seatbelt feels tight around my chest, and I frantically release it. I'm not sure what I'm trying to do, but it's clear that I want to mean something to Asher. But I don't, and now I feel stupid. I tighten my hand around the door and watch my knuckles turn white as I squeeze tighter. I think about jumping out of the car and finding my own way home. Why had he invited me if he was going to tell me he wasn't any good? Didn't he expect me to console him? I can feel tears coming to my eyes, and I want to blink them away. Maybe Mom was right about my spending time with him. We're halfway to Bellingham, and I settle into the reality that I can't get home on my own. I promise myself to play it cool, but once we're home, I won't see Asher Blair again.

He exits the store, and I check myself out in the mirror. I don't think he'll be able to tell I've been crying. He jumps into the car, and we don't say anything.

Eventually, he shifts in his seat and looks straight at me. "Close your eyes."

I do. Asher stretches out his hand and drops a cold object into my palm. His hands rest on the top of mine. He doesn't try to quickly pull away, and for a few moments, the warmth of his hand radiates onto mine. He presses both hands into the top and bottom of my own.

"Now open your eyes." When I do, he gestures toward our hands and then moves both of his back to his lap.

"A Hershey's—" I want to say *kiss* but he beats me to it.

"Hug," he finishes. "White chocolate, not milk. That's the difference from the kiss. I think they're better."

Not the only difference, I want to say.

"A hug to say I'm sorry. I know you mean well. The band is a tough subject for me, and I'm sorry about that. Umbrella was the best and worst time of my life. But it's over, and I don't know how to move forward. Tonight is a hard night because it's the first time I'm trying again since... we broke up."

I nod because I know a thing or two about break-ups. "I get that. Can I ask you something though?"

His eyes grow serious, and I feel like I can ask him anything. I want to know if I'm his rebound, while in the back of my head, I'm wondering if he's mine.

"Why did you invite me?"

He breath stills, and then he exhales heavily. I'm afraid of what he has to say. He looks away from me, and I find my hands squeezing tightly around the hug.

"I really liked talking to you, and listening to you, and listening to music with you. Music is my thing, and I had these people to share it with, but when Umbrella stopped being a band, I stopped having someone to understand this part of me with. But today, it felt like I could just be me, with you."

He glances back at me and lets out a small, kind smile.

"As for the gig... while I'm back helping my grandma, I thought I'd try music again, solo this time, but most of the people I know live in Bellingham, and so I only was able to get a show up there. I had planned to go up earlier today and stay with my brother tonight, but then you kind of ruined that for me when you came over."

I feel a pang of guilt, which must translate into a look on my face.

He shakes his head. "I'm not complaining that you did." He lets a smile sneak out and then looks away from me again.

We take a moment to settle into the silence. I can't stop a huge smile from smearing across my face.

"Plus," he continues, "I want to know more about you, and why you can drink at noon and go see a show at eleven p.m. on a weekday."

"Seriously?"

"Seriously." He grins confidently while starting the car.

We're back on the highway, and I can't believe I'd almost sworn him off entirely.

"Now, it's your turn to be vulnerable. Give me the short version of why you can and why you want to be here."

"I'm not sure we have enough time."

"We do if you get started now, plus we have the whole drive home." He chuckles to himself.

"What can I say? Girl goes to college, girl doesn't know what she wants to do with her life, and then some. The *then some* you can learn about later."

"Okay, well there's enough to work with in that sentence alone. What did study in college?"

"Business. As my mother always said, I can do anything with business."

"Including doing nothing, apparently."

"You, you're a funny guy. Sure, comedy isn't your thing?"

"Maybe I'll give it a try if things go south tonight." He winks at me. "So, Reagan Wilde, what do you *want* to do with your life now?"

"I don't know. And even sometimes when people do know, they can't even do it. So, I guess why does it matter? I've just got to find something to do, whatever that means. I know I need to get a job. But I don't want to hate my life once I have a job. Too many people do that. And I don't understand why."

"Yeah, you do that a lot."

I snap my head in his direction. I like staring at his profile while he watches the road.

"Do what?" I ask him playfully.

"Wonder."

"Do I?"

"Look. There you are wondering again."

I shrug like there's nothing I can do to stop that. He takes his eyes off the road and turns them to look at me. We pass the time with small talk until suddenly we're there.

"Well, Reagan Wilde, enough chitchat."

"Did you just say... chitchat?"

"Sure did. I think you have more to your story, and we need to crack this case on the whole what-you-want-to-do-with-your-one-and-only-life thing, but in the meantime, we're here."

Asher steers the car into a spot and jumps out without another word. He unloads the back seat, leaving the napkins untouched, and then we march inside. The first thing I notice about the Barrel Wheel is the fish tank centered in the restaurant. It's a dark space with an eclectic group of musicians and patrons. The band on stage includes a woman who must be in her late fifties, wearing pigtails and strumming the last of a country-western cover. Asher says he'll be right back and rushes toward the stage. I find a stool near the bar and settle in as the stage transitions to a new band. They all look to be in their early twenties but are dressed only in black. There are six of them, but it looks like the music is coming from a computer one of them is using. I'm not sure if it's a joke, but I don't dare ask anyone in the bar.

Asher sneaks up behind me and the hairs on my neck dance around excitedly. He whispers, "I have to set up. I'm on next."

"Oh, okay. And I should stay out here?"

"Yeah. Why don't you grab a drink? No backstage access for you until I know you're a real groupie." He raises his eyebrows and winks. Then he's gone.

I look around the Barrel Wheel and realize it's a thin crowd. There are four of us sitting at the bar and a few booths that are full. Otherwise, people are spread out across the room. It's a good room to practice on, I think. While the computer band starts up, I spin around and decide to get a drink. Before I have a chance to make up my mind on what to order, the bartender is asking what I'll have. Her name tag says Tina, and she's beautiful. She has long, dark hair and bright red lips. I panic.

"Uh, just a beer please?"

I don't specify which kind, and she doesn't ask.

"Sure, anything to eat?"

"Uh no, I had pizza earlier, thanks."

She looks at me like I've already told her too much, and then she turns abruptly away. I notice a long tattoo decorating the length of her arm. I bet she's the kind of girl Asher would date. I suddenly feel very plain, and very certain he wants someone adventurous and beautiful. He probably wants someone who is certain about where they're headed in life, and she seems like the type.

"Fuck it," I mutter under my breath. "Tina, can I also get a shot of tequila?"

She smiles an almost cruel smile and starts pouring from the bottle. The guy sitting two stools down was almost ready to order from Tina when he hears my order, spins his barstool in my direction, and shouts directly at me, "Tequila? I like where your head is at. Make that two Tina." He seems drunk but harmless.

"Sure, Martin, coming your way." Tina's smile seems more genuine when she's looking at him.

Martin gets up and asks the guy sitting next to me to swap places with him. I notice Martin is young, maybe my age. He has a short buzz cut and is wearing circle-rim glasses that look too hip to be worn here. The guy next to me looks like a scary Santa Claus, and Martin bribes him with a tequila shot. It doesn't take much convincing. When Martin's settled, he introduces himself. "Martin Caravan." He stretches out his hand to shake mine. It's a sure sign he isn't a Barrel Wheel regular. "And you are?"

"Reagan Wilde. Thanks for jumping on the tequila train."

"It is my honor." He bows theatrically.

Tina saunters over with three limes in hand, a shaker of table salt, and three shots of tequila. Bad Santa doesn't wait for us, throws it back, and immediately looks again to whatever he's watching on the bar TV, decidedly not interested in getting to know us better. Martin counts us down from three, and we throw back the shot in unison.

"Another?" Martin shouts. It sounds like a question, but Tina is already pouring.

We have another shot and order another beer all before Asher comes out on stage. While we drink, we talk, and Martin tells me he is from Canada. He used to be a drummer in a band, but that didn't work out, as it doesn't sometimes, and now he's living in Boise with his girlfriend, who is a local reporter. He says she is terrific and repeats it over and over throughout the conversation. I wonder if Oliver ever said anything like that about me.

Martin explains he's in town because his girlfriend, Jess, is working on a piece about a player from Idaho State who was set to play against his twin brother in some big basketball game against Western Washington.

"Except, they only just found out they were brothers," he elaborates. The story sounds made up, but he's so excited when he's telling it that I decide I don't care if he's lying.

"One twin was given up, the Idaho one, but the other was kept because the family could only afford one kid. It's sportsy, yet emotional. Truthfully, she's weaseled her way into dinner with the parents."

His grin drips with pride. He stares off into the distance, and it's like he's momentarily left the room. He takes a long sip of his beer and then suddenly, he returns to our conversation at the Barrel Wheel. "While she's doing something she loves, I figured I would too. I used to come to this bar with a friend of mine. Figured it'd be fun to see what kind of acts come through here now. And let me tell you, I am not disappointed. That lady in pigtails? Amazing."

I notice Santa Claus give Martin a death glare, and I wonder if maybe the country-singer is his much younger Mrs. Claus.

Martin doesn't notice and continues with his life story. He graduated, somewhat recently, and is now working as a bank teller. He can take time off when he likes, but it isn't paid. He says he doesn't care; he needs the time to think about what is coming next in his life. Marriage and stability, or maybe he'll quit his job and travel the world with his girlfriend. A man torn in two directions. I like Martin. He's easy to talk to and easy to drink with. I think about telling him my life story, but then I hear a guitar on stage.

"Ha. Asher. Look, he *is* really up there. I was still doubting if he really knew how to play the guitar." I laugh out loud to myself. I can't wait to tell Martin about how I know Asher. I think that maybe I'll ask him to give his perspective on our budding friendship. The good thing about strangers is you can tell them anything. Maybe I'll even tell him about Oliver, and not knowing what I want to do with my life. I, too, am a person torn in two directions. But as I spin around to start telling Martin, I realize he has no interest in listening to me. He looks like he's seen a ghost. "Uhm, Martin, are you okay?"

"Is that Asher Blair?" His eyebrows furl quizzically.

"You know Asher?"

"*You* know Asher?"

We both shout yes, but it is too loud to find out how because Asher starts to slam down on his guitar. He strums for the first song with a good energy, but not an infectious one. As he finishes up the first song, he searches the crowd. I wonder if he's looking for me, or someone else, but whoever it is, he doesn't find them and starts on another song. By the final song, his guitar strokes are so soft, you can hardly hear them over the lyrics. The crowd politely applauds, and Asher sulks off the stage. I almost don't want to spin around to start the conversation with Martin again. We both know Asher, somehow, but at this point, neither wants to brag about it.

Martin breaks the silence. "So, are you like his girlfriend?"

"Woah, no. We're just neighbors, well kind of. I'm, like, his grandma's neighbor and yeah, we just met really. Are you like, a fan?"

"A fan? Ha, hilarious. You were awake for that performance, right?" he whispers as if not to alert the others at the bar. "We went to school together at UBC and I used to play in this band with him... Umbrella?"

"What? *You* were in Umbrella? I just heard them—well, you—and I loved it."

"Really? I haven't played much since we broke up, but we really did have something. It's good Asher is still playing... I mean, he sorts of sucked tonight though."

I didn't know I could say bad things about Asher Blair, so I didn't. Plus, he was walking this way.

"Reagan." Asher shouts as he walks across the room toward me. Martin spins around, and Asher looks as if he's the one seeing a ghost.

"Asher." Martin screeches.

"Marty?" Asher looks flustered. I can't tell if Martin—Marty—is good or bad news.

"Hi, Asher..."

"Reagan, Marty, how do you know each other?"

"Great set, Asher." Marty exclaims.

I panic. By the look on his face, I realize that isn't what he wants to hear.

"Thanks, uh Marty." He goes in for an awkward hug. "What are you doing here?"

Marty proceeds to explain how his girlfriend, Jess, is a local reporter, how he works in a bank now, how he is a good guy living in Boise, but really misses drumming. And then how we ended up drinking at the bar.

Marty asks how Asher is doing, and he explains all the things I already know about Asher Blair. Both forget they told me any of this first. I sip on my warm beer and realize I'm spinning.

"Wait, I almost forgot to tell you." Asher grabs us both by the shoulders. Finally, he remembers I'm there. "I ran into a guy in the back who booked this show. He said there's an amateur showcase coming up, and the winner gets $20,000. He said I should check it out, and if I'm interested, he can connect me with the local booker. The only thing is it's in Los Angeles, in six weeks, but it's at the Echo. Can you imagine how cool it'd be to play there?" He doesn't stop for confirmation. "I think this is what I need to get back out there."

Marty and I exchange a quick glance, hoping it's quick enough that Asher won't pick up on it. But of course, he does.

"What was that?" Asher points between the two of us.

Luckily, Marty is up for clueing him in. "Look man, I love you, and you are really talented, but that was not a good set. Not a $20,000 set. More like a charity set." Marty doesn't leave any room for Asher's ego. "It reminds me of freshman year when I heard you singing sad songs to Lucy O'Malley in the laundry room. And what did I tell you then?"

"Well, after you convinced Lucy I wasn't worth it, you so kindly explained that I was good, but not great."

"Exactly, but by the end of college, you got pretty great. And you're welcome for that."

"You know exactly why I got good. Because I had you by my side."

"I did always make you better."

"So, what if we did it again?" Asher is smiling. He knows he has the same power over Marty as he harbors over me. It's his damn charm.

"When's the show again?"

"Six weeks from tomorrow."

"I've been telling Jess for a while that I'm an artist, but she doesn't believe me. I guess it's time to show her." Marty's grinning bigger than I've seen all night.

"Looks like you are my good luck charm, Reagan Wilde." Asher pulls me into his chest, but I'm still trying to understand what I've done.

"The band's getting back together. Tina, can we get some more tequila?" Marty shouts.

Tina spins around without a response and starts pouring. Her long, dark hair is two seconds behind her and flows back and forth before settling just about her waist. She's back with three shots in her hand before we can change our minds.

I look at Asher and find his eyes are locked on me. He throws me a wink like he was planning this all along.

Six

Marty's hotel is only a few blocks away, so we decide to stay the night. Considering I had four tequila shots, I don't disagree. But I have a few questions.

"Won't Jess care that we're just showing up in her hotel room?"

Both boys spiral their heads in my direction. Asher raises his eyebrows and makes eye contact with Marty. Marty nervously bites at his bottom lip in contemplation. He releases his words slowly, like air leaking out of a balloon.

"No way. Jess is super cool. She won't mind." He says with a hint of hesitation.

Asher's accepts Marty's response at face value, and then declares we should get hot dogs. This time, I give him a look of concern. I'm not sure why hot dogs are the next step. He points to a stand at the end of the street with a short line of drunk college kids. Without another word, Marty runs to the stand. His preppy Sperry's squeak against the wet pavement. He shouts that he'll get one for Jess, too, like a hot dog is ample consolation for bringing home two drunk strangers.

Asher must sense I am dubious and assumes it's about the hot dogs. "It'll help with the hangover. Trust me, Ms. Wilde."

He places his hand between my shoulder blades, and I lean into him. I decide to leave my worries here and give into the hot dog idea.

"I can see this is why they pay you the big bucks."

"Just you wait and see." He winks at me.

I pretend I don't notice the wink and skip over to Marty, who offers to pay for us.

"Can I have two please?" I say with a big smile on my face.

"I'm sorry, I'm not sure who the authority is on hot dogs, but two seems unhealthy." Marty declares.

"Let death take me swiftly and full of hot dogs."

They burst out laughing. It feels so good.

"Get the woman what she wants. Eight hot dogs, please!" Asher shouts.

I assume the extra two are for Jess. The man working behind the stand doesn't flinch when we order eight. He's seen worse in his time. He has dark bags under his eyes and looks like he could benefit from a night's sleep. He passes the eight over, two at a time. Marty leaves the cash on top of the stand, mutters, "Thank you," as he bites into his hot dog. Wordlessly, we follow him down the street.

The hotel is only a block away. We get into an elevator, and as soon as the doors open, Marty looks to both of us and puts his pointer finger to his lips, signaling we should be quiet. Asher opens his mouth to say something sassy, but Marty firmly shushes him. Asher's face turns a bright shade of red. We tiptoe inside, but quickly notice all the lights are on and it's clear that Jess isn't here. I don't spend too much time thinking about it because a wave of exhaustion hits me. Without another word, I finish my second hot dog, climb onto the sticky hotel sofa, close my eyes, and let a smile grow across my face.

***

I wake up to the repetition of bells. *Ding-dong ding-dong.* And then it stops. My eyes blink open, and I struggle to remember where I am. I'm lying on my side with my face stuffed into a leather couch. I roll onto my back and shake my left arm back and forth until it wakes up, and I remember where I am. I suddenly feel very nauseous and role to the other side only to assume the fetal position with the great hope it'll stop the nausea. When it doesn't, I pick my head up to look for the guys but only find a messy, and seemingly empty hotel room. I don't have time to focus on that for too long because I hear the bells again, and this time, realize it's coming from my phone—specifically, it's my mother. I ignore the call. The screen displays the apparent seven missed calls I've had from just this morning. All from Mom. I forgot to tell her I wasn't coming home, and she was of the opinion Asher was more harmful than harmless. I'm now beginning to worry about how much she'll harm me when I finally call her back.

"Hey there, stranger," sings a friendly voice, though I'm not sure where from. "No literally, we are strangers."

She strolls out of the bathroom casually, and the first thing I notice is that she's perfectly put together. Her hair is braided and tied together with one red ribbon at the bottom. She's wearing a baseball tee under a pair of overalls I only wish I could pull off. She has two cups of coffee, and I'm praying one is for me. I scramble to sit up on the couch as quickly as possible and frantically pull my hair back into a messy ponytail.

"I'm Jess, and you are?"

"Hi," I quietly squeak out. "My name is Reagan. Nice to meet you. Marty said a lot of nice things about you yesterday."

I'm hoping she's seen Asher and isn't thinking that Marty brought me home.

"That's always good to hear." Her voice sounds kind, like a Disney princess. She blinks at me like there's more I need to say.

"I'm uh… I'm friends with Asher. I guess Asher and Marty used to play together in—"

"Umbrella," she says while smiling at me, and then takes a long sip of coffee.

I wince as my head lights up with a sharp, searing pain.

"I got you some coffee. To help with the hangover." She passes it over, and I take a long sip out of the cardboard cup.

"Sorry, I'm moving slowly today. I really appreciate the coffee."

"Yeah, I figured you'd need it. It sounds like you all had quite the night." She giggles sweetly.

My cheeks flush with embarrassment.

Her lips curl upward. "Don't worry, you were far from the worst of it. Asher passed out with his pants half on and spooning Marty. It was quite the sight to come back to. You leave your innocent boyfriend at some random, rundown restaurant and come home to a bunch of half-naked strangers in your hotel room.

"I'm so sorry. That is beyond embarrassing."

Jess takes a sip of her coffee and then sets it down. She has this calm, yet playful energy about her. She stands up and walks to the mirror in the front of the hotel room, where she gently untucks some hair from the front of her braid. She begins to twist it around her finger and then let's go. The hair bobs up and down and then settles in a place that looks better than before. She smiles at herself in the mirror, then spins on her heel back towards me. Add wildly confident to the list of her characteristics. I take a sip off coffee while wishing I could be anything like her.

"It's not embarrassing, it's adventurous and I love adventure! So I think I'm really going to like you. Plus, it seems I owe you and Asher a big thank you."

I choke on the warm coffee. "What are you talking about?"

"Marty has decided to take a chance on his dream—it's something I've asked him to do for years, but he could never do it on his own. Now he gets to try again all because of you."

She must mean the band. I can't help the huge smile that escapes.

"I have hardly anything to do with that."

She answers me with a nod, though I wish she'd instead insisted I played a role. When she doesn't, I change the subject.

"So where are the guys?"

Before she can answer, the bells start ringing again. *Mom.* I hit ignore again, and text quickly that I'm okay and will call her later.

"They aren't wasting any time. They found a music store in town. Apparently, Marty needs to buy a new drum set. Shall we go track down our musicians?"

I want to tell her that they aren't *our* musicians. They may be hers, but not mine. Before I've said anything, she bounces into the bathroom and turns the shower on, then returns to plop down on the bed. She looks up at me only briefly, and then turns on the TV without a discussion. I take the hint and disappear into the bathroom.

Sliding into the shower, I feel stiff and icky. I am too hungover to think about anything other than the warm water beating down on my body. Each drop soothes my alcohol-soaked skin.

She clicks off the tv when I enter the room in a damp hotel towel. I notice she's set out a dress.

"I figure you don't want to wear something that smells like cigarettes and tequila today."

"That is actually my personal scent," I counter.

She giggles with a lightness I envy. I throw the dress on and ignore that it's a little too long to be cute. We head out the door, and slowly slip into conversation. I ask her about her job because it's the only thing I already know about her.

"Yeah, it's a good gig. I get to do local stories for our city newspaper. Sometimes I get to travel."

I ask her about how she got into it—did she always dream of being a reporter? She explains that she never dreamed of the life she has now. In college, she studied abroad in Spain and met a boy who was living in a rug shop in Morocco. Jess followed him there. They lived in the shop, pretty much just drinking tea and trying to sell rugs. Eventually, the romance fizzled, and the money ran out. Her parents flew her home to Boise and made her promise she'd live a life of dullness.

"I got a job, and met Martin on a dating app. Ended up falling for him, even though he doesn't have a bad bone in his body. And guess what..." Her eyes lit up like she had the biggest secret in the world. "None of it feels dull. I couldn't be happier."

"Wow, and the best part is I actually believe you."

"Well, of course you do. Everyone wants to believe in love." She puts her arm around me and steers me to the music shop.

Once inside, I notice that the room is covered from head to toe with all the happy sounds and sights of music. Guitars, drum sets, violins, and saxophones line the walls. I can't help but think about Jocelyn and Oliver, and how they'd react if they saw me now. Asher and Marty are in the back room of the shop. It's called the Jamming Room and is evidently where one jams while trying out the possibility of new equipment. Glass lines the room walls from floor to ceiling, so all the other musicians can *ooh* and *ahh* while watching those inside the room. I see Asher before he notices me. He's strolling back and forth across the room. From the side, he almost looks concerned. Marty notices Jess and rushes out to pick her up.

I hurry inside to Asher.

"Well, hello there. How are you feeling, Ms. Tequila Tornado?" He greets me happily, but something feels off.

"What an original name. I'm just happy to see you wearing pants."

"Are you really now?" He winks.

My knees feel like they may collapse, and I can feel my face grow red. I take a breath and pray Asher doesn't notice. "So, are you really doing this thing? Starting a band again?"

"Honestly? I don't know what I'm doing. I don't think we're going to be ready in six weeks or maybe ever. And I feel like Marty's starting to have second thoughts."

I look outside and Marty's kissing Jess all over her face.

"That doesn't look like a man having second thoughts to me." I use my eyes to point towards Marty.

Asher groans. "But you didn't know us before, Reagan. We were *good*. And last night... that wasn't good."

"I know you were really good. Remember, I used words like *love*, though I won't repeat that again."

He chuckles and the room lightens up by a few degrees. "I'm just going to call that guy and tell him I can't play the showcase. After last night, I'm doing him a favor."

"Self-deprecating Asher is by far the worst version. Forget twelve-year-old Asher losing in tag."

"I never lost in tag."

"You lost. And then you flipped your shit."

"Hey, I just care. And it turns out I care about this almost as much as tag."

I can tell he's serious. "So, let's do it. You said we were going to confront your biggest, greatest fear, so let's do it."

This is important to Asher. The only important thing to me in the last few weeks has been avoidance. Avoiding thinking about my future. Avoiding the picture that replays in my mind where Oliver is pressed against my ex-best friend's stupid, perfect face. And then it hits me. "Didn't Marty say you weren't a solo act?"

He nods.

"And didn't I say Umbrella was amazing?"

"You said something like that."

"Well, you already have Marty. What if you could bring the other members back? Umbrella was some of the best times of your life, right? What if you could have *that* exact experience again?"

He slumps his shoulders over like he can't stomach to hear what I'm about to say.

"Come on. What's there to think about? They know all your music. You've played together before. You said your songs were good, but you couldn't play them without the band. That it wouldn't be right. Well, this is a chance to play those good songs in the right way. And maybe win $20,000 too."

He shimmies his shoulders back and sits up straight but still doesn't smile. "I think it's a good idea, Reagan, but we'll never be Umbrella again. There's a history there you don't understand."

This time, I feel deflated, and it shows.

"I think it's a really good idea, honestly." He moves across the room, closer to me now.

I look up to meet his eyes, and my stomach does a backflip.

"It won't be Umbrella, but we can still go get Phil. I'm sure he'll do it. It'll be different, but it'll be better. We're smarter now. Hell, we can even road trip and play a few shows along the way."

"See—I have good ideas sometimes."

"You have the best ideas, sometimes." He smirks. "Plus, now we have our secret weapon."

"Which is...?"

"You, of course."

Suddenly I feel *hot* and maybe a tad confused. Before I can find out what he means by any of this, he rushes out of the room, and over to Marty. Through the glass, I see Marty light up, and Asher point to me. Jess gives me a big thumbs up, and I float out to the group, feeling honored but also like I'm a few steps behind.

"Okay, so Marty's going to buy that set, and then we've got to get started planning our trip to Denver."

Asher leans hard on the word *we*, and I realize I need to ask a follow-up question even though I don't want to.

"What do you mean we?"

"Phil lives in Denver. I'm sure we can find a few shows to play along the way. Kick it at his place for a little while and get into performance shape. If we tell him now, he can start playing again, too, so we don't lose time with him warming up." Asher puffs his chest out. Marty takes a hand off Jess to fist bump Asher.

"I'm excited for you guys. That'll be great." I try to smile, but my unhappiness shows.

"I did say *we*. Minus Jess. She's got to go back to work."

Asher pouts like a puppy, and Marty looks genuinely sad. I'm caught in the moment.

"Asher, I can't go to Denver."

I can see his joy floating away again. Both Marty and Jess look at me like I am no longer a part of the cool kid's club.

"I'm sorry, Asher, but I need to get a job, and find a place to live." The responsibility in my voice surprises me.

"But why?" He looks at me like I've missed the point.

"Asher, come on, if she can't go, she can't go." Marty reaches for him, but Asher shakes him off. I'm glad to know I'm not the only one he does that to.

"If it's about your mom, I'll tell her I'm hiring you as our manager. People management experience."

"Dude, what? We can't pay her," Marty starts to say, but Jess grabs him by the waist and pulls him away.

"Asher, you don't need me, and I *do* need to get a job."

"Look, this can be a job, and it isn't a boring job that you'll end up hating. You love music. I could tell that the first night we met. And if we win money, we can pay you. Think of it like commission, eh? You help us get better, and if you do a good enough job, there will be money in it for you too."

I'm not sure why he is trying so hard to keep me around. They don't need me.

"Listen, it's not about the money."

"Then what's it about?" He doesn't wait for an answer. "You said you want to figure life out. You want to find a job you like. You like music. And besides, you said you'd come with me to confront my biggest fear."

I'm not sure if the reasons are good enough, but I call Mom anyway.

Seven

"It's eighty-five degrees today. Can you even believe it? Late September, and practically in the nineties in Seattle."

I did not believe it. I had told Mom I stayed the night in Bellingham, and we now had plans to road trip across the country, while I held the title of band manager for Asher Blair, and she didn't explode. So, the eighty-five degrees in Seattle thing didn't shock me.

"Are you sure you're okay with this? I know I didn't call you back, and you called me a lot. I'm sorry about that, I just, I was trying not to be the only person calling their mom back."

"Listen, I really wish you would've called me to tell me you weren't coming home. I want you to respect me and understand that I'll always worry about you. And I *am* angry, don't get me wrong, but I've also seen you live inside your room for months on end."

I want to tell her it had only been eighty-eight days, but I don't dare interrupt.

"Now you're getting out in the world, and I'm happy to see it. But next time, seriously, just send me a text." She says firmly, and I promise I will.

"And while you're on tour, I want lots of photos and updates. I'm really excited for you, Reagan."

"You are? Are you sure? 'Managing' a band can't be what you pictured for me. I thought you wanted me to become like a CEO or investment banker type."

"Listen, I would be thrilled if you were a CEO or like on the *Forbes* 30 Under 30 list, but only if you're happy. Plus, music makes sense. You always loved it, and you may not be a great musician, but I'm certain you can help those guys get famous."

"Hey. I'm an okay musician. What about all those years of piano?"

"Can you still play the piano?"

"Well, not exactly. But I could try."

"You certainly could try. But management is also a good path." I can hear her smiling on the other side and smile too as I think about Asher offering to call my mom earlier. *People management—isn't that what matters?* Apparently, the answer to that question is yes.

"Maybe this is a one-time adventure, maybe it's the start of the rest of your life, but whatever it is, my love, I'm happy you are doing it."

I feel like I don't know this version of my mother, but maybe it's the person I get to know as an adult.

I look over at Asher and Marty, and they're picking up and playing different instruments. Asher's picked up a blue guitar, and Marty's on a drum set that I think is meant for children. They look so happy. Jess is laughing and videoing them on her phone.

"Thanks, Mom. I'm excited. And it feels good."

"Good, that's all we want."

The phone line goes silent, and a peace overwhelms me that I haven't felt before. It feels like I have reached the first day of the rest of my future. But like all bubbles, it bursts quickly, and without warning.

"Reagan, there's one more thing I think I should tell you. I don't want you to think too much about it, but..."

I lean further into the phone while all the possibilities of something horrible run through my mind. Did my grandma die? Are my parents getting divorced? Did they revoke my diploma because I'm a real-life failure?

"Oliver is in town."

In the fall semester before graduation, Oliver had accepted a job in Eugene as a finance analyst for some environmental company. It wasn't ideal. We wanted to live in Seattle, but it was a job and that was something I didn't have yet. So, the plan was that Jocelyn, and I would rent a two-bedroom apartment in Seattle and find jobs in the city. Oliver would keep his job in Eugene, and eventually request a transfer to Seattle. The transfer wasn't approved, as far as I knew.

"Oh. That's strange." The back of my throat feels very dry. "Where did you see him?"

"At the market. I was surprised to see him too. We talked a little. I guess he was in town for the weekend. He was with a few friends."

"Did you know the friends?" I ask, knowing it's a leading question.

"That's the thing—I did. It was Jocelyn, but I wouldn't think too much about it..."

She continues, but I stop listening. My heart feels like it's fallen out of my chest. This means they are still together, and when I get home, I will probably run into them together. Why did it take him so long to find a way to be with me, but he's already visiting her? Didn't they know people would see them together? And they grocery shopped now? Grocery shopping is a deeply personal thing, reserved for people who love each other and are in long-standing relationships.

"Darling, I really think a few weeks away will be good for you. Disconnect, adventure, try something new. I'm excited for you. And please remember, we love you."

I nod into the phone like she can hear me. When I don't say anything else, she continues.

"Do you want to say hi to your dad? Tom, I've got our band manager on the phone. Yes, I said band manager. No, I don't know if that's a real title. Reagan, what is it called again that you're doing?"

We chat for a few minutes. Dad gives me a list of all the places we should stop for food and sightseeing while driving to LA. I can tell he thinks this is just a vacation, but he's still supportive. Mom must've told him about seeing Oliver.

When we end the call, I'm ready to show Oliver what he's missing. I storm over to my new friends, who are still living in a bliss bubble. "Let's get this tour started."

"Woah, I love the confidence." Marty snickers.

Asher looks at me like he knows I've made the right choice, and I feel like I have. He starts to say what he's thinking about where they should play, but I stop him short.

"I thought that was my job."

"Oh, my mistake, Ms. Tour-wide."

Asher is beaming, but Marty, Jess, and I all look at him with disgust.

"Is that a play on Mr. Worldwide? I know you sucked last night but thank God you didn't try comedy." I wink at him. Whatever it is between us, I'm suddenly very glad it's happening.

"And besides, it's Mrs., not Ms., to you. Now, let's get planning. This is what I'm thinking..."

Before I can say any more, Asher chimes in that he made the right decision about bringing me into this wild plan.

"Well, I have to prove you right after you put your neck out on the line for me. I know Marty wasn't so certain."

Marty starts to argue, but I don't listen. I'm smiling at Asher like we're the only people in the room. I tell them that after coffee, we'll head back to Seattle, pack, sleep, and hit the road. Surprisingly, they all agree. The three of them go to grab all of us coffee, and I spend a few minutes doing research. We'll drive down through Oregon, Idaho, Utah, and on to Colorado. We'll stay in hostels. We'll crash at Phil's for a week or so, and then on to LA.

I'll be the best at this, I say to myself, wishing Oliver could hear.

Eight

"I heard someone once say that every experience these days begins and ends with a photo. I don't know what it is about social media, but we all feel the need to show the world what we're up to, even when nobody cares. Like on the Fourth of July, when everyone watches the same variation of a firework show, and yet posts a video like someone's suddenly going to care about their angle of the firework."

"Are you just saying this because you saw me post a picture?" I quickly click out of Instagram where I've posted a photo of the two-lane highway, and a sign that reads "Boise 372 miles," in the background.

"Well, did you caption the post something about being on the *road again*?" He leans on the word's *road again*, and I think he may break into song.

"No?" I say as if it's a question. I hope he doesn't catch on, but of course he does.

"Well, I'm going to see it, so I'll know you're lying."

"No, you won't." I think quickly. "You don't follow me, and you don't even know my Instagram."

"Sure, I do. It's @wildeaboutReagan."

"What? How do you—?" I sigh, feeling defeated. "Never mind. I'm going to make it private. Ha-ha."

"So you admit it. You posted it. You're as predictable as I thought you were."

I smile at him; I don't mind being predictable to Asher Blair. It means we're spending time together. Asher makes me laugh. He makes me forget what was going on in my world. He makes me feel like I am making the best possible choice by just choosing to be around him. Maybe Mom is right to be worried about me. I shudder at the thought and shake myself out of my head. This is about more than just a boy. It is about finding what I want to do with *my* life.

I look in the rearview mirror, and see Marty and Jess passed out in the back seat. They're just like me, trying to figure out what their life should look like. In a few hours, we'll drop Jess off so she can go back to work. It's hard to believe that just two days ago, we were getting the idea for the trip.

After leaving Bellingham, we stopped in Seattle. Jess and I stayed the night at my house, where my parents fed us leftover pizza and we stayed up painting our nails and talking like a childhood sleepover. The guys stayed at Mrs. Blair's, where they put together the perfect set list, and picked up Mrs. Blair's minivan When we left the next morning, my mom waved goodbye from the front porch. I felt like my life was just getting started. The moment felt free, like the first day of summer, when you can choose your own adventure, and the days feel infinite.

Asher adjusts the volume on the radio, and it's enough for me to snap back into reality. As his arm reaches from the dial back towards the steering wheel, he starts to nod his head back and forth to the new beat. He looks happy.

"Hey, smile." I shout before snapping a photo of him.

"What, me? I'm driving, lady." Asher's dark hair falls in front of his face, his nose wrinkles ever so slightly, and he pretends he doesn't want to smile, but does anyway.

"You're good at smiling, even if you are a tortured artist."

"Are you flirting with me?" He looks at me from the corner of his eye, and I melt. Before I can decide if I'm flirting or not, Asher makes a funny face and I snap another photo, immediately posting it on my Insta.

"It shall live on @wildeaboutReagan for the next twenty-four hours, and you'll have no way to look at it because I'm officially private."

“I’m going to make a secret account and start following you. It’ll be dedicated to tiny dogs and their unlikely friend combinations. You’ll be none the wiser.”

“It feels like I may figure that one out.” He smiles at me, and I try not to listen to the butterflies beating around inside.

It’s only six p.m., but fall is pushing itself upon us, and with each passing day, the sunset is forced to set earlier and earlier. We got a late start this morning but had time to get coffee at a hipster shop in Ellensburg. They must have thought we were hipsters too because they were very nice. Jess, Asher, and I all ordered Americanos, which I think helped the hipster persona. Marty got a pumpkin spice latte, which I think the mustachioed baristas found funny, and not offensive. The rest of the day has been a beautiful blur, and soon, we’ll stop to get something to eat before arriving at Jess’s. We’ll chat and laugh and be the epicenter of whatever restaurant we’re at while we’re there.

A few buzzes on my phone bring me back to life in the van. "Oh, would you look at that? Notifications are already rolling in on my little on-the-road photo.”

“So you admit it. There was an open road cliché.” He claps both hands on the steering wheel.

But I can’t respond to him, because then I see it. It isn’t a comment or a like on my photo. It is everything I hoped for. I suddenly feel very sick, and apparently, it’s obvious. I can feel the blood rush out of my face.

“Woah, Reagan, are you okay?” Asher says as he reaches for me, grabbing hold of my arm.

“Can we please pull over?”

“Uh.” He looks around, probably for safe place to stop. He doesn’t realize we don’t have time for that. “There isn’t a rest stop nearby. Can you wait?”

I take another look at my phone to make sure I’m seeing it correctly. I may have deleted his number, but I can’t help but recognize the digits anyway. I surprise myself when I start to hyperventilate, and it surprises Asher as well. He looks panicked, like I’m a bomb waiting to explode. Or rather, exploding. He doesn’t wait for me to say anything else.

"Okay, we'll pull over. Okay, just two seconds."

He puts on his blinker and zooms across two lanes of traffic before pulling off to the side of the road. By the time we get there, a measly ten seconds later, I'm spinning. As soon as the car stops, I burst out of it. I run up onto the hillside of the highway, and squat down behind a tree where Asher can't see what I do next. Maybe he thinks I'll hurl, but all I do is cry.

I open my phone, but I'm not ready to read what he wrote. I know he's with her. Why does he want to talk to me now?

Maybe he needs something from me.

Maybe he wants me back.

Maybe he wants to remind me he's with her and doesn't want to run into me in town.

The maybes are making me spiral even more. I need it to stop, and the only certainty I have is whatever exists in that text message.

I can hear voices from down below, and see Jess and Marty pop out of the car. There's some comfort in knowing that Asher won't be able to explain what's going on because he has no idea. I know I can't explain it to them. I don't want them to know that Oliver has this sort of control over me. I don't even want them to know who Oliver is. I only want them to know the version of Reagan after Oliver. I need to get it together before one of them inevitably climbs up the hill and finds me hiding behind this tree.

But I also need to know what he said. Like I said, he has this control over me. I click open the text.

Hey Reag, it's been a while. I'm in Seattle so naturally I'm thinking about you. I hope you're doing okay.

My first thought is fueled by anger, and I'm proud of that. *After all this time, after all these unanswered text messages, you're just thinking about me? How about the fact that you're with my best friend, in my hometown, and I know this because you ran into my mom.*

But also, he's thinking about me. Which means something. I was more than something. Of course, I was. I was with him for *years.*

The anger hits again. Then sadness. Then a line of bubbles, like he has more to say, and I quickly close my phone. I don't get a second to breathe because then suddenly Jess is there.

"Hey Reagan, it's Jess. Just coming to check on you?"

She has no idea what's going on, and she seems like she genuinely cares. Problem is, I have no idea how I'm feeling, so I decide to lie.

"I'm so sorry. I just got really car sick, and I thought I was going to vomit—I just didn't want any of you to see that. It comes on quickly."

"No worries, I figured that was it. Asher was concerned that something bad had happened, but I'm glad it's just motion sickness. That sounds bad—not just motion sickness. I know that sucks. Can I bring you anything? I have some water and snacks in the car?"

"No, no, I'm fine. We should get going. Again, I'm so sorry."

"Don't be sorry. It happens."

We start down the hillside with Jess a few steps ahead. It gives me a chance to check my phone. His mysterious bubbles have stopped. I can't help myself and quickly text back.

Hi. I'm doing great. How are you?

Jess is almost back to the car but stops to look for me. She waves, and I speedily scurry down to the car.

In what I assume is an effort not to embarrass me, Jess mentions to Marty and Asher that I'm fine, just car sick, before I have a chance to join them. She's loud enough that I can hear, which I appreciate because it means I don't have to explain myself.

"Another reason not to Instagram and drive." Asher chuckles.

His eyes smile at me as he waits to see how I respond. I give him a shy grin.

"We can stop at the next real rest stop and, and get some air," he says as we both hop into the front seats.

He waits until I'm situated in my seat and then delicately put his hand on top of mine.

"I was worried. I'm glad you're okay," he whispers, only to me.

I wish this moment could be enough to pull me out of my head, but then I feel a buzz and I'm back to thinking of Oliver. I stare at my phone for two seconds before Asher reprimands me.

"Hey, what just happened when you were staring at that thing? Maybe leave it alone?"

"It's fine. I'm fine," I say, looking at Jess and Marty like I'm thankful that they care so much. And I remind myself that I *am* fine. It doesn't matter that Oliver reached out. His text was pointless. He's with *her.* He is in the past and my future is ahead of me—this trip, and whatever comes after it. He was a bad dream, and I am finally waking up.

I open the text with a confidence that I can handle it this time.

Cool, that's good to hear. I'm glad you're doing well. I was worried about you after the last time we talked. I'm doing good too.

I roll my eyes when I read the word *worried.* And then he sends another text.

I'm back in Seattle. I wanted to see if you're around and wanted to get a coffee or something?

Before I start to spiral, I check one thing. I have a feeling he knows exactly what he's doing, and I prove it when I look at my story and see he's already watched both stories. He knows I'm not in town right now, and he has no idea who I'm with. But he knows it's a guy. It's possible he missed me or was jealous, but two days ago, Mom saw them together. Whatever he's doing in Seattle, he's with her.

I'm surprised when we pull into the rest stop. I mumble something to the three of them about getting some air, but don't look anyone in the eyes as I jump out of the car and head quickly down the sidewalk.

It's almost dark, but I can see there's a small park in the back of the parking lot. I walk as quickly as I can, without physically running, in that direction. The streetlights flash on, and I become very aware that we're not the only people stopped here. There are huge semi-trucks with drivers jumping inside. There's a family carrying a little one to their car because they've fallen fast asleep. There's a dog barking. I decide to keep walking.

I still need to figure out what I want to say back to him. But what is there to say? I've desperately wanted him to want to see me for months. I also wanted him to say he made a mistake and wants me back. Maybe he *will* say that, and he plans to when he sees me in person. But Mom saw him with *her*, and clearly it made such an impression that she needed to tell me about it.

The phone buzzes again and I jump without reason. This time, it's my mom. She's sending a picture of wine at dinner.

Drinking a good bottle and watching the Voice. Hope you're having a fun time. Love you.

I ignore the text and keep speed walking. *Good for you, Mom,* I think to myself. At least one of us is having a good time. The sidewalk around the park ends, and I near the car again, but I'm not ready to face my new friends, so I turn abruptly towards the bathrooms and circle back through the park. I see a bench and shift my strategy from walking fast to sitting and breathing. But that's impossible because I've got another text. Another buzz. This time, it's not Mom.

And I know you probably think you know why I'm here, but it isn't just that. I'm visiting a few friends. I realize it isn't the same here without you. It would be great to just see you, so this city feels more like the city I know. I miss you.

Is there a word for when you're feeling giddy, dreadful, and torn all at the same time? If so, that's the one that describes me.

I have to go home. *I can't go home.*

Does he really mean it? *He's still with her. He doesn't mean it.*

He was with Jocelyn. *Why was he with Jocelyn?*

Does he love me still? *I still love him.*

I do. *I still love him.*

I look up from my world for a moment and notice the darkness has fully taken over for the day. The family is gone, the trucks are getting back on the highway. I can't see Jess or Marty, but the car is turned on and there's no one in the front seat, so I imagine the two of them are in the back seat, waiting for me to be ready to go. This is going to be hard to explain, and I don't have much time.

Suddenly I see Asher is walking my way. "Don't tell me it's car sickness, because I won't believe you." He shouts before he reaches me. "You don't have to talk to me, but you should if it'll help. It's better than storming around the block or making us stop fifteen times every five minutes after you look at your phone." He gestures to the device, which lights up as if it's been cued. "Speaking of which, it looks like you got another text."

"Another text?"

"It's hard not to notice with you in the front seat, glued to that thing. Is it your mom? Is she upset you're here? I know she hates me, but I thought we were moving past that."

He sits down next to me and lets me take a moment to put together a thought. He looks concerned, but it's like he knows there's nothing he can do, like when you see someone drop their groceries in the parking lot and don't know how to help them clean up spilled milk.

"Asher, I'm heartbroken."

His eyes go from concern to understanding. "And whoever did that, they're the one texting you now?"

I press my lips together and squeak out something that sounds like affirmation.

"And is that what happened in the car too? Is that why you were glued to your phone?"

"Glued seems harsh." I laugh, but he doesn't. "Yes, that's why."

"I didn't know—" He starts, then stops. I'm not sure where he's going with this. There's a lot he doesn't know about me, and that makes me worry that he's starting to second-guess having me here. There's a chance this whole trip could come to an end because of me. And then if I come back to Seattle like this, then Oliver will see I haven't changed, and will change his mind about me—again. He'd realize he never should've missed me.

But then Asher finishes his sentence.

"It's just, I didn't know you were seeing someone recently. It didn't come up when we were talking."

His eyes dart away from me. I don't want him to feel uncomfortable, but I can't hide my pain.

"I mean, I'm not surprised. That's not what I mean. You are great—fantastic, really—so it makes sense. It's just. I didn't know. So I didn't expect it."

"Well, we haven't had a ton of time to talk about it. I mean, I don't know that much about you, Asher. I don't know what you did before I met you, how you have the time to do this now, who you've dated, *if* you've dated, or even what happened to your band."

"Yeah, you're right. But this isn't about us, and if we make it about us, then we'll be focused on the wrong problem."

I want to know what he means when he says "us," but I don't ask because my phone buzzes again.

"You can check it if you want to," he says casually, like he's offering me the last bite of his sandwich.

"I know I can."

"Well, are you going to?"

"Not yet."

"Do you want to talk more about it?"

"I don't know."

His eyes dim, just a little.

I continue, "I haven't told anyone about what really happened. Not even my mom."

"Well, mothers tend to be bad secret keepers. Not me, though. I'm essentially a vault of secrets. You wouldn't believe what I know about Marty. And if that's not enough, I'll even offer you an Asher Blair pinky promise, insured by Asher Blair himself."

He sticks out both pinkies, and I loop each with my own.

"Okay well, with an argument like that, here we go. I loved someone, and they loved me. For a long time, I thought we were destined to be together. I figured we'd be living together right now, planning our future. And instead, I lost that person, and lost track of my future. I also lost a best friend along the way, but that was just collateral damage."

Asher doesn't say anything, so I continue.

"I prayed and begged and bargained with the universe that I would hear from him again. The months kept passing, and now I'm trying to move on. It feels like I've just started to."

I can't help but lean my body towards him when I say this. It's obvious to me now that he's a big part of my moving on.

"But when I talked to my mom, she told me she ran into him and Jocelyn, the ex-friend. Which means they're still together. Oh yeah, they got together, by the way. Kind of the whole catalyst for the breakup. Nothing like finding your boyfriend and your best friend… together."

His face twists into a look of disgust, and I feel justified.

"And despite the heartbreak, the future that didn't come, the praying for him to come back, I was moving on. Except he must've sensed that, because here he is, texting me first for the first time since before the breakup."

"I'm pretty sure exes have sensors in them that can tell when you're life is just getting good. If you reach any level of sustainable happiness, then the sensors go off and said ex realizes they need to make an appearance," Asher says, as if he's explaining a scientific theory, and I almost can't tell he's joking. "What did he say?"

"Ugh, what does it matter? He's with her."

"It could help you understand what he wants now. Plus, if you want him back, then maybe this is your chance."

And for some odd reason, hearing him say that hurts. I tell myself Asher is trying to help, but if Asher helps me get Oliver back, then he doesn't have feelings for me. Whatever butterflies I have been feeling for him are misdirected. And yes, while I am still confused about Oliver, part of me wants Asher to use this moment to confess his love for me. But when he doesn't immediately change his tune, I decide to read the text. Oliver's sent two more.

I hope it's OK I reached out, it's been a few months and all, so I figured we're both in a good enough place to see each other.

The second one was sent twelve minutes later.

Anyway, LMK if you're free this week. Maybe we can get a cup of coffee or something.

Asher's watching me closely, maybe studying for signs of a further breakdown. I won't let that happen.

"I guess he wants to see me, he figures it'll be fine to see each other because so much time has passed—but if you ask me three months isn't that much time. Whatever, he's only in town until Tuesday anyway." I groan like maybe if I groan loud or long enough, Asher will solve this problem for me. When he doesn't even try, I continue. "Asher, why are your human counterparts such shit?"

He scoots closer, wraps his arm around my shoulder, and I can't help that it feels good. "Well, my dear friend, you can't see him, so this really isn't a problem. Physically, I mean. I need my manager with me as we get the band back together. It is going to be a very long journey, with lots of twists and turns and no vacations. At least for the rest of the month. You feel me, human counter-counterpart?"

"Can we please not make human counterparts a thing? My brain just stopped working for a minute."

"Eh, I don't know, I personally think it's kind of cute, counterpart."

"You're overusing it." I sigh, pretending to be annoyed.

"Reagan. I understand heartbreak as much as the next tortured musician. You deserve more than this guy gave you. Whether you realize this or not, you are in luck, because good fortune gave you an out. You aren't ready to see him, but he doesn't need to know that. Tell him the partial truth—you're on tour right now with your new band that you manage. Sorry. Can't see you now or ever, Mr. Ex." He chuckles humorlessly. "And please, *please* realize that he shouldn't get to hold this much power over you. Let him know seeing you isn't something you'd consider. Not right now. Make no plans, leave no openings. If in the future you change your mind, you can reach out to him and do it amicably, but him springing this on you is not cool. And no offense, but you're clearly not okay. If the texts you've sent him before today are a tenth of the breakdown you had tonight, well, he should know that not enough time has passed."

"What are you? Some kind of breakup guru?"

"I've been there, done that. If you tell him no and shut that door, it'll keep him somewhat interested, but also give you time to reflect on what you really want. You win."

"Wow, I had no idea it's so easy. Can you help me write that wining text?"

He takes my phone and starts to type away. I wonder if I'm making the right decision, but Asher has a point—I won't be home by Tuesday.

"So when do I get to learn about your heartbreak?" I blurt out.

He's silent.

I struggle to cover it up before it gets awkward. "It doesn't even have to be romantic. Could be things like jobs, the band, global warming?"

He spins the phone back in my direction. "How's this sound? *Enjoy a cup of coffee for me. I'm working with a band right now, and we're on tour. Not sure when we'll be back.* No exclamations points, no openings for the future. No joy. No questions. No answers. Nada." He's waiting for the okay. The text seems too simple to me, but I'm too wounded to help myself, so I give him a thumbs up.

"Alright, then I'm hitting send."

"Wait, no, don't send it please." I grab for my phone. "I should be the one to do it." I take a deep breath and hit send, like my sending it will make all the difference.

"It's sent?" He raises his eyebrows suspiciously.

"It sure is."

I look at him under the glow of a dim streetlight and notice freckles dancing across his nose. His arm is still draped over my shoulder, and I turn my head to rest against his chest. He squeezes me into him.

"Thank you, Asher. I'm really sorry about all of this."

"No problem. And going forward at all gigs, I'm taking your phone. Prime drunk texting territory. Again, trust the professional on this one."

"Ha. I can't make that promise. But maybe you can bribe me. You can start by telling me a little bit about your own heartbreak—ya know, make it even?"

"Mm, maybe another time, my human counter-counterpart." He pulls out his phone and checks the time. "We've got to get going. Is the 'motion sickness' officially gone?" He uses air quotes around the words motion sickness.

I check the text thread again and feel disappointed when I don't see three dots waiting on the other side. "Yeah, I don't think I'll be getting motion sickness any time soon. Especially if you let me drive."

Without another word, he tosses me the keys.

Nine

"I'm really glad I peed." Jess smiles as she finishes her second bottle of water. She knows we all regret not using the bathroom at the last rest stop.

"Yeah, well keep on drinking like that and you're going to wish you made us stop—again." Marty gruffly mutters. Jess sticks out her tongue. Marty pulls gently on her ponytail.

"Okay, I'm with Marty. This is torture. We need to stop." Asher chimes in, and I nod vigorously in agreement.

Thanks to my Oliver freakout, we are trying to make up for lost time. It's now nine p.m., and we still have another hour to drive before we hit Boise. We are also on the verge of hanger because we planned to eat dinner at Marty and Jess's to try and save some money.

"Another stop wouldn't put us too far behind," I add.

Jess begrudgingly agrees, and we pull off when we see a sign for a city called Ontario, Oregon. I pull into the first gas station parking lot before anyone has a chance to disagree. I'm determined to make this stop quicker than the last two.

Jess decides she'll run inside with me. "Better safe than sorry," she says.

We're in and out of the restroom in minutes. If peeing were an Olympic sport, we would've medaled, but when we get back to the car, the guys are nowhere to be found. After five minutes of idle conversation, we head back inside and find them looking for their names on niche keychains designed to look like different types of motorcycles.

"I found a Jess-ica."

Jess shudders when she hears the -ica, but Marty doesn't notice.

"The rest of us may be out of luck."

"I'm starting to think we're going to lose them here," Jess whispers to me. She has to return to her adult job in the morning, and I have to imagine Jess is somewhat stressed about the time and housing us all tonight, but you wouldn't be able to tell that. She is either very good at hiding stress, or not easily bothered.

"If they decide to stay, that's okay, because I have the keys." I pull them out of my pocket and shimmy them back and forth. Neither guy responds to the jingling, and Jess is forced to interfere. Without speaking, she takes the keychains from Marty's hands and puts them back on the spinning rack. Before he can protest, she kisses him, and he's hooked. He leans in to kiss her again, this time more aggressively, but she wiggles her fingers back and forth as if to say no, not here.

"Jess is right. Let's get out of here." Marty rushes out the door and Jess isn't far behind.

"Don't make me do that, Asher." I gesture towards the door, hoping he finds me humorous.

"Yeah, like that would be so bad." Asher blushes at his own comment, puts down the keychains, and strolls outside.

The remainder of the drive to Boise is quick. Jess and Marty make us breakfast for our very late dinner, and we all fall asleep in the living room. When I wake up in the morning, I can hear someone getting ready in the bathroom. Jess and Marty are gone, probably in their own room. Eventually, I stretch out my arms and decide to wake up. I stumble into the kitchen and start making a pot of coffee, knowing we could all benefit from caffeine. It's still early morning and the sun isn't up, but Jess is.

"Good morning," she whispers sweetly, floating out of the bathroom and into the kitchen. "I hope I didn't wake you up."

"No, you didn't. But I hope this doesn't mean you were planning to slip out without saying goodbye."

"It's not goodbye, Reagan—it's see you later. I'll meet up with you in LA. I won't miss our guys."

I wonder if she can tell by the way I'm looking at her that I know they aren't my guys, but it's kind of her to share them. I tell her I'm going to take a shower before *those guys* wake up. It feels good to have a moment alone, and by the time I return to the kitchen, both guys are awake, and the coffee is gone. Marty offers us breakfast, and I accept a piece of toast and peanut butter. It's almost 7:30, and we need to hit the road.

As we pile into the car, I can tell the mood is changing. Marty is probably wondering if he's making the right decision, and I'm sure Jess reassured him that he is. She waves to us as we leave, and I think about my mom waving goodbye to us just a day before. *It's the start of summer, of new adventure, not goodbye,* I think to myself, and wish Marty could hear.

Asher climbs into the back seat and instantly falls asleep. As we drive down the street, Marty keeps checking the rearview mirror to make sure he's the last one waving goodbye to Jess.

"Twelve more hours, and we're there," Marty mumbles.

"Yeah, only twelve more to go until we meet... what's his name again?"

"Phil. Great guy, you're going to love him. There's nothing to dislike. He runs his own business, he's a great musician, a nice guy, and super chill because of all the drugs." Marty chuckles and flashes me a mischievous grin. "He owns a pot shop in Denver, just to be clear."

"Ah, of course." I nod like that clears it all up for me.

I can tell Marty is sad but trying to push himself to be happy. He's probably excited to be doing this thing just for himself, to have time to enjoy his life, but is also scared about the future, and what this could mean for him and Jess. Or maybe I'm projecting.

"Do you think we can stop in Salt Lake? Jess was saying there are some cool record stores there. Maybe we could get her a few? What kind of music does she like?" I assume talking about her will help both of us pass the time.

"Oh, she likes it all. That's a really good idea."

He's silent for a moment, and I settle into the quiet until he's ready to talk again.

"Thanks, Reagan. For coming with. We're lucky to have you. This time will be different. And for the record I won't be mopey the whole trip. Can't let it cramp our style."

He shimmies his body towards the steering wheel like that is a sign of style. I laugh out loud and agree that he won't cramp our style, he's the most stylish one here. When our conversation slows again, I check my phone again, only to confirm that Oliver hasn't responded. I guess I "won," but it feels more like rejection. I put on a playlist so if Asher wakes up, he doesn't think we've just been sitting here in silence. Though Marty and I probably would've been okay with that, I know Asher wouldn't approve.

While the whole drive is twelve hours, we've decided to break it up into shifts so we can try to play a few shows along the way. Phil won't be able to get time off at the shop until later this week, so it makes sense for the guys to play a few shows. If we can book them, that is. As we drive, I notice the colors outside our window shifting from deep greens and blues to lighter shades. In a few days, the colors will become browns and oranges as we move from the Pacific Northwest to the dry desert of Los Angeles. The drive reminds me of when I was a kid, and my parents flew us to Arizona so we could go see the Grand Canyon and road trip back home. The canyon held colors I'd never seen before in nature—oranges and reddish browns, colors so unfamiliar to Washington. I'm startled when Marty pulls off into a gas station because my thoughts had inconsiderately consumed the passing time.

Asher slowly wakes up, realizing he's been asleep this whole time. He offers to go grab snacks and doesn't wait for us to say okay.

When Marty finishes filling up the car with gas, he jumps back in and doesn't waste any time. "So, what's going on with that?" He points towards the gas station, and then to me. I only assume he means between *us*. "Are we going to get down to the truth now that it's you and trusty old Marty?"

"Trusty old Marty. Pretty catchy. Maybe the name of your next solo album?"

"Asher was *so* right about you and your sass."

"What's Asher saying about me?" I gasp, skeptical that Asher's talking about me when I'm not around.

"He's your biggest fan."

"What? Shut up."

My insides blush, but I deny it. I know Marty's teasing, but it feels good to think that Asher could be talking to him about me. I wonder if his opinions changed based on what happened yesterday. Marty wouldn't know about that yet. I imagine if Asher had felt anything for me before yesterday, it has changed now, but it doesn't change my being here, and that part is confusing. He seems to still want me around.

"Fine then, trusty old Marty. Nothing is going on with that," I say, pointing towards the gas station. "But I don't get it. What am I doing here? You guys don't need me."

"Reagan. You're our manager—you manage the band. Duh. The fact that you don't understand your job description is a bit unsettling though." He jokes like he may get away with avoiding this conversation, but I'm determined to get a response from someone.

"Yeah, except I have no experience and no idea what I'm doing. I hardly know Asher, and I know you even less."

He shifts in his seat and shrugs his shoulders before beginning. "Well truthfully, I don't know why Asher decided to bring you along, but I can say with confidence that I'm glad he did. You keep him grounded, and excited. He needs both. And the three of us need help being better this time. I mean, we could do it, but it's better to have you here. And I imagine you think it's better to be here than somewhere else."

I wonder if Asher told him about Oliver, my somewhere else, but I trust him to keep my secret.

"Reagan, I think you give him confidence, and he trusts you too. Which, dare I say, gives you some much needed confidence too."

It stings a little to know he doesn't think I'm confident.

He looks at me seriously. "Do you want to talk about what happened yesterday? At the rest stop?"

I didn't realize it was so obvious to everyone that I wasn't okay, but I didn't want to talk about it anymore. Luckily, I don't have time to explain.

"Maybe another time then." Marty smiles. "Here comes our lead singer."

Asher dances into the parking lot and starts shouting at us. We can't hear him, so Marty opens the car door. Asher is shouting and pointing to the gas station speakers.

"It's 'Come On Eileen'. It's a classic!"

Ten

There comes a point in every road trip when the group runs out of music, leaving only the radio or the thoughts in your own head. Both can be a little scary, so it's at this point that we scoured the car for a change of ear scenery. We locate five CDs in the back seat pockets of Mrs. Blair's van. They're labeled with the same blue marker and identical penmanship. Asher's face blushes when we find them, and he's adamant one of his brothers must have made them. I pick the one titled *90's Hits*, but it's vetoed because it has, and I quote, "too much Britney Spears."

We make it to Salt Lake for lunch and visit four record shops so Marty can get Jess those records. It's at the third shop that I feel a sense of unease run over me. In between obsessing over Oliver, driving, and trying to play it cool, I haven't had the time to learn how to manage a band.

"I'm going to sit this one out, guys, see if I can get some work done."

Both boys look at me like I just told them I might grow a second head, but don't argue. They wave as they walk into the next shop, realizing the work I'll be doing is for them.

I'm not sure where to begin, but I assume finding a venue to play at isn't a bad place to start. I settle down on a bench coated in sunshine situated across the street. The sun feels warm against my body, but when I exhale, I can see my breath. It's another reminder of passing time, as summer becomes closely acquainted with fall.

I open my Instagram and start searching for venues in the Explore tab. When I find one that looks cool and has a good following, I DM them. I reach out to a few venues in Salt Lake and a few more in Colorado, but at some point I've stopped paying attention to what I'm doing as I find myself thinking about Oliver.

I flip back to his texts. It feels good to read what Asher wrote, and I do like winning, but I can't stop there. I stumble into our earlier text messages.

There are several messages that say something along the lines of: *Please can you call me? I think we just need to talk.* Because if we talked, I could make it make sense.

Then one that says, with a fake confidence: *You know what, this is really good for me. Really. You were holding me back. So best of luck. With her. She's a nightmare too, you'll see.* I cringe at the thought that she was my best friend, but I read on.

Another says: *Despite everything, I'm glad I met you. You made my life better. So, thank you for being a part of my life. Although briefly.* I recognize that one's a little dramatic.

And finally, too many to count saying: *I still love you.*

Each message left without a reply. Until the one a few days ago. I wonder if I misplayed my hand, and suddenly feel the urge to go home.

I don't dwell on too long, because my phone lights up with a number I don't recognize.

"Uh, hi," he says when I answer, his voice deep and unrecognizable. "This is James from the Rock. Did you still want to play a gig tonight?"

My mind is racing—the Rock? The Rock. One of the venues I messaged.

"Hello? Is this Reagan?"

"Hi. Yes. Sorry." I realize I'm too excited and try to settle into a response that is a little less desperate. "Yeah, we'd be down."

"Six p.m. tonight work? Dinner set?"

I didn't know what a dinner set means but figure the guys—or Google—will.

"Yes. Yeah, we'll be there."

"Make it acoustic," he says, and then quickly hangs up, like that is an appropriate way to say goodbye.

I don't mind the abrupt end to the conversation. I'm doing it. Managing. Booking gigs. I quickly Google the venue and confirm that the Rock is a real place. I get up to dance around and catch Asher's eyes through the record store window. I send him a big thumbs up. Maybe he was right about me.

He coolly strolls outside. "What's all this about?" he prods while miming my bad dancing.

"Guess who has the best damn manager in the world?"

"Harry Styles? Beyoncé? The Rolling Stones?"

"Uh, no. Obviously it's *you*." I shout. "Tonight, half of the band formerly known as Umbrella takes on *Salt Lake City*."

"Really?" Marty cries before I can see him. He's exiting the store with two more bags of records in hand.

"Yes, tonight you're playing *the Rock*." I'm practically yelling.

They look at me like they have no idea what that means.

"It's a venue in town. Can you at least *pretend* to be excited?"

Asher shrugs his shoulders like he can't be convinced, but Marty is beaming. I write off Asher's lack of enthusiasm as teasing.

"It's an acoustic set. You can do that, right?"

"Of course we can. That's what I did in Bellingham, my sweet, innocent Reagan Wilde."

I look at Asher and hope he reads the look as me saying, *I've had enough*. He smiles, and my annoyance melts.

"Maybe we can go over a little early to get set up and play through a few songs? Did they say?" Asher says.

"I'll call them back." I light up knowing I can do this thing. Looking at my phone, I see it is already 4:30. "Maybe just head over and I'll text you in case there are any issues, but let's just plan to get you in there and practicing. Ask for forgiveness sort of thing. In the meantime, I'll find us a place to crash tonight."

"See. This is why we need you. You are the brains we need to be creative geniuses."

Asher picks me up and spins me around in his first display of happiness. I feel butterflies start to fly around my body and ask them to get back into place. He sets me down and I try to ignore the flutter as he looks at me, grinning, like he knows what he's doing.

Marty breaks the tension. "You really *are* the best. I told you so."

"I think *I* actually told you *both* so," Asher chimes in.

Before I can argue with either of them, they head off for the venue. I find my place back on my lucky bench and start searching for a cheap place to crash tonight. I book a modest Salt Lake City hostel with a private room and two beds just a few blocks away. When I get there, the lady at the counter acts like she's been waiting all day for me. Her hair is a white blonde, but her face is tanned with freckles.

"Glad you found us okay. You're just here for the night?"

"I think so."

She looks at me like I need to be sure.

"Yeah, just the night."

"Your room is up through those stairs." She points to a staircase across from the desk. I can see she's wearing a sparkling wedding band, but she looks too young to be married.

I nod gratefully and turn toward the stairs, taking them two at a time. Shuffling into the room, the beds look small, but can fit two broke musicians, no problem. I claim my bed near the window and let my head rest against its pillow.

I'm there for a moment before I get a text from Asher.

Hey, we got to play through a few songs and do a soundcheck. Looking good, I am anyway. We sound pretty good too.

I smile and send him back the emoji attempting to roll its eyes. Checking the time, I quickly shower. I take a few minutes to pick out an outfit. I have only my small bag, but I bought a new shirt while we were out today. It's a gray and black tie-dyed baseball T-shirt with a slit down the center. I don't recognize this Reagan Wilde when I look in the mirror. I scrunch my hair, hoping it will curl, and call a Lyft.

***

The Rock is noticeably different from the Barrel Wheel. It has large circle tables placed thoughtfully in a semi-circle around the stage. They serve dinner under bright lights. The patrons are a mix of young and old, but they all looked excited to be there. I think about angry Santa and how he never turned away from the TV. I rush to find someone who works here so I can ask him where the guys are. I want to see them before they go on stage. The employee behind the bar is wearing a gray polo and an apron with cursive blue writing that says *The Rock*. He also has a bowl cut. He's no Tina.

"Hi, excuse me."

The non-Tina looks at me like I'm already wasting his time.

"I'm here with the band."

"Great?"

There's no recognition on his face. It's clear this is not as big of a deal to him as it is for me, but before I bother to explain, I hear Marty shout at me. The patrons give him a dirty look, and I want to ask if they realize they came to a show. Instead, I rush over to Marty.

"Great attitudes here tonight."

"What's that?" Marty shouts.

It's loud in here, and he's clearly excited. I realize he hasn't noticed the loud patrons or angry bartenders and I decide not to ruin his mood.

"Oh nothing, nothing. You look great."

He's changed into a button down, and I'm convinced he's never had a bad boy bone in his body.

"Where's Asher?"

"He's in the back. Doing lead singer warm up stuff," Marty says while rolling out the rest of his gear. Even Marty seems too busy for me.

"I'm woefully unaware of that singer stuff, but should probably go acquaint myself. Good luck, Marty."

And without another word, I slip back to find Asher. He's sitting on a crate of boxes behind the curtains and has his headphones on. It looks like he's sing-talking to himself. I tap him on the shoulder, and he spins around to greet me.

"We really should stop meeting like this." Asher says with a smile that stretches across his face.

"If we did that, then some would argue I'm not doing my job." I shoot back with a wink.

"Well, we can't have that."

He runs his hand through his hair, and for a moment I think he can tell I'm watching him. I scramble to change the subject.

"So how do you think middle school Asher and Reagan would feel about today? Do you think they would've known we'd end up here?"

"Ha. They would. This is our destiny."

"You really think so?"

I want him to say yes, but he doesn't have to. His eyes are shining in a way that I recognize—a way that reminds me of how Oliver used to look at me.

"Anyway, here's the room key."

"Keep it. We're going back together, right?" he asks, like he needs to ask.

"Fine. If you're sure, I'll hold onto it. I'm starting to think I'm basically your purse."

"You're more than that." His lips curl upward ever so slightly.

I stumble over my words. "Well, I better get out of your way. Can't keep the dinner crowd waiting."

"Oh, you're so right. How will they ignore us if we aren't on stage??"

"Don't think you get to be picky now. Play a few shows, maybe win that showcase, and then we'll talk."

"We'll make you proud, don't you worry. At the showcase, and tonight."

And with that, Asher Blair rushes on stage with a grin I haven't seen since we were twelve and he was winning the neighborhood soccer game. I decide to stay backstage tonight, admiring the guys as they play like a real band, not one we assembled a few days before. Over the set, I watch as the crowd moves from eating to singing along to full on dancing by the end. For a dinner show, most people pay more attention to the music than their meal.

Afterwards, while the guys pack up, a few people saunter over to them. I try not to take notice of any pretty girls. Instead, I stroll over to the bar, and try to find James. There's a guy furiously texting on his phone. He doesn't look up when I walk over.

"Hi are you James?" I ask, after standing their awkwardly for a few minutes.

"Yeah." He turns to look at me, then back to his phone. "And you must be Reagan."

Before I can confirm or deny who I am, he continues. "The guys were good tonight. Better than I would've thought."

"Uh, thanks." I say, taking the half compliment.

"They can play again if you let me know in advance. You're lucky my band tonight canceled last minute, otherwise I'd never have responded to your message. Oh, and next time, message me from the band account." He peppers in good advice despite his rude tone. "Anyway, the guys get a free entrée and drink." He slides some paper coupons across the counter, throws up a peace sign, and walks away.

"Okay bye, great chat," I grumble under my breath.

He was right about a few things. We need social media accounts, and I need to be more proactive. I make a mental note to do both, grab the coupons James left on the bar top, and rush over to the guys.

Asher is talking to a group of people when I walk over. I notice one of which is a brunette in a full-length dress. Her hair is cut short and falls just below her ears. She's laughing hard at everything he says, and I try not to take it personally. I make another mental note to stop any feelings I was starting to have for Asher.

"Reagan." Marty cheered. "What did you think?"

"You two crushed it. I mean, as much as one can crush acoustic covers at six p.m."

"We're getting the magic back," Asher chimes in. I look up to find him standing next to Marty and feel relieved when I notice the girl is gone.

"Time to celebrate." I say.

We drink, we eat, we celebrate. Marty calls Phil to let him know we are a few days out. He calls Jess to let her know we miss her. Asher and I talk like there's nothing going on between us, and maybe there isn't. When we get to the room, we fall asleep right away, Asher and Marty in one bed, and me in another.

***

We say goodbye to Salt Lake early in the morning and make our way to Colorado. We plan to stop in Grand Junction and pull off for dinner when we see a sign for all-you-can-eat fish and chips.

"I can't believe I've gone all my life without this." Marty is practically jumping up and down from the moment he gets out of the car.

"I can't believe this is a thing that exists," I say in disgust. I elect to order a hamburger and opt out of the all-you-can-eat situation.

"Okay, but now that you know it exists, can you imagine your life without it?"

Asher is on his second plate of all-you-can-eat. Some local country band is up playing covers of Big & Rich songs. He asks if we can play here next, and I hope he's joking. Otherwise, we have different visions of our future. He heads back to the buffet, and I stick out my tongue like I may vomit, but chuckle as he walks away. I'm just about to start mocking him with Marty when I notice he's hardly touched his all-you-can-eat plate.

"Seems like now it's time to talk to trusty ol' Reagan Wilde." I use a country twang to describe myself, then flip out of character. "What's going on, Marty? Is it Jess?"

"Not everything is about love, Reagan Wilde." He's serious, and I wonder if I've overstepped. He catches his tone quickly. "I'm sorry. I do miss her. I'm just starting to wonder if this is a good idea."

"What? The band? The shows? Are you kidding?"

I thought I was doing a good job, but if Marty doesn't, it will crush me.

"Last night was good, but what if we aren't good enough for the showcase and this ends the same way it did last time? Broke, disappointed, and not speaking for years. Would you be okay with that?"

"I mean, no, I wouldn't, but I don't think it would get that bad. I mean, we're all friends. We'll figure it out together."

"Yeah, you'd think that. I did too. But last time, things didn't exactly go that way. Asher can be... difficult."

"It was Asher's fault you broke up?"

"Woo, I take it back. Forget it."

"What? No, that's not fair. What are you talking about?"

"Look, you're like his number one fan, and he's yours. I don't want to burst that bubble. Or get on the bad side with either of you."

"Marty, what are you talking about? We wouldn't put you on any side. Seriously? Please tell me what's going on."

"I'm sorry. I'm just stressed. I want this to go well, but my boss called me and told me he needs to know if I'm quitting, I can't just take the time off without pay anymore because it's going to be a few weeks. And of course, Asher thinks I should because he thinks this time, we're going somewhere, and it's better if I'm dedicated to the band. But he doesn't get what it's like to quit your job."

"I think he's quit jobs before, Marty. That's not fair. Is it Jess?"

"No, Jess gets it. She thinks I should do it. She thinks maybe we'll move anyway, so I may as well take this chance."

"Well, there you go. You have everyone's support, so what's the issue?"

"I'm worried, Reag. I'm worried about Asher and what happens to him after this. And I'm worried about what Jerome will think when he sees us all together. I mean he's going to see us together somehow with the way everyone's freaking connected on this freaking planet thanks to freaking Mark Zuckerberg."

"Wait, Marty you're all over the place. Who is Jerome?"

"Ha! Classic. He didn't tell you." Marty breathes out heavily.

"Asher?" I search the room to find him talking to two older ladies at the salad bar. They are looking at him with adoration. He is easy to adore. "I don't know that he really tells me all that much."

"Let's be real. He tells you more than he tells most. But he keeps a lot of the bad stuff to himself, so you don't see it until it's too late."

My heart rate accelerates, and my palms start sweating. It's like that when you don't expect bad news. "You're talking in riddles, Marty, and it's scaring me."

"He's different with you. He really seems to care about you, which is great, I'm not taking that away. I just think he's really focused on the band, and every time we move forward, he gets more and more focused. The last time he was focused, he hurt a lot of people, and he really hurt one of our friends."

"Jerome?" I ask, hoping to put together the puzzle pieces.

"Yes, Jerome. And Jerome won't be part of it this time. I guess I'm just worried about how he's going to react if we do this without him."

"Can't we do this *with* him?"

"Not likely. Asher and him? They don't really talk anymore."

Before I can figure out why, Asher strolls back to our table, and we put our happy faces back on.

Eleven

I wake up in a motel room with a groggy body and hair that smells like regret. I push myself to remember that we found a Super 8 in Grand Junction to stay the night after Asher suggested we move from bottomless fried fish to bottomless beers. After my conversation with Marty, neither of us turned that down. To save some cash, we got a room with a pull-out couch and a twin-sized bed. Asher and Marty are spooning on the bed while Marty clutches most of the ratty motel blanket.

Today, we finally meet Phil, and in true rock star fashion have dinner plans at his parents' house at 6:30. They've graciously invited us to stay the night, and I plan to be professional, which means arriving on time. We agree to meet Phil at his shop around four, and then check out downtown Denver until dinner, so we don't need to leave until noon, which lines up perfectly with checkout time. In Denver, the guys can practice at Phil's parents, and I hope they'll be able to play some shows in Denver, as we plan to stay in town for at least a few days to maybe a week. We'll see how long Phil's parents can tolerate us. We still have a few weeks until the show, and the more time we can stay in Denver, the more time the guys have with a dedicated practice space, and a guaranteed bed.

I've been at this "manager" thing for a little over a week now and we've already had one successful show. I have no idea how to measure my success in this role, but that seems like a pretty good start. I haven't heard back from the other venues I messaged, so maybe the Salt Lake show was just beginner's luck. I need to take James's advice and create a social media presence, then reach out to venues beyond Denver so we can plan the rest of the trip.

I hope to sneak out of the room so I can get some planning done. I look over to the guys and find Marty cozied up against Asher with only his feet covered by the blanket because Asher's managed to pull it all off him. I wonder what Marty meant when he said Asher could be difficult. Is this a sign? Is it worse than this? Stealing all the covers says a lot about a person's subconscious. Plus, everyone seems to have some opinion on Asher Blair. From the mothers in the cul-de-sac to one of his best friends, they all see signs that I don't. That has to mean something, but it's hard to predict what. I need concrete proof.

On the counter next to the TV sits Asher's phone. It's lighting up and buzzing. I think about maybe looking to see who it is, but I know that would be wrong. Then it buzzes again. Three times. Four. Now it's taunting me.

Asher and Marty are cozied up on the bed, unaware of the buzzing. I get a sense that I can learn a lot about someone from four buzzes, and I don't think about the complications, or the possible invasion of privacy. A simple check to see if anything is out of character could help me determine if I should be worried. I'm sure the Asher Blair I know isn't like the Asher Blair they know. And wouldn't I sleep better with a little peace of mind? I sit up and try to make some noise to see if either of them wakes up. When neither moves, I gently tiptoe across the room.

As I pick up the phone, I notice the buzz isn't from just one person. First, he has an ESPN update, which throws me, as I can't imagine Asher caring about sports. But I guess I'm wrong. The second buzz is from one of his brothers—a group text with their grandma. Maybe he isn't the only Blair who cares about his grandma, and he's ignoring her while using her car. That could be a bad side of Asher, but maybe I'm reaching. The third and fourth are from someone named Kitty. I can only see the first part of the texts on his home screen. I read the first text quickly. It feels like I'm being punched in the chest.

I miss you. Even though we are...

Even though we are, what?

Even though we are friends?

Even though we aren't together anymore?

Even though I'm way older than you?

Even though it's forbidden?

Even though you're in love with someone else?

Did I hope it was the last one? Maybe a little, but I doubt it was true.

At some point, Asher started talking to Kitty, or maybe he was all along, and he never told me a single thing about her. It seems like if this Kitty character is sending messages like this to him, it would have come up in one of our conversations. Somewhere between my gushing over Marty and Jess, and having my heart broken. Somewhere between the hours on the road, and the hours drinking and talking together.

"Ooooh, tell me I'm not dead."

A groan escapes from one of the spooning men, and it startles me. I drop the phone directly onto the desk, leaving evidence behind that I'm not in bed.

"Loud noises. Why must you torture me? Don't you know they could kill a man?" Asher rolls over and our eyes lock. His eyes stay on me for an extra second, and then he sees the phone resting face up on the table. I expect to be called out right there. He'll think I'm crazy, and he'll tell me to go home. And the worst part is I'll never learn about Kitty. But I still have an ounce of beginner's luck.

"Well, aren't you an early riser? Could you toss me my phone? But do it gently. I think if anything touches my body too hard, I'll break. Maybe you can just walk it over and gently place it into my hand with the grace of a cloud?"

He hasn't put it together.

"Wow, you are a diva." I take a deep breath and try to steady my hands from shaking.

Play it cool, Reagan. He doesn't have to know.

"So, what are you thinking for breakfast?"

He's oblivious. And I'm...

Even though we are...

Not good for each other.

Destined to be together.

Living in different cities.

I'm spiraling.

"Hey, I'm talking to you."

"Oh sorry, I'm in the fog."

The fog became a phrase we use to describe the suffering that comes with a hangover.

"Sounds like we need a coffee."

"I don't know if he's going to make it to coffee." I point toward Marty, who hasn't stirred, even though our voices are growing louder.

"He'll be fine with breakfast in bed. Should we go get something?"

I don't respond right away. I'm still calculating what Kitty means to Asher, and where I fit in.

"Hm, you *are* really in a fog today, my friend."

Friend. I'm a friend.

"Yeah, sure coffee sounds good. But talking to James made me realize I need to do some more work. Proactively. So, I should probably go do that, and it's better if I do it alone so I can really focus. I can make a few calls, pick up the coffee, and bring something back in an hour or so?"

"I don't know if I can make it an hour." He's smiling at me, but his eyes keep darting back to his phone. I doubt he's looking at that ESPN update.

"You should shower and pack while I'm gone. That way we can hit the road when I get back."

"Wow, the real rock star treatment. Sure, Mrs. Manager, that'd be great. But this time, remember, no gluten for breakfast.."

"I forgot you're on a no inflammation diet. Don't worry, my star performer, I'll bring back peeled grapefruit and black coffee for the group."

"You really know how to treat a guy."

I slip into the bathroom without a response. Maybe my mother was right. This whole thing is about Asher. I've jumped onto the next best thing. Maybe Jocelyn was right, too, and guys don't like me like that. Oliver was a fluke, and I'm imagining it with Asher.

Maybe the tour is stupid, and I would've been better off staying at home, finding a job, or going back to Oliver. But then I remind myself, it doesn't have to be about him. I'm learning. I'm growing. I love music, and I love trying to figure this whole thing out. And if I can move past the hurt with Asher, then we can move to something amazing together. I won't allow myself to break at the expense of someone else's love story.

When I get out of the bathroom, Asher's back in bed fast asleep. I grab my jacket and walk out the door. Out on the street, I'm determined not to think about this morning. The morning is bright, the air is crisp, and I wish I'd brought a beanie to cover my ears.

Grand Junction is not a big enough town to have many choices for coffee. I quickly search Yelp and find a coffee shop only a few blocks away. Charging inside, I catch the eye of a barista who chooses not to respond with a smile. He's wearing an orange bolero hat, a patterned silk shirt, and a thick gold chain. He can't be over the age of eighteen but has better fashion sense than most of the city of Seattle. As I take in the remainder of the outfit, I manage to trip over the carpet in front of the counter. He appears to be offended.

"Oops, I'm so sorry about that."

"It's fine." he snaps back. I realize I shouldn't apologize for tripping, but we're past that now.

"Thanks. Uh, could I do a coffee now and then order more food and drinks in a few minutes? I have a little bit of work to do but need to take some food home to feed my band."

Feed my band? Have I kidnapped them? Are they a pet?

"Okay, what do you want?" he says.

"Uh, just a drip coffee."

"Americano, okay? We don't do drip."

I strain to smile but remember my politeness. "Sure, yeah, coffee is coffee."

I see him shutter. "It's Ethiopian. Roasted yesterday."

"Great." I smirk and walk away, thinking coldness may work better for us both.

"Did you say band?"

Coldness works. I spin around, ready to show how hip I am to bolero boy. "I certainly did."

"Cool. You should check out the artist wall."

"Artist wall?"

Two customers walk in, each wearing more jewelry on their faces than I own in my whole wardrobe. He lights up when he sees them coming and wordlessly points me in the direction of a chalkboard in the back of the shop.

I stroll over and start reading articles about local bands, shows, and all things I wish I'd known about a day earlier so we could have played while we were here. If only I had more time to plan, then Asher would see what a great manager I could be. I shake my head. *Stop thinking about him. Start thinking about the band—your band. That's what comes next.*

And then I see it. A show in Denver in two days. I write it down, and then I write down all the local bands on the board and start to research where they're playing. Bolero boy yells at me to grab my coffee. I ignore his tone as I grab the cup and keep researching. There are thirty-five venues across Denver and LA, all with ties to the local artists on this wall. I add a few in Albuquerque and Phoenix in case we decide to expand the tour.

Next, I start on the social media. Umbrella is obviously out of the question. We hadn't discussed a name, so I panic and go with the one thing that both Jess and I resonated with: My Guys. My Guys on Instagram, on Facebook, and on Twitter. I upload the videos and the photos I have from the trip with messages about following us for our next gig. I type and retype, trying to think of something that may appeal to bolero boy.

My phone buzzes and breaks the momentum. It's the man himself, the main guy. I feel nothing. That's a good sign. I don't need something to happen between Asher and me. Clearly, I was confused. I was reading into a connection and that put our relationship at risk. But now we can settle on friends. We work together. We are still creating something together, and that is meaningful. When I've almost convinced myself, I read his text:

Feed me? Please. I'm useless without carbs and caffeine.

I finish up the last post and decide to call it a morning. I stroll up to bolero boy with a newfound confidence. "Any chance you have a grapefruit?"

"What?" he utters, shocked and exhibiting more emotion than I knew he was capable of.

"Never mind. Can I just have three more Americanos and three of those fancy croissant things?"

"They're called Cronuts." He rolls his eyes, and I realize I'll never be eighteen-year-old hip.

"You know what? I'll just have three muffins."

"Makes sense."

"Okay, now wha—" I feel the phone in my purse start buzzing and let the buzz save that barista, and maybe me, from myself. "You know what? Never mind." I answer the call without checking the number. "Hi," I say abruptly. I grab all three coffees with my two hands, a talent that deserves more respect than the huff and puff of barista bolero boy.

"Uh, yeah hi, maybe I have the wrong number. Is this... well, I'm calling to get in touch with a Reagan? She left me a voicemail about her band playing at our venue in Denver. Well, I just had a cancellation for a gig tonight and I wanted to see if we could schedule you or her in."

I quickly adjust my tone. "Yeah, hi, this is she." *Less professional Reagan, less professional.* "Yeah, I left you the voicemail. My band—well, the band I manage—they'd love to play. What time, and where?"

"Oh, cool. Larimer Lounge. Get here at like 6:30 for sound check. Can they play at 9:30?"

"9:30?" I notice myself leaning on the word thirty like it's a national treasure I'm hoping to find. It isn't the midnight shift, and it isn't the dinnertime show. It's practically the main event. "Yeah, that would be perfect. The guys will be thrilled."

"Is that what they're called? The Guys?" He chuckles.

"Actually, it's My Guys," I say, trying it out for the first time.

"Alright, we'll see you at 6:30."

"You didn't mention your name. What is it?"

After James, I'm determined to get on better terms with the bookers up front. James may have been grumpy, but he had some good advice.

"But of course – I'm Nick. Pleasure to meet you, or I guess to meet you in person tonight."

"Pleasure's all mine, can't wait." Was I flirting? Maybe a little.

"Hm, that could be true. The pleasure *could* be yours." He was definitely flirting. "I'm booking a few shows for the rest of the month. If your guys do okay, we could schedule a few more shows."

"Well, if you have anything going on this week, we'd be interested. We're only in town for a week or two."

"Really? Where are you heading next?"

"Uh, maybe straight to LA, or Phoenix. It's not totally decided."

"Hm, well if the guys are any good, I know a few more folks in the Phoenix area and LA that may be able to help book you some gigs."

"You'd do that? Really?"

"Well, you sound cute, so why not? But only if they're good. I figure I can embarrass *myself* with a bad band, but not my buddies."

I blush at the mention of sounding cute. I try not to let that show through the phone. "They're good. You'll see for yourself."

"Well, if you're so confident then I'm confident. Sounds like you're making my job easy so maybe we'll have time for a drink tonight?"

"Tonight?"

"At the show... Won't I see you there?"

This guy really *was* booking his night blind.

"Well, uh..."

Oliver, Asher, Oliver, Asher.

"Maybe not then."

Neither are interested, remember? That's why we're feeling sorry for ourselves.

"No, I'll be there. So yeah, let's have a drink. It never hurt anyone. Well, wow, I guess that's not true..."

"Ha, you are a trip. I'll be the guy behind the bar. See you then, Reagan Wilde."

And with that, the mysterious Nick hangs up before I have a chance to say any other stupid things out loud. I feel another buzz and quickly looked down to see that another thirty people have followed and liked the videos on the band account. Chalk it up to beginner's luck.

Twelve

The drink would be a good thing. It would allow me to stop obsessing over how I felt about Asher and Oliver. I should never have checked Asher's phone, but maybe that was a good thing too. I can admit I was feeling something for Asher, but more importantly, it isn't going anywhere. Now, I *had* feelings for him. Nick would be a single drink—a one-night thing—and really, it was just meeting people in the industry. Everything is as it should be. And the guys will be thrilled.

I climb the steps to our room, repeating again and again that it will be okay, and then I fling the door wide open—a grand gesture to help me climb out of my head. "Lucy, I'm home."

I hear a shriek and stumble inside.

"By the beard of the KFC man. What are you doing? Some of us are *dying* in here. And terrifying the living alcohol shit out of us doesn't help *anyone*," a voice hisses.

"Well, good morning, Marty. Sounds like you're still feeling the effects of the gallons of beer you drank far too much of last night. Here, have a muffin." I take one out of the bag and toss it in the direction of blankets and pillows, assuming he must be under there somewhere.

"God bless you; I never give you enough credit." He reaches from under the covers to catch the muffin, and then tosses the blankets off his body.

"Well, that's high praise. What's gotten into you?"

"I think Asher's rubbing off on me..."

"Where is he anyway?"

He points towards the closed bathroom door, and mumbles, "Shower," with his mouth still full of muffin from that first bite.

"Still? He was headed there when I left. What a diva."

"I think he had a phone call; he took one outside for like forty-five minutes, maybe an hour. I have no concept of time. I could really benefit from some more ZZ's."

He chuckles, like trying out the word "ZZ" was new for him and felt foreign in his mouth.

I'm thinking about Kitty again and can't help but wonder if that's who he was talking to. Maybe it was his grandma, his mother, or a landlord. It could be anyone, for all I knew. Whoever it was, it doesn't matter to coffee shop Reagan, so I need to move on.

"Well, I have some news."

"News? Oh no." Marty gulps down the rest of his muffin in anticipation.

"No, no, it's good news."

And so, I tell Marty all about my morning.

"Hell, yes. You really are the best. We're doing the damn thing!" Marty shouts while attempting to work up the energy to high five me before warning that he may blow.

Asher hears us cheering, and flings open the bathroom door with only a towel wrapped around his body and another around his head. He finds the bag of muffins and rips into it with little emotion. He doesn't seem like the same person I left here, and I wonder if he knows about the phone.

"Two towels. Such class, my man," Marty chuckles.

Asher takes a bite of muffin, unfazed by Marty's comments, and points in my direction. "What's she done now?"

"She's been working on social media all morning; can you believe that? We are officially live on all the tweet, like, share pages, my man. That's not even the best part—she even got us a show in Denver tonight."

Marty's building me up, and I feel like I could burst.

"Well, look at you. I knew I picked you for a reason."

Asher's smile melts my heart, and I try to quickly rebuild a wall between us. "I also have a date." It comes pouring out of me like I have no control of the words.

Marty practically chokes on air as he quickly turns to survey Asher's reaction. It makes me feel like maybe they've talked about me, but I can't assume that anymore. Not when there's at least one Kitty out there.

"Cool..." Marty trails off. When no one says anything, he adds, "Well, I'm going to go shower now." He charges towards the bathroom without looking either of us in the eyes.

"Mm, yeah, probably a good idea. We need to leave in—" I check my watch, "—twenty?"

Asher hasn't moved or responded. I've gone back to staring at my phone, but I'm just opening and closing the same apps, waiting for him to say something. And then he does.

"Is it Oliver?"

I gasp, and hope that Marty can't hear. I don't know why, but it's embarrassing. "No, of course it isn't Oliver," I whisper, then quieter, "Why would it be Oliver?"

"Well, why would it be anyone else?"

"I got asked out. Is that so hard to believe?"

There's a big pause this time.

"I'm not saying that. It's not about you—"

"How is this not about me? And why are you trying to fight me on this?"

"Reagan, can you just stop? I'm not fighting you on this. I'm just—"

"It really seems like you're trying to fight me on this. Someone who wasn't trying to fight me would probably say something like, 'Cool.' or 'Congrats, good for you, Reagan. Get back out there.'"

"Stop interrupting me." He breathes out heavily, and I can tell he's frustrated. A new side of Asher Blair. "Can you just tell me how you plan to go on a date? How did you meet this guy? Where did you even meet him?"

He's peppering me with questions like a protective older brother. It's so not what I expected, and it makes me mad. Why did he get to know every detail of my personal life when he hadn't told me any about his.

"He'll be at the venue. He booked the show," The words slip out, and I'm hoping that'll be the end of it, but I quickly see something change in his eyes.

"Are you kidding me, Reagan? *Seriously*? You're sleeping with the guy who got us this show? How cool of you. Do they even want us to play or do they just want to get in your pants?"

"Woah, Asher? I didn't say anything about *sleeping* with anyone. I booked us a show, the guy thought I was funny, he asked if I wanted to get a drink. It may not even really be a date, okay? Just a drink."

"I don't get it. Honestly, tell me—is this, like, just a game to you? Because this is *my* life, this is *my* dream, and you're here because I thought it was important to you too. But maybe you just want to party until you get even with a guy who doesn't even care about you anymore."

We catch each other's eyes, and his are filled with a look of disgust. It's a quick moment, then he turns around to face the window. I feel all alone.

I manage to get out, "I didn't think it would matter."

"Well, it matters a lot. You're associated with us, and this looks like I'm getting gigs because my manager is sleeping around. That's disgusting and it makes not only *you* look bad, but Marty and me too. I don't even think I can look at you right now." He's shaking his head back and forth in disapproval, but I catch a glimpse of sadness in his eyes. "Can you just leave so I can finish getting ready?"

"Asher, come on. I wasn't trying to hurt you." My eyes feel heavy, but I don't want to make him feel uncomfortable.

"Yeah, I wouldn't say I'm hurt. Clearly, this isn't what I thought it was. Maybe this wasn't a good idea."

"What does that even mean? I did a lot of other things right today. This is still a good idea." I feel panic wrap around me like a scarf that's too warm for the weather.

"This isn't just a party, okay? This is important."

I feel the sadness and regret inside of me start to churn and move closer towards anger. Before I know it, I'm mad and I'm letting him know. "I told you; I understand that. I never said I think it's a party, but like..." I take a deep breath and feel a rage bubbling up inside that I don't recognize. "Like,

I'm so sorry I must be confused with the constant binge drinking every night, the lack of a plans except for the one I piece together when you give me just a drop of information, or free rein. This is your second shot? I'm sorry, but at what? Having me do all this grunt work so you can pretend to be important?"

"Fuck you, Reagan."

"Right back at you, Asher. I'll give you some privacy."

I don't want to give him a chance to say anything else, so I storm out of the room. I also don't have anywhere else to go, so I collapse on the carpeted floor across from our door and fall apart.

I expect Asher to rush out, to tell me he's sorry, like Oliver did whenever we had a messy fight, but when he doesn't, I implode. The connection I'm building with Asher, romantic or otherwise, feels cheap. But relationships like this shouldn't implode overnight because someone makes one bad decision. And going on a date *isn't* a bad decision. I can see why Asher would be nervous about those boundaries with the bookers, but I would never embarrass them or ruin relationships. I thought he knew that part of me, but this is proving we don't know each other well enough. I burst into tears just in time for Asher to abruptly open the front door. I try to collect my emotions as quickly as possible, like gathering Easter eggs in a basket, but it doesn't matter because it's clear I'm not okay, and he is. I wipe tears out of my eyes, hoping he hasn't noticed. My face feels hot, and I'm sure it's bright red. The thought embarrasses me more, and I can feel it growing redder.

He has his jacket and sunglasses on, his bag is packed and next to the door. Mine is there, too, and I assume he collected it. He brushes past me, lifting the bag over my head, while refusing to look at me. He leaves the door open long enough that I can slide my foot in before it shuts.

"Marty texted me and said he'll be done in five minutes," he says without looking at me. From down the hallway, he hollers, "I'll be downstairs."

"Okay," I respond. I let the door close and plan to slink in when Marty comes out.

Asher's at the end of the hallway, and then spins around. "Do you remember the year of the baseball tournament?"

"What?" I'm not sure if he's talking to me, but who else could he be talking to?

"The year of the baseball tournament. It was the year before the summer I spent at my grandparents'. We had the neighborhood baseball tournament. One of the tall fourth graders was pitching and was shockingly good."

"Kyle Peters."

"Yeah sure, whatever. Well, the loud, pudgy neighbor with the glasses—"

"Bryan Wilcox."

"Him—he was up to hit. He was right in front of me. He goes up to hit, and he hits it, and wow, it's a home run. It's going, going, gone. He's running the bases and we're all cheering. And then we hear a *smash*. We're freaking out. We look over, and it came from that mean neighbor's yard—don't tell me his name. The mean guy who had all the cars parked out front.

Mr. Richards, I think, but I don't say it out loud.

"Well, as you likely recall, our friend Bryan smashed out one of the windows of the trucks in the yard, and everyone is panicking. Kyle's freaking out, Bryan's freaking out, and I'm freaking out because I'm next in line, holding the bat, and I know all the adult neighbors already hate me. So, we start to scramble. People are running everywhere, but what I remember next is that you're there. You—twelve-year-old you—are standing there trying to convince us that we need to go talk to the mean old car hoarder of a neighbor and explain what happened. You're begging us to do it, and I think you might cry. No one wants to do it, but you're smart, and you know they'll figure out it was the kids who smashed the window. You want to get ahead of it. No one wants to listen to you, but I'm dumb. And so, we do. The two of us go over to his house. We knock on his door. And do you know what happened next?" While he talks, he's walking back towards me.

"I think we ended up getting yelled at by him." I straighten in my spot on the floor as he gets closer.

"Yeah, he yelled at us, but that was it. He didn't come after you, or me, and I think he liked us better after that." He moves over towards me and squats down next to me on the floor. "That's what you do, Reagan. You take a situation and make it better. You control the chaos. You help me make better decisions. I trust you. I have since you were twelve." He slides his hand on top of my left one, resting on the carpet. "Reagan, I'm sorry. I don't want things to be weird. This is important to me."

"I know it is. I don't want to fuck it up either. This is important to me too."

He takes a deep breath. "I know it is. That's why I want you here. You improve a situation just by being in it. And you're good at this. If it weren't for you, this would be a big party, and I'd be wasting away, pretending that my second shot could never happen. But because of you, I think my second shot could be better than my first. I'm sorry. I really want you here."

We let a silence settle between us.

He squeezes my hand tight and then stands to go. "I never would have thought I'd see the day I leave you speechless."

"Well, I guess you still surprise us both." I smile. He blushes and changes the subject.

"So... My Guys? That's what we're calling this now?" He points in between the two of us and back to the room.

"Is it really that bad? I mean, listen, my first choice was Cronut's Revenge. This seemed... better."

"I don't even know what to say to that. I'm taking away your creative liberties."

"Yeah, well, I didn't go with that. Nick liked My Guys, so I think I made a good game-time decision."

"Seems like a smart guy. Is that who you're, you know... with later?"

"Having a drink with? Yeah, but honestly, it isn't a date, Asher. I don't know why I said that." I lie. I did it to make him jealous, but I regret it now. "It really is more business than anything. Get to know him and get to know who he knows thing. He said he can set us up with a few contacts to play shows on our way to LA. If you're any good." I let a small smile escape.

"Well, we don't need to worry about that last part. Just don't drop the ball, Wilde."

"I'm a team player. No need to worry about me, Blair."

I want to say more about all the things I've been thinking about this morning, but before there is any more time, Marty flings open the door.

"Hey, do you guys know we have to leave in ten minutes? I lost track of the time."

I figure he was hiding inside, listening through the door, waiting for us to kiss and make up.

Thirteen

After checking out of the hotel, we start on what feels like a fast journey by comparison of all the drives before. In a few hours, we'll be in Denver, and we'll stick around the city for the first time in a little while. Our plans are loose, but we'll finally have a place to stay for the days we decide to stay. The guys will get to practice together and will keep practicing until we play—and presumably win—the showcase. That's the plan, anyway. Even now, I don't think about what comes after.

Marty offers to drive, and I call shotgun, which leaves Asher in the back. I catch his eyes in the rearview mirror, and he offers a kind smile in response. Asher and I are on good terms. He is teaching me that there can be disagreements and we do not have to lose each other. But it's clear Asher thinks I'd put the band at risk.

I know in my heart I would never do that to him, or to any of us. We've moved past it for now, but I'm not sure how long he'll keep trusting me. Asher and I have slipped quickly into knowing one another and he now knows my heart better than anyone else. This gives me a small bit of hope that his outburst is bigger than the band, and that maybe he is afraid to lose me to someone new. As much as I want that to be true, there is still Kitty to think about and what she means for the two of us. Whatever there is between us, I can at least hold on to the fact that Asher stuck around, even when he was afraid his most important thing may be at stake: the band.

With Oliver, it was different. Things got tough, and distance doubled between us like we were standing at a starting line where I stayed put and he ran as fast and as far as he could. When our relationship started to fracture, the best he could do was shut down. I still haven't heard from him, but I know someone who hasn't been so silent: I open my phone and navigate to Jocelyn's Instagram.

The first two photos are selfies. She looks pretty in an obvious way, like the dozens and dozens of other selfies you've seen that day. The selfies are followed by yoga posts with inspirational quotes to serve as comments, as if she holds some sort of wisdom, and it doesn't mean she totally lacks any creativity. I keep scrolling until I'm stopped short.

Three nights ago, at our favorite bar in downtown Seattle, the two of them sit at a booth with their hands intwined. A painful twang reverberates throughout my body. There are others in the photo. It isn't an obvious example of their being together, but it's close. His text makes less sense to me now. He's been with Jocelyn long enough to realize it was a bad decision. The honeymoon phase has to be winding down, and the enjoyment they shared of mutually destroying me can't keep them flying high in love forever, and yet here they are, showing signs of their togetherness for everyone on the internet, and whoever took that photo.

"Hey, can you tell me when my next turn is coming up?" Marty utters without taking his eyes off the road.

I shake myself into reality. "Yeah, it looks like your second-to-next left and then it'll be on the right-hand side. Half mile."

"Oh man, you are going to *love* Phil. Don't you think so, Asher?"

I suddenly realize Asher's been silent too.

"Yeah, Phil's hilarious. You'll love him, Reag." He reaches around the seat, squeezing my shoulder, and I feel chills light up my spine as his fingers linger for a moment.

I stay in my own head until we pull up to Phil's shop an hour or so later. If the GPS hadn't told us we'd arrived, I don't think we would have stopped. The corner that houses Phil's shop is not particularly inviting. The buildings are stocky, old, and brick. They look beat up, and a bit forgotten. The other businesses in the center include a liquor mart with a few lingering patrons, a sub shop, and a Hawaiian poke restaurant, all of which are empty. I can see employees buzzing around the front door of the mattress store, just waiting for someone to enter. Then there is Phil's shop. You can smell it before you can really see it.

The Cannabis Kings sign hangs out front, the crisp blue letters illuminated. I burst out laughing, unable to control myself as I see excitement spread across Marty's face. I can't tell if he's more excited to see Phil or what Phil's selling. I chuckle harder as I watch him dart inside without saying a word to us.

Asher sneaks up behind me, clearly noticing me notice Marty. "I used to call Marty our big puppy dog. It's good to see the years haven't changed him."

"He's a good guy. Jess is lucky."

"Yeah, she sure is, but so are we. Getting to be his friend and all." Asher slides his hand over my shoulder, and I feel the tingle in my body light up again.

"Well, aren't you sentimental."

"Hey, I just know when to be grateful. Marty knows how to be a good friend, even without me asking him to be."

I slip out from under his hand and begin to walk inside before I'm stopped.

"What's going on with you, Reagan Wilde?"

"Oh, using the full name. Aren't we formal?"

"Sentimental and formal. You know me. So, are we talking again?"

"We never stopped talking."

We exchange a look that says something like, *well, we almost did.*

I answer his question. "I guess there are a few things going on, but none of those stop me from wanting to be here or talking to you." There is a lot I don't know, but I know that much for certain. "I hate the way our conversation went earlier today. I'm glad we talked about it, but I still don't feel good about it. I don't want you to regret having me here. More than anything, I don't want things to change between us."

He looks down briefly, and when he glances back up, he's smiling. I think about asking about Kitty but can't bring myself to do it.

"I guess Oliver is also on my mind because I haven't heard from him in a while, and I saw a dumb photo of him and... her."

This time, his smile drops. He shifts his weight and looks away from me, towards the store. "Yeah, I can see why that would put you in a mood."

I want him to talk to me now. To tell me how he's feeling, and what's going on with this Kitty. I don't want every conversation we have to be about Oliver and me, because it isn't just about that anymore. But he doesn't know I know there's a Kitty, and if I tell him, he'll feel betrayed. I'm on thin ice, and it's melting.

"Well, at least you're doing a good job with us. Booking us gigs, naming our new band, getting us on that *youthful* social media."

I raise my eyebrows at the mention of youthful.

"What?" He smirks.

"I guess I'm just not used to you being nice to me." I grin widely, a natural response to Asher Blair sass.

"Yeah, well, get used to it because I hear some of that social media is blowing up."

"What are you talking about?"

"Okay, maybe you aren't a *great* social media manager."

I stare at him blankly, and then remember I switched out of the My Guys account to my personal account to stalk Jocelyn. I flip open my phone and navigate back. We have 3,000 followers already. "What? How did this happen?"

"Again, I'm worried about you being our social media manager."

"I'm you're *everything* manager."

"Good point—maybe I should be worried about that too."

I punch him on the shoulder, and he reels back in pain, acting as if I could hurt him.

"Yeah, it's crazy right? I guess the video on Instagram got reposted on some indie music accounts. It made it's way over to Intsa, and a friend sent it to me when they saw it on their discover page."

I sigh, relieved that that's what had been holding his attention. But then I also wonder about why he was so quiet in the car and obviously unexcited.

I let that emotion pass and decide not to overthink it. Instead, I let myself get excited. "I can't believe it. I'm looking at the tags and see that Nick reposted it." I cringe as I say *Nick* and hope the mention of his name doesn't send us backwards.

"Well, now we know how she saw it."

She. I want to ask about her, but I don't. I already know who *she* is.

He whispers, "You are the best."

I want to let that be enough, but I feel insecurity creep in.

"Asher, are we okay? You said all that stuff about Marty being a good friend, and I want to be a good friend."

He reaches for me again and lets both of his hands rest on my shoulders. His eyes lock with mine. I'm not sure what he hopes to find. "Of course, we're okay. We're better than okay. We just had our first fiery band meeting. Happens to the best of them. Do you know what the Beatles went through with Brian Epstein?"

I have no idea, but I just add it to the pile of questions left outstanding.

"You two. Are you going to come inside or just stand outside all day? It's legal here friends, nothing to fear," Marty shouts while laughing at his own attempt of a joke.

"Just handling some business," Asher shouts back. He turns around and gently waves me on with him towards the shop.

Phil's shop is like equal parts modern and hippy. The entire shop is one large room. Every wall in the shop is white, except for one, which is painted a deep red. The shop is easily lit up by large industrial lights overhead. All three of Phil's employees are wearing tie-dyed jackets. Two of them are helping customers, and one is lighting incense while simultaneously watching a movie on a computer, making me think they're getting high on their own supply.

Marty points Phil out to me. He's one of the two helping a customer. His tie-dyed jacket is blue and green with some bright yellow. After he finishes helping the customer, he gives them a firm slap on the back like I've seen football players give one another at the end of a game. He gives them a deep laugh and then spins around to find the three of us. Once turned around, I instantly notice his long, lumberjack-like beard. When he recognizes Asher, he issues him a toothy grin.

Marty practically skips over, embracing Phil with a big bear hug. Phil is taller than me and Asher but looks shrunken next to Marty. As Phil comes up for air, he combs the beard with his hands, like he's afraid it got out of place. Once it's perfect again, Phil walks over to Asher, grabs his face with both hands, and lands a large kiss directly on his lips.

"The man, the myth, the magical beast. Come here to get me back in my music pants. Good to see you, brother." Then he turns his attention towards me. "And who do we have here?"

I know I quickly need to establish myself with Phil or lose ground with all the guys. With a confidence I don't recognize, I try my best. "Reagan Wilde, pleased to meet your acquaintance." I stick out my hand, and hope he'll embrace it for a handshake. "But you do that to *me* and I'm going to give you a lot more tongue. As much as I'd like that, Asher doesn't approve of me kissing the talent."

Asher gives me a disapproving look, and then nods his head like he agrees.

"Oh, and I'm your manager."

Phil looks at Marty and raises his left eyebrow. Then to Asher, who is still nodding as if to say, *yeah man, she's the real deal.*

"Manager? Okay, Asher, I guess this really *is* our second dance for success. And every good success story starts with a good leader. Nice to meet you, madam manager." He curtsies and offers me that toothy smile. "I'm just surprised Asher is letting someone *else* lead this time, but after our last dance, that's probably a good idea." Phil breaks into a loud laugh.

I try not to let my confusion at that show while Marty quickly changes the subject.

"Alright, friend, well it's time to get down to business. We have a gig tonight; hope you remember some of the old stuff cause we're playing a prime-time show."

"Well, shit. Let's do it. We can head back to mine, get a little jam in before dinner with the folks. They are very excited to see you guys. And of course, we expect you to crash there for as long as you're in town."

I find it funny that this legal drug dealer is living with his parents, but then again, so am I. And only one of us is a business owner.

"Perfect." I chime in. "We also have a show tomorrow, and the booker was clear that if we do good tonight and tomorrow, that we can book some more shows through his network. Maybe a few gigs on the way to LA."

"Ah yes, tell me more about LA. How has that come into the mix?"

"Let's get your stuff and head back to the house. I'll tell you on the drive." Asher claps Phil on the back and steers him toward the door. The room feels tense, but I'm not sure if that's just me.

"Can you leave now?" Marty asks, looking around the shop and gesturing towards the handful of customers still milling about.

"Hey, Cesar, I'm gonna head out. Can you finish out the day and close?"

Cesar is hiding in a chair behind the counter. Without calling his name, you would've missed him completely. He spins his chair around from behind the cashier counter, poking his head up. "Sure thing, boss. Catch ya—"

And without missing a beat, Phil shoots back, "On the flip."

We head straight for Phil's parents' house. Pulling into the driveway, I notice how perfectly normal the house and neighborhood look. It is a neighborhood of tract homes, kids riding bikes, people walking their dogs and waving as cars go by. It reminds me that we have been living in this bubble for the last few weeks, and I shudder at the thought of having to leave it.

Phil's mom, who is introduced as Karol, must have expected us, because she's outside when we pull into the driveway. She spends a moment embracing each boy and reminding them of the last time she saw each of them. Then she turns to me, "Oh and I can't wait to get to know you. I'm a hugger. Bring it in." She embraces me warmly, and then pushes me back, like she suddenly has better things to do. "Let's get your stuff inside."

After we unload, the guys quickly disappear downstairs, where Phil had his own space to live and *jam*, a new term I've learned and am trying to use. Karol takes me into the kitchen and invites me to sit at the counter to watch as she "whips us up some snacks before dinner."

It was almost as if I've been transported back to elementary or middle school, and my friend's mom has picked us up after school. She treats me like she's known me for all of Phil's life.

"Alright, so I'm thinking we do grilled cheese sandwiches, or I have Bagel Bites. I know it's not gourmet, but they always liked them in school."

"You should see what we've been eating. I'm lucky if our dinner isn't found at the gas station."

She chuckles lightly in response.

"So, you knew the guys in college?"

"Yes, of course, they were very close. We would always go get dinner when I went out to visit Phil. There was one Christmas break where they stayed with us for two weeks and would wake up to scarf down breakfast before heading up the mountain to snowboard all day. It was like having four Phils." She seems to think that would be a good thing. "And then of course, there was when the band started to take off. I honestly thought they were going to make it into something big, and not just because I'm Phil's mom. Perhaps even despite that. Have you heard them play all together?" she asks.

"Well, yes, but not live. I've seen Asher play live, and Asher and Marty attempt to do what they all did together live. Asher got a lot better with Marty, even if it was quickly, so I'm excited to see what they can all do together."

"Ah, is Jerome coming too?" Her eyes light up, and I instantly understand Jerome means something to her.

"Oh, um, I don't think so. I've never talked to him... and the guys haven't really mentioned him. So, no."

"Mm, okay, well not *all* together then, but I guess I'm an original Umbrella fan." She chuckles to herself, and I feel like I've offended her.

"Yeah, the original stuff was really good." I want her to know I mean it, because I do. Plus, I don't want things to be awkward between us if we're planning to stay here for at least a few days. "We actually amended the name, for the *time being*." I lean on the words *time being* like there is still hope of a reunion.

"Oh, is that so? What are they going by now?"

"My Guys... I picked it in a panicked moment. I don't know if it will stick."

She takes a long pause to respond, and I'm afraid I've offended Karol again. But then she lights up. "My Guys? Huh, I love that. They *are* my guys. I'm sure others will feel that way too."

"Ha, yeah exactly. I feel like they really *are* My Guys, in a way too."

"Lucky you." She gives me a smile, and I instantly recognize the toothy grin. "It'll take me a minute to get used to though."

I nod and hope she can't tell that hurts my feelings. It's a reality check that I'm still on the outside of what once was between everyone else here.

Sounds of music dance into the kitchen from downstairs. I decide to keep the conversation going and ask her exactly what I want to know. "I know this isn't really my place, but no one will tell me about Jerome. What happened to him?"

She turns back to the freezer and ruffles through it, moving ice bags and frozen vegetables as if an answer could be found there. Then she starts in like she planned to have this conversation.

"It's sad, but I guess I'm not surprised they still aren't talking. It's funny because you get to meet your children's friends throughout their life, and sometimes you become attached. How are they doing? What are they doing? It's all a reflection of your own child. And then sometimes, they become so important to you that even when their own reflection says nothing about your child—because of time or distance or good habits or bad—you become attached."

She shuts the freezer and spins around.

"Well, anyway, you're smart to ask me about it. Marty is a bit of a cowardly lion and may not feel comfortable sharing. Phil would probably share too directly, and the risk of Asher hearing is too high. Then that'll lead to another fallout. It's a very good thing you haven't asked Asher about it—he can be the most sensitive of them all. I'm just glad he'll see Phil, even though he still talks to Jerome. Asher's got a real short fuse, as I'm sure you have seen by now."

I don't give her an indication either way. I've seen Asher get angry, but I understand it. The stuff with Nick was painful for him because he thought

I was jeopardizing our band and all that we are working towards. That was reasonable. He lashed out in an unreasonable way, but who hasn't done that in their life? I debate if that qualifies him as having a short fuse, but then I notice that the music has stopped. I need to get at least one of my questions answered, so I nod to give Karol some indication that she should continue. The music starts again, and so does Karol.

"When the boys first met, there were, of course, four of them—Phil, Marty, Asher, and Jerome. They met in some silly school course about the Beatles— I couldn't believe it was a college class, and of course they all loved it. Phil has always been excited about trying new things and was a good musician. He loved the bass. Marty, you'd never guess it because he's so sweet and timid, but he played the drums *loud*. Maybe the noise gave him the voice he wished he had, or he just likes beating things, but wow, my ears are ringing just thinking about it. Then, of course, Asher played guitar, and the band was his dream. He wanted to be a lead singer, he wanted to run the band, he wanted the band to go places. He couldn't stand the thought of doing something normal for his whole life. He went to school, but it seemed like the band was the only thing he cared about doing.

"So, it was great that they met Jerome, and Jerome decided his talents could fit into the band. He had been playing guitar since he was seven, and his entire family was musical. His dad played in a bunch of bands growing up, and even went on tour. He knew more about music than any of him. It was in his blood.

"Asher was also a guitar player, a pretty good singer, an obvious teenage heartthrob, but he didn't have the same talent. Music was something he pursued on his own, whereas music was in Jerome's DNA and always around him as he grew up. So, while Phil, Marty, and Jerome joined this band because it was college and it was something to do, Asher was doing it because it was a shot at his dream—and I think he hoped to get some attention from his family."

All I could think about was Asher's grandparents. He visited them over the summer each year until he couldn't. Maybe it was harder on him than I thought.

"And listen, I know this is a lot of detail, and you can think, 'Karol, you crazy old lady,' but I think it's important for you to know the story. You're like the band mom, and maybe you can keep them on track this time around."

I grimace at the thought of being a band mom. It makes the Asher dynamic even more uncomfortable.

"They played together, they had fun, and they started playing a lot of shows. They even caught the ear of a few record labels, and we all thought maybe it *was* going somewhere.

"For Marty and Phil, it always was just fun. For Jerome, it was family. When we talk about Asher's family being difficult for him to please, it was a cakewalk compared to Jerome. Yes, he had music around him as a kid, but his parents were not reliable, and he was essentially raising himself. He hardly ever saw his father. His mother lived in New York and had no interest in him except when she needed a few extra dollars or wanted to introduce him to her new boyfriend. They had both been musicians before, very passionate people, and very self-involved. Jerome really became like a second son to us, coming home for every holiday. And for whatever reason, he really wanted to please Asher. I don't know if he saw some sadness in Asher that felt more treatable than his own, but all he wanted was to make him proud. But Asher didn't really seem to notice how hard Jerome was working for him. He saw Jerome as someone who had the same dream as he did. At first, they got along great. Asher believed in the band, mostly because of Jerome's belief in him."

She's moving across the room, fluttering about, getting out cutting boards and knives to chop something up for dinner, throwing Bagel Bites into the oven, finishing sandwiches. She can't stop moving, but she slows down as she gets to the next part of the story.

"Listen, I don't blame the guys for not wanting to talk about this. It's hard for any of us to understand. Marty feels like it's just a big understanding, but didn't want to upset Asher further so he'd never say it to him. Phil's caught in the middle, wanting to be loyal to them both. Asher, he pretends it never happened, like he never caused the chaos that came next. I do love them all, but I don't forgive him for that."

Her face is serious. The look of a loving mother is gone, replaced with a protective mother bear glare. I take a deep breath, like I'm about to plunge into dark water.

"Asher finds people, and he makes them feel like something. He did that with Jerome. Maybe you've caught a glimmer of that too. Phil and Marty, they were already something, some sort of people. They weren't reaching for greatness like Asher, and they weren't looking for love like Jerome."

I shift in my seat anxiously. The music stops again, and I'm afraid I've missed another opportunity. She catches the look in my eyes as I turn my head to hear if they'll keep playing.

"Don't worry, they're probably going over notes. They do that after every practiced set. We probably have another twenty minutes. Plenty of time."

She sets down the knives and cutting board, and stares straight into my eyes. I hate that she knows about how they practice and that it's the same after all these years. The way she talks about the past feels dark. It makes me fearful of Asher in a way I haven't been before. I fear heartbreak, I fear not being enough, I fear not being loved by him. I don't want to admit that, and simultaneously begin to think I may already be in too deep to get out without a few scrapes and bruises. She's acting as if whatever happened to Jerome is a warning of what could happen again.

"Asher and Jerome, and the whole band got bigger. They got a following, started playing more shows. Asher decided he didn't need to get a job after graduation, and Jerome decided he wouldn't either. I pushed Phil to finish his degree, find a job he wanted to do. Marty was an anxious love, fearful of what would happen if he *didn't* get a job, so I didn't worry as much for him. But the divide grew stronger. Jerome and Asher were serious about it all. The thing was, Jerome was *better* than Asher. He was a better guitar player, a better singer, but played second guitar without a second thought. Then they played a show in Seattle, and it just so happened that this big-time singer, Sharkee, I think—it was somebody from Larger than Caves—was also at the venue that night."

"Wait, Larger than Caves? What would someone from a band like that be doing at a random venue in Seattle?" I break my silence, questioning why one of the world's best rock stars would be watching a local band.

"Ha, fate? Social media? Who knows, really? But he was super impressed, and it turned out he was looking for a new guitar player because of a fallout with his current one. He found Jerome after the show and let him know he thought he was amazing. He wanted him to audition, and that if he was picked, then he'd get to tour with them over the next year. Jerome knew instantly he couldn't try out. The silence of who was better would finally be broken, and with that, Jerome knew it would destroy Asher. He'd lose Asher if that happened. There would be other opportunities, but for him, there wouldn't be another Asher. He passed on the opportunity and suggested Sharkee speak with Asher instead. I'm sure Sharkee tried to talk some sense into Jerome, but Jerome was a loyalist.

"But I guess Sharkee thought Asher was good enough to talk to after all. Asher was thrilled when Sharkee gave him the details. I can guarantee you Asher didn't think twice about what this would do to the band. He just felt chosen. When I spoke with Phil about it, even he was disappointed at the thought that this could be the end of Umbrella. It did make him glad to have a job."

She chuckles to herself. I wish I could push her to finish the story faster. She must feel the shift in my energy because she promptly stops laughing and begins to apologize. "I'm sorry, I know this must seem trivial. I'm almost there. The background is important, without it, you'll misjudge the situation."

I want to tell her I won't, but how do I know that to be true? I let her continue at her pace.

"The guys were disappointed, but they were excited for Asher. Of course, he asked them all to come along so they could play a few shows while in LA. They agreed, and set off on a short trip, much like yours, through Portland to LA. They arrived the day before the tryouts and had plans to play that evening. Asher was so certain it would be the last time he played with the band, so the guys had a great day running around LA. They went out partying that night, and I guess Asher took it too far, ended up stumbling home early the next morning with a black eye. He got separated from the group and made some poor decisions. He was not in good shape for the audition. He tried to sleep it off, but he was still irritable and insecure the next morning. He pushed the guys out of the room so he could sleep until late afternoon. Eventually, the guys woke him up to get him ready for the tryout, and off he went. Problem was, he forgot his guitar.

"He had about a fifteen-minute head start when Jerome found it in the bedroom, so he grabbed the guitar, and ran as fast as he could to catch up with Asher. He never caught him on foot, so went to the venue.

"When he walked in, the first thing he saw was a frustrated Asher fighting with someone at the door. Asher didn't see him at first, so he kept arguing with whoever it was. Jerome froze. I think he started to see Asher for who he really was at that time—lost, out of control, consumed with himself."

I feel my heart drop. I had dreamed Asher was someone different, and this reminds me of the conversation I had with my mother. I tried to defend him then, before I knew him. Even knowing him now, he isn't like this at all. I want to tell her that he has changed, but I can't get it out because she was right about me wanting love. She was right about Asher putting himself first. He was so angry with me about the possibility of wrecking the band, while I had hoped his anger was really fear about losing me masquerading as something with a bite.

"Then Asher saw Jerome, and instead of feeling relief, he flew into a fit of rage. He came screaming down the hallway at Jerome, screaming that Jerome was backstabbing, had no talent and no reason to be there, the worst things you could possibly say to someone who loves you. Asher and his misdirected anger could not believe that Jerome was there to give him his guitar, and instead, assumed Jerome was there to audition behind his back. He didn't waste time trying to find out the truth.

"He started yelling and only stopped to try and start a physical fight. Jerome refused. Eventually, Asher was ushered out. And then, as Jerome explained to me, Sharkee comes out, and says he will never work with Asher and begs to Jerome to audition. So Jerome *did* audition. He was fantastic, so of course he got the spot. When he got back to the hotel room, Asher was already gone. Phil and Marty were waiting for Jerome to get back, to tell him Asher had headed to the airport. Jerome tried to call Asher, and Asher never picked up. He disappeared, and for the longest time, none of them heard from him. When Jerome finally got the spot, he texted all of them, even Asher. And it was radio silence.

"Jerome had been alone his whole life. In a world where so few people cared for him, he remained caring, loving, and loyal. When he met Asher, he thought he found brotherhood, but it came with conditions. Phil and Marty remained friends with Jerome, and distant with Asher, who would ever so often pop into their lives. I guess Asher met some girl at the airport and moved in with her for a while."

This time, I *do* feel my heart break. I don't want her to notice. I don't want her to think I'm just another Jerome.

"Jerome started to tour, but his heart wasn't in it. For him, it was about brotherhood, and that was broken. For a while, the band toured all over the world. Europe, South America, and the whole dang United States. Jerome sent me a postcard every month to catch me up. I watched his social media, proud as I could ever be of this boy who felt like one of my own. For a while, he was good, until he wasn't."

This time, it's *her* heartbreak that crosses her face.

"Jerome fell into the lifestyle. He started abusing it. He mended his broken heart with drugs, alcohol, and who knows what else. After the tour finished, he didn't know where to go. He could have come here—I swear, it would've been fine—but I don't think he wanted to show how bad off he was and so honestly, I don't know where he lived. I heard he was in Portland, then Los Angeles, and New York for a little while. There were no more postcards, and that's when I knew there was a problem, but there was nothing I could do. We all tried to reach out—well except for Asher—but we didn't know where to find him and never got a call back.

"After a few months, we found him. He turned up at a bar in Portland, got in a fight, and he spent the night in jail. I have no idea how he ended up there. He got one call, and he called us, the house—I have no idea how he remembered the number. We—my husband and I—flew out to see him in

Portland and picked him up. We didn't get there for two days, but I paid his bail. He was shaking in the morning when we got to see him. Withdrawal."

There was the sporadic banging of drums coming from downstairs. Maybe they had started to play again.

"We checked him into a rehab center, he got better, and then he relapsed. We moved him to a facility in Phoenix. He's out of the facility, but still living in Phoenix. I think this time it will stick. He's working in a kitchen; he's learned to cook, and he's quite good at it. We'll go see him in the spring, just like we did last year. I think he and Marty have exchanged a few calls. Asher still hasn't spoken to him. Jerome is fragile, but strong. If—I guess, when—he hears about this, I don't know what it will do to him." She glances up with a worried look adorning her face, but lovingly takes my hand in hers. "To see them all together, to see him replaced by you, it will be... painful."

Fourteen

The room starts spinning and I attempt to excuse myself, but all that comes out is a wordless mumble. She must sense I'm anxious to get out of the room because she squeezes my hands tighter and then lets them go. She turns back to the vegetables in front of her and proceeds to chop them up. The moment is so normal, it's almost as if I've dreamed the conversation up. I manage to get something out like, "I just need a moment," and she says, "Absolutely, take all the time you need," like I'm ordering dinner at a restaurant and need some time to peruse the menu. I give her the type of grin that leaves all my teeth hidden and walk with meaning up the stairs. Her gaze follows me like she's studying my reaction to gauge how far I am under Asher's spell. I turn up the next set of stairs and catch her eyes. She's twisted her face back into that of a loving mother. I wonder if Asher knows she hates him. Then I wonder if she's right to.

Once upstairs, I fling open the first door and am relieved to find the bathroom. I turn the water on and splash it onto my face. Staring in the mirror, my eyes are red. I may not have told her how I was feeling, but my face made it obvious.

Getting to know everyone's opinion on Asher is exhausting. The opinions have never been solicited, and I never anticipated one ounce of what I've been told. The Asher I see never matches the Asher I've been told about. Who has the authority to make the final judgement?

What Mom said, or what Marty said when he was worried, was one thing, but if what Karol said about Jerome was the truth, then there is a side to Asher that has the potential to destroy. He destroyed the person who was closest to him, the one who gave up everything for him. And now Karol thinks I've put myself in the same place.

I turn the faucet off and allow myself to collapse onto the tile floor. I pull my legs in for a hug and slump over in the fetal position. It's hard not to realize that only a few months ago, I was feeling this same sort of devastation for a different boy who had broken my heart in a completely different way.

Suddenly, I'm back in my parents' house studying carpets and lamps, feeling nothing except for disappointment and betrayal. Wondering if I will love again, be loved again, or ever leave that godforsaken room. And you know what? I had. I hadn't lost myself completely to Asher. This warning has arrived in time. I can walk away from him unscathed.

But then, on the other hand, can I? He's the reason I'm here. Yes, I love music, but they don't really need me. He makes me feel interesting, adventurous, and smart. I wake up each day excited to live my life and spend another day with him. Without him, what happens to the Reagan I've become?

My heart has been in a perpetual state of heartbreak for months, and there is no end in sight. First, it broke for Oliver, who walked away from me like it was easy to throw me out and get a newer model. For Jocelyn, who broke my trust and tossed aside years of friendship. For Asher, who chose me, not because he cared about me, but because he cared about being loved. Most of all, my heart broke for Jerome, who fell the way that I did for Asher Blair. At first, slowly, and then suddenly, all the way.

I've allowed my heart to break a few too many times, and I don't know if I can go through this again. If I fall for Asher, he may destroy me. But if I can get in front of it, stop any feelings from progressing, then I can save myself and everything we've been working for. I want to be a part of My Guys, and Asher's life, and shutting off my feelings for him is the only way.

We can keep the shows going. I can push aside this feeling, fight through it for the betterment of the band, and chalk it all up to a crush. People survive crushes, and bands survive them too. It could be the sort of thing we laugh about over the years. We need to be a team. Whatever happens next, we have to do it as a team. “I can do this,” I whisper out loud to myself.

“Reagan, is that you?” We're only four words in, but Asher’s voice sends my confidence sprinting away. Maybe I can't shut my feelings off. “Dinner’s almost ready, so Karol wanted me to come and grab you.”

“I’m not feeling very well. I may skip dinner,” I say calmly, and curse Karol for sending Asher upstairs. I’m sure she thinks she’s doing us both a favor.

“Did she feed you too many Bagel Bites? She didn’t even bring us any. Classic Karol.” Asher giggles like he’s simultaneously too old to be served Bagel Bites, and too young to call Karol, Karol. All I can think is that if he knew what Karol was saying about him, I doubt we’d be in this house. When I don’t respond, he clears his throat and then says seriously, “Okay, well I’m sorry you don’t feel well. Do you think you’ll still come to the show tonight?”

“I don’t know.”

“But Reag, what about that guy?”

“You didn’t want me to see that guy. What should that matter?” I say snippily.

“Well, he said if we did good tonight, maybe there’d be more shows. Right? I just think you should be there for that.”

“Of course, you do.”

“What did you say?”

“I said of course you do. Of course you care about the band and me getting us another booking, but you’re perfectly capable of doing all of this without me.”

“Reagan, what’s going on? Listen, if you want to see that guy, I’m over it. Go for it.” He’s silent for a moment, maybe hoping that’s enough for me to stop pouting. It isn’t. “Reag. Please. Can I come in? Can we talk?” He jiggles the handle, but it’s locked.

I think about Jerome and know I don’t want to end up like him.

He rattles the door harder. "Please?" He taps his foot, and I can see the shadows from under the threshold dance up and down, quicker, quicker, quicker, as he grows more anxious. "Please," he whispers quietly.

Without a word, I twist the handle and crack the door open. His foot stops tapping, and he slowly pushes the door open, like he's nervous to find out what lies behind. I prop myself up against the tub, and mentally prepare myself to have an honest talk. But when I see his eyes, my heart stops, and the fact of the matter hits me hard.

I think I'm falling for you, Asher Blair.

I stop breathing, and then I let out a heavy sob, surprising both of us.

Asher rushes to my side, cups my face in his hands, and shuts the bathroom door with his foot. "Hey, hey, hey. What's going on? It's okay, you're okay. I'm right here."

He tries to catch my tears with his fingertips, but the floodgates are open and more than I can count are flowing out, only to come colliding with the floor. He doesn't seem to care about the ones that sneak by, and instead, he's shushing me now. Not in a harsh way, but in a calm one. He runs his hands through my hair, and then maneuverers his body behind mine so his back is pressed against the tub, and mine is against him. He feels warm, and my body feels electric, which only makes me cry harder. I think about my mom, and her not wanting me to follow a boy just because he is a boy. I would plan my whole life around him if he'd only ask. What an impossible thought to me only a few days ago, and now it's my reality. Asher is reminding me to breathe like I've only forgotten the word and just hearing it will help my body function. He strokes my back with his hand. His head is pressed up against my ear. Eventually, we're silent, and our breath is in tune.

Calmer me has questions I need answers to. What does he feel for me? What does he think about me? Am I just a lighthouse to help him navigate his way to shore? Is he manipulative? Evil? Why didn't he call Jerome when he was hurting or any point over the years? How can he make me feel so safe and so loved in these moments that I forget about all the bad in him? How can I trust him?

Asher Blair holds me, not knowing that the sadness I'm releasing is because of him. Eventually, my sobs steady. I have no concept of time and I am grateful no one has come to bother us. I'm breathing now, emptier than before, the sadness gone. But my mind feels steady.

"Reagan, can we please talk? What's going on?"

I can't tell him everything I've learned, not while we're in Denver. And truthfully, I don't want to pop the bubble we've built. Karol's story hurt, and I know I'll have to ask questions about Jerome, but part of me believes the only true version of Asher is the one I know. There is a trust between us that no one understands, not Karol or Mom, or even me at times, but that trust makes me believe he's looking out for me.

Asher doesn't wait for my response. He starts in. "If it's about the text you saw, then I want you to know she doesn't matter to me. She's just someone I know from before."

I panic. He knows I know about Kitty.

"Marty told me you've been off since this morning. At first, I thought maybe you weren't feeling well, but then I remembered you were looking at my phone. And that she texted me this morning. I know what she sent, and I'm sure you saw part of it." He stops, like he's waiting for me to clear the air and confess. I don't. "Okay, well, I'm sorry I didn't tell you about her when you told me about Oliver. A long time before I met you, I met Kitty. Back when we were Umbrella, not My Guys." I feel his lips turn upwards in a smile as if to accentuate the difference in situation. "The band had just broken up."

I have a moment of hope. He wants to tell me the truth, and that means we *are* different. I hold on to the hope and sit up so I can hear more clearly, but don't have to look him in the eyes. My body presses further against his.

"Kitty was the first person I thought I loved. I'm sure you don't want to hear this, and I'm sorry if this makes you feel anything other than trusted. I didn't want to keep her from you. I just met her at a really bad time. We moved quick. After the band broke up, I had to let something else fill my life, and it was Kitty. That's why I understand Oliver. I saw the hurt when I first met you, and that's why I wanted to be around you. I recognized the pain and wanted you to know that it ends." His voice gets quieter, and I lean in closer, so my temple is nearly pressed against his lips. "I don't need to go into the detail because it doesn't matter. But she broke my heart, and I guess I deserved it. I moved from one heartbreak into another, from a band to a girl. And I didn't write a single good song afterwards, which is the real tragedy."

He turns his head and strains to look at me. "Reagan, she didn't want to be with me. She thought I was a loser because I wasn't going anywhere. And I *was* a loser, so I left heartbroken, and tried to figure out my shit. I tried to get a real job, but I hated it. I felt useless and bored. I woke up and did that for days on end. Then my grandmother called me and asked if I could come home. I quit my job, determined to take some time to figure this life thing out, and then I met you. And we've been having the best time figuring out this life thing together. That matters a lot to me."

"So why are you talking to her?" I manage to ask. I'm surprised by how annoyed I sound. I almost forget if I'm upset because of Jerome or Kitty.

"We talk occasionally. We're better broken up than together. But the random texts over the months became more frequent in the last few days because Kitty saw the video you posted. I think she was surprised to see me playing again, and maybe a little upset. I think she wants to be a part of it this time around. For her own stupid reasons. I told her this time, it's going to be different. *You* are a big part of that being different."

"Maybe."

"Reagan, I thought it was done. From the moment I met you, I didn't think about her again. I know who we've been to each other. You and I have a connection, and it's a once in a lifetime thing. You understand me in a way that no one else ever has. I feel for you deeply, I want to protect you, and I want to be there for you. And of course, I've noticed you're beautiful."

I can't help but blush, and hang on to those last few words. He continues.

"But, I don't want you in a lustful way. You're more precious to me than a one-night stand. I wanted to see where this was going to see. I wanted to be sure it made sense for us to be more than friends. But then you had him, and each time I saw what he did to you, I felt what that did to me. So, when I heard from her, it felt good. It felt like I could focus on something other than you. And then she asked to see me."

I feel part of me break off like an iceberg melting away. "What did you say to her?"

"I told her yes. I'm different now, and so is she. I thought it would be good to get some closure on whatever happened between us."

Suddenly, I'm angry. I can't explain it, and there's no time to. I push his hands off me and slide back across the bathroom floor. I run my hands through my hair, hoping it looks less stupid than it feels. What does it mean that he's seeing her but he told me to push Oliver away? Was he doing that to hurt me or did he really never consider my feelings? Didn't he know that by going to see her, it felt like he was picking her over me?

"You didn't even have a conversation with me. You didn't even let me know how you felt about me, and you've decided to go see her. What happens after you see her? You just leave and never talk again or better yet you're suddenly friends? What can you possibly gain from seeing her?" I'm trying to keep my voice low so the others don't hear me, but I'm losing control. "And now you're telling me there was a point in time when this all could've gone differently, if only, I'd known? But how would I have known if you never told me? I guess that is the clearest message you could send a girl."

"Reagan, I didn't think I was picking. I was just doing what you were—trying to reconnect. I wasn't thinking about hurting you when I said yes. I knew I didn't want to screw anything up with the band. I would never intentionally hurt you. I'm sorry. I just..."

The anger is getting louder. It breaks out of my body.

"You know what? I don't care, Asher, I really don't. You've never told me what I meant to you, and you had a million chances. So, I'll be first. I think I'm falling for you, Asher, and I didn't know it until tonight when you walked in here, but now it's as clear as a bright light. I feel this way for you even though I never thought I could love again. But when I met you, you wanted to be around me, and all the hurt in the world vanished into the background. People I never thought would support me supported me in things I never thought I could do. And as I ran away from pain, I ran closer to you. But you wreck people. You've wrecked *me*. And I get it, it's my fault. You didn't ask for me. You didn't want this. You had to pick, and you didn't pick me. I only have myself to blame."

"Reagan... please, I'm sorry." He pushes his body further into the tub, like he wants to get further away.

"Ha, that's it. You *are* sorry. Just sorry for doing this to me. I'm sorry, too, Asher. I'm sorry I thought this was a good idea. I should go."

I stand to go, and he grabs my wrist, pulling me down off my balance. I fall slightly into his lap but push my body quickly away from his. This time, there's no electricity.

"Please, Reagan, I need you."

"You don't need me. You need Kitty. Or maybe a therapist."

"Reagan. Please. I'm sorry I said anything about her."

"You should be. I wasn't even upset about this. Way to make it all about you. Whatever, you need to get ready for tonight. Let's just move on."

"But you said you have feelings for me."

"I think—or I thought—I was falling. That's different."

His body stiffens. "Okay fine, well, what were you upset about?"

"What?"

"If this wasn't it, what were you upset about?"

I know it's a cheap shot, and that he needs more time to be evaluated before I judge him as the monster that destroyed Jerome, but rage is blinding. I can't help the words that tumble out of my mouth. "Am I just another Jerome to you? Another person to treat however you like while I'm loyal and then as soon as I do something you don't like you'll just throw me out?"

"What are you talking about?"

"Don't play dumb, Asher. I know what happened with Jerome. I'm surprised I didn't see you for the person you are before today."

"First of all, you clearly don't know shit, because if you did, then you'd know damn well that you and Jerome are nothing alike."

"I know Jerome mattered to you until *you* didn't matter to *him*, and then you destroyed him. I know that when I got asked out, you came for me in a vile way. And now I know that even though it was clear to everyone how I felt about you, you decided to ignore my feelings and go see Kitty anyway. At least I already know you're capable of abandoning people when they need you most. Thanks for saving me from learning that lesson the hard way."

He takes the longest pause in the conversation yet and uses the silence to run his hands through his long hair. It has grown noticeably longer since we left Seattle. His face is tired, and his eyes are sad. I almost feel bad about what I've said.

"Reagan, you don't know anything about what happened. I don't know who you talked with or how you know about any of this, but it isn't any of your business."

"Fine." I press my lips firmly into one another but can't stop from hurting him one more time. "At least I know I shouldn't fall in love anymore."

"What?" His face grows bright red, and then he lets out a large rush of angry air. With it, the redness lessens.

"Never mind. Just forget it." I shift my body, so I don't have to touch his, and I try not to think about how good it felt to be close to him before. I wish I could go back and replay the scene from the beginning. I don't know how I would've done it different; I just wish I had the chance.

"Reagan, I don't *want* to forget it."

"Asher." I look him in the eyes, trying to see what's in there. "It doesn't matter. You told me you had to pick, and you picked."

"I chose to *see* her one time. I didn't pick anything."

"Sure, you did."

He gets a text. He ignores it but checks the time. "Listen, we've calmed down now, so let's talk about this later, please. I *want* to talk about this, but we need to go. Let's go to the venue. Please, still come?"

I want to ask him why, but I also don't want to fight, so I agree. He brushes his hand against my shoulder and lets it linger. He's testing me to see if I'll lose my mind again. I don't. I let him sweep my feelings under the rug and know he's planning to pull the feelings out the next time they're convenient for him. I decide to tell him what he wants to hear.

"You should go get ready for sound check."

"Okay. Are you coming though?" He's cautious, like he knows this conversation is a bomb he narrowly defused.

I nod and stand to signal we should leave. I tell him I'll be late, and he understands. Asher disappears and I head to the guest room Karol pointed me to when we first arrived. She was thoughtful enough to put me in my own room, right before blowing up my life. Maybe she is a gossip, maybe she was trying to protect me, or maybe she didn't know what she had done. I try not to think the worst of her. Laying back on the bed, I take in a deep breath of air. I try to calm down by counting, but that just reminds me of Asher and then I'm angry again. I decide it can't get any worse, so I find Kitty on social media.

Lucky for me, there aren't many people named Kitty following the band account, and so when I see the handle Kittys_Paradise, I annoyingly know it must be her. The account is public, and her profile picture is her in a rainbow crochet halter top. Her bio says something annoying like *live, laugh, love*, but in a hip way. I disregard it and start to scroll. So many of her photos are landscapes of cool places she's been recently: Mexico City, New York, Costa Rica. She has photos of dogs, of nature, of her home cooked meals that look like they've been prepared by a chef. It takes me fourteen photos before I finally find one of her.

She is sitting in a restaurant she neglected to tag with a plate of cheese and a glass of wine in front of her. Her dark brown hair is curled effortlessly, which makes her piercing blue eyes stand out. She is mid laugh and looks like she holds all the joy in the world. Of course, he loved her, and of course she broke his heart. I could easily see she was that kind of girl.

I scroll to the top of her page and not so accidentally allow myself to click her story. If she views her followers, she likely won't think twice about some random girl watching her page. She's out at dinner with friends. It's relatively harmless until I see the location. Los Angeles. There is no way he can avoid seeing her there. Then a horrible thought crosses my mind. Maybe this is what this had all been about. The band, playing the show in LA, trying to be the absolute best he can be, all so he can see his ex and win her back. It isn't the craziest idea—after all, half, or maybe even all, of what

I've done over the last few weeks has been to hurt Oliver so badly he begs for me back.

There is another knock on the door. I respond, "Asher, I'm coming." I quickly close out of the app just in time for the door to swing open. It's Karol.

"Hey, Reagan, dear. They guys just left. They had to scurry on over. Asher said you weren't feeling well, so I wrapped up the sandwich and I also have some ginger ale, if you'd like. If you don't want to Uber, I can drop you off. I don't mind."

I suddenly feel like I'm fourteen again. I'm the type of girl Kitty would make fun of. That, coupled with the thought of spending any more time with this Asher historian, makes me realize I will most certainly break into tiny pieces if Karol drives me anywhere.

"Oh, I couldn't ask you to do that. I'll be fine grabbing an Uber. Thanks for being so hospitable." I use adult-like words, hoping she'll remember I'm an adult.

"Alright, have it your way." She's doesn't walk away.

"Okay, well thanks. I think I'll take that ginger ale while I get ready, if you don't mind." My eyes travel to my suitcase, where I began to mentally plan out my outfits. By comparison to Kitty, I'm going to come out looking like a librarian.

Karol must have been watching me stare at the suitcase because she immediately breaks into another offer. "Got it. I'll go grab that. I also was just thinking I had bought a new top the other day, and it is way too young for me. I was going to see if you wanted it. Lord knows Phil won't."

Great, a mom shirt. This should complete the vibe.

"I'd love to look at it," I utter, hoping I don't accidentally roll my eyes.

"Be back in a moment." She practically winks at me and I wonder what ulterior motives hide behind that mischievous look.

I start with hair and makeup. If things are crashing with Asher, at least I can look forward to seeing Nick. I send him a text before I have too much time to think about it.

Hey, can't wait to see you tonight. My bands going to blow your mind. ;)

I put the phone away in my purse, determined not to check for his response until I get to the venue. If Nick is a bust, I try to remember about all the work I've put in to get here tonight. Yes, the guys could've done it without me, but they didn't. And despite the bullshit from today and yesterday, the adventure has been well lived. I smile to myself in the mirror and try to push past the unease I'm feeling.

When Phil's mom returns, she hands me the sandwich and ginger ale, and I realize I'm starving. I quickly scarf it down as she pulls out the shirt from a department store bag. I ready myself for something awful and try to think of ways I can let her down easy.

"For the grand finale, ta-da." She whips out a sequined gold blazer. If I get creative, I could wear it as a dress with a plunging neckline.

"Wow. That's cute."

"I *do* have quite good taste. Now, get out of this house and to that venue. Tonight is as much your night as theirs."

Fifteen

I can't stop myself from checking my phone in the car. I'm hoping I missed a vibration and I have a response from Nick that will make me forget about the last few hours. The drive to the venue is quick, and thankfully the prayed-for vibration comes as the car is dropping me off out front.

We'll see about that.

I don't know what I hoped for, but I know those four words are not enough to make me forget about today. I anxiously pop out of the car, uttering a quiet, "Thank you," to my driver. The air is cold, and a breeze is blowing the weather in. I should've brought a coat, but a coat can be a liability. It can cover up your cute outfit or easily get left behind. The pros and cons of bringing a coat can only distract me from the present moment for so long. Tonight, a band I manage will play a real show. And the best part about it is that I played a role in getting them here. I didn't owe this moment to Oliver, Asher, or anyone else. The thought gives me the spoonful of confidence I need to walk into the bar.

It's quiet, but it's still the busiest venue we've been to, and the crowd is growing by the minute. My eyes search the room for the stage, and that's where I find Asher Blair buzzing around. He's wearing a white T-shirt with the sleeves rolled up around his muscular biceps. His hair is pushed back. I hate that he looks so good, but I remind myself that I look good too.

Marty sees me before Asher does. He waves me over. Asher looks up and our eyes lock. I'm not sure if he's happy to see me. The moment feels long. I want to know what's going through his head. Finally, he releases a smile. It's the type of smile that makes me realize that we can get through this night, and maybe even enjoy it. It's everything we've worked towards. We're building something, and it isn't worth throwing away.

"Well, hello there."

I'm intercepted by a short man wearing a plunging black V-neck. I notice he is balding, but also growing a thick mustache. I wonder if he can sense the irony.

"I suppose you must be Reagan; you look absolutely stunning."

"How do you— Wait, are you Nick?" I try not to seem disappointed, but this man looks more circus ringleader than sexy band booker.

"Me? Wow, what a flattering thought, but no. I'm Cyrus" He chuckles like he's often confused for Nick. "Nick told me about you. He just ran out back to sign for our beer delivery. Told me to stop any beautiful ladies from leaving tonight until he had a chance to stay hello." He throws me a wink, and I'm afraid he thinks he has a chance.

"Cyrus, get away from her."

I'm grateful this conversation is ending before it's started. I spin around to find my hero, and this time, I'm hoping this person is Nick. He doesn't have a mustache, but he has a very attractive five o'clock shadow. He's also wearing a black V-neck that fits snug against his muscular chest. He has light blond hair that's cut tight around the sides and long on top. I can tell he is attractive in a problematic way, meaning that he's likely *caused* problems with all that attractiveness. Maybe Asher had a reason to be concerned after all.

"Sorry, he can be such a flirt."

Cyrus skulks away like a reprimanded dog. I almost feel bad for him.

"I'm half assuming, half hoping you're Reagan."

"I can confirm you're 100% right."

"Lucky me. Well, it's wonderful to meet you. The guys sounded sick during soundcheck. I'm glad we were able to make this work."

I cringe at the word "sick." Does he think he's a surfer? It doesn't matter, because two seconds later, he reaches for my hand and asks if I want to grab a drink. I nod yes because I lack the word, and he steers me towards the bar. As we float there, he shimmies his hand to the small of my back. I push Asher far from my mind, and instead fantasize about how much Jocelyn would hate to see me here looking so good with this entirely too-sexy-to-be-alive man. The best revenge *really* may be living good.

We grab a drink and begin to chat. He is funny. He's so funny, I'm almost surprised. I throw my head back in laughter and I catch a pair of eyes staring this way. When I return the look, Asher hastily looks away. Marty must sense I'm staring at the guys, and he waves again, oblivious, like a kid who doesn't know his parents are fighting. Phil yells for the guys and they all vanish behind the curtains.

Nick picks up my drink and leads me back to a high-top table. We talk about my band, and the bands he's played in, and booked. He asks me if I've ever played in one, and I'm honest when I tell him that this is the closest I've been to making music. He doesn't think that's weird. He understands what it's like to make music happen without playing. He's not in a band anymore. He likes booking gigs. He likes being on this side of making music happen. He doesn't ask what I did before this. It's like all that matters is happening right now. He tells me that he'll introduce me to a few more bookers he knows in Denver. I blush because I realize I'm making this happen. *This* is what it feels like to build something.

"You were right, Reagan, they're good. With what you're doing on social media, and the people you'll meet if you keep networking, I think you guys could go places." He smiles, and warmly places his hand on top of mine. I ignore the fact that what he said is a cliché. He makes me laugh, and I almost feel that the worst of the night is behind us, but I can still feel the harsh gaze of a hateful lead singer looking this way. Strike that—walking this way.

"Excuse me, can we borrow *our* manager for a moment?" Asher leans on the word "our," and I almost want to remind him not to be rude.

"Of course. Can't keep a boss lady from her business."

Nick reaches between Asher and I to lean in for a hug. He smells amazing, like pine trees and a good time.

Once he's out of earshot, Asher starts in. "Boss lady," he mimics, and makes a stupid face. "Super cool dude."

"Hm, I thought you didn't care."

He either doesn't hear or just chooses to ignore me, and instead says the most devastating thing he can think of. "You look beautiful."

My stomach does a backflip, but my brain reminds me we aren't on good terms with Asher. I'm silent for a moment, hoping the silence means we don't have to address that comment, or what happened tonight. I give him a smile and a meek, "Thank you." I'm hoping he's forgotten that I told him I was falling for him, but I also don't want him to forget it all together. If we pass over it too quickly, it will be obvious there was never a chance for us. It's so complicated with him. I also can't put Jerome out of my mind. If we're going places as a band, like we all want, it will only be a matter of time before Jerome finds out about My Guys.

"This is what we're planning for the set." Asher pulls up a playlist on the notes section of his phone. It has a few covers, and a couple Umbrella originals that people won't recognize. He's never shown me their set list before. I accept it like a peace offering.

I smile, wanting to return the offer. "Hey, can you do me a favor?"

"Anything."

"Knock 'em dead."

A smile grows wide across his face. "You can count on it."

I watch him walk away, and he turns back once again to wink before disappearing behind the stage. I'm reminded of how important this night is for him. Despite everything, I want him to be happy about tonight. Sure, this is just one show at one random bar, but it's also a shot at the future he dreams of.

I saunter over to the bar and ask for another drink before shuffling to the middle of the floor facing the stage.

Four minutes later, exactly on time, the guys come on stage and start their first song. From the first strum, the energy is noticeable, and a crowd grows around them like the opposite side of a magnet, drawn together with force. It's clear to me that we need all three of them to make this happen. I try not to think about what a fourth could do to the group, and instead let myself get lost in the crowd.

By the sixth song, the entire venue is dancing. Strangers in the crowd make eye contact with one another and mouth, "Aren't they so good?" loud enough for me to hear. Suddenly, we have crowd surfers, and I whip out my phone to take an Instagram live video from the crowd. I want people to feel like they're here in this moment with us, where time stops and everyone in the crowd is reminded of what it feels like to be alive. I can feel the music reverberate in my chest. We all dance with strangers like there aren't any differences between us. If the whole world knew how good it feels to be here, they'd never miss a show.

As I'm recording, a phone number pops up on my screen. I ignore it too quickly to notice who it's from. It doesn't matter because I'm here in this moment. I slide my phone into my pocket, but I feel it buzz again, and again, and again. I whip it out, determined to turn it off so I can be fully present in the moment, but when I see it again, I think I recognize the number. I beeline out, brushing past sweaty, happy bodies. I see Nick and make a special attempt to brush against his muscular arms. I mouth, *I need to take a call*, and he mouths back *Okay, boss lady*. I picture Asher mimicking him again.

Before the ringing stops, I answer, but I'm not quite outside. "Hello?"

The person is talking, but it's still too loud to hear.

"Hey, hang on, please. Just a secomundo—like a second but a mundo one." I chuckle, and realize I've had too much to drink. I finally find a spot outside and try to quiet the ringing in my ears. "Okay, hi, hello, how can I help you?"

"Reagan?"

"Mm, yes this is Reagan Wilde." I say, chipper, wondering if I recognize the number because it's another venue. But of course, it isn't. It's 11:34 p.m., and anyone who books a band is probably at a show.

"This is— it's uh, Oliver."

Suddenly I'm sober.

"I hope it's okay I called. I thought you'd know it was me, but maybe you deleted my number, which is also okay. Is it okay I called?"

"Uh yeah... well no, wait umm, I guess, why are you calling me? Is everything okay?"

"No not really."

"What happened?" Immediately I feel panic pull me under, running through all the bad things that could have happened. Maybe someone died. Maybe my mom invited him over for dinner. Maybe he's going to marry Jocelyn. He takes a long pause, and more bad things come to mind like popcorn popping in a microwave. I'm spinning, and I'm not sure if it's the impending bad news or the alcohol.

"I miss you."

That's it. I'm going to throw up.

"Reagan? Are you there? I said that—"

"You— you miss me?"

"Yes."

"Really verbose today, aren't we? Well, I just find that interesting since you haven't even responded to my te*x*ts." I feel myself really annunciating the "x" in texts and realize I'm quite drunk.

"I'm sorry, but I didn't know what to say to that. I was trying to reach out and well, you shut me down."

"Gee, I wonder why that is. How's your *girlfriend*, by the way?"

"Jocelyn isn't my girlfriend *anymore*." He almost whispers the word anymore, like maybe I won't catch it slipping out of his mouth and that'll make all the differences. "We were never like you and me. I almost don't want to call her my girlfriend."

"Well, you're in Seattle with her. You *left* me for her. Seems like she meant a lot more to you than I ever did."

I'm surprised at how angry I feel and wonder if he's surprised too. Maybe he's regretting making the call, and my anger will change his mind. I'm startled when I see someone lighting a cigarette outside, staring at me and looking somewhat terrified. It's Cyrus. I decide I don't care what Cyrus or Oliver thinks and send Cyrus a wave. He waves back and turns around, but he's still close enough to hear everything I'm saying.

"Listen, Reagan, I messed up. We were perfect. *You* were perfect, and I didn't see it. I really—"

"You really fucked my best friend."

Cyrus must be loving this show.

"I'm so sorry. I'm so sorry that I did that. I don't know who I was when I did that, or what came over me. You were the most important thing to me, and I made a mistake, and I pushed you away because I didn't understand what I was picking. Then I didn't know how to say that I made a mistake. I didn't know how to recover from it. I'm trying to say— I'm saying— I'm sorry. That was the worst mistake of my life. I miss you; I've missed you for weeks now."

"We've been broken up for *months*."

"It's been months. I'm sorry, I know nothing I can say will be right or enough, but I love you, Reagan. That has to mean something."

It almost feels insulting to hear that. I decide not to fixate on his words. "Where are you right now?"

"I'm... I'm in Seattle."

"Why are you in Seattle, Oliver? Were you with her? *Are* you with her?"

"Yes—"

"Ha, great, wonderful. Sounds like you *are* really broken up, now, doesn't it?"

"Reagan, I broke things off with her tonight. I couldn't do it, and she knew I was still hung up on you. It's over. I'm out at our place, the bar downtown by the Pike Place. Do you remember we came here for that one anniversary, and you got a candle in your hamburger? I asked if they did that still, and they looked at me like I was crazy. I *am* crazy, but I know I want that again. Candles in burgers, and you and me again. But for now, I just want to talk to you."

"You're drunk."

"A little, but I mean it. I want you back."

My mind is spinning. For months, this is the exact call I've needed. This is the reason I was burning time until I could be with him again.

I let him keep talking as I look up to find clouds whirring past the moon. The light is bright, and it's hard to believe everything that has happened today has happened in only one day. Soon the moon will set, and I'm not sure what tomorrow will bring.

From inside, I can hear the faint playing of "Sweet Caroline," and know we're at the cover song before the encore. I need to get back. I press the phone back to my ear, and he's pleading.

"Oliver. I have to go."

"Reagan, please don't go. Can we just talk about this?"

"Not now. I need to go. I have something to do."

"Please, I love you. I know I messed up."

"Go to bed, and you'll feel different in the morning." It rips a part of me to hear myself say it out loud.

"I won't. I promise, I won't."

"Fine, then. Let's talk in the morning."

He's slow to respond, but finally agrees. I begin to say goodbye, but this time, he interrupts me.

"Reagan, I love you. I'm sorry."

"Tomorrow, Oliver. Let's talk tomorrow. Good night."

I hang up the phone and walk back inside. I feel Cyrus's eyes following me and try to ignore them. I rush inside, hoping I don't miss their encore, and I'm relieved to find they are just about to start. I pull my phone out and began to record. I add a caption to the video: *Packed room in Denver for us tonight, who wants to see us next?* The guys start in on their final song, and I dart towards the bar.

Cyrus finds his way next to me and doesn't waste a minute before shouting. "Everything okay? I heard a little of your call out there and well, it didn't sound so great."

I'm annoyed that he's asked, so I respond honestly. "Yeah, it's fine. Love isn't always the greatest."

"Are you in love?"

I want to tell him that's a weird thing to ask, but it's a good question. I *was* in love, and then I was hurt. I loved Oliver once, so fiercely I thought I could never recover without him. Then I thought I loved Asher, but it was probably just the heat of a moment. Now I'm moving on from Oliver and confused about Asher. And suddenly, Oliver loves me again.

"Maybe. I don't know anymore."

"Well, tequila then?"

I smile wide. "Yes, tequila then."

We take a shot and then I drag Cyrus out to the dance floor to dance to the last song, and wipe my brain clear of the day. All the questions can be a problem for future Reagan.

When they finish playing, people cheer for another encore, but the bar is trying to close. Nick appears behind the bar, and I saunter over to him with a confidence that can only be explained because of alcohol.

"Hey there. Do you work here?" I wink, and he smiles. It's fun to flirt with him, but I'm realizing that's all this will ever be. I continue before he can say anything. "Thanks for letting the guys play here tonight. I'm glad we were able to make this work."

"Me too. They rocked, and you weren't so bad yourself. I wish more managers could get down like you. Plus, the screaming on the phone outside was very cool."

I feel like my body is overheating. "Oh, I'm sorry, I—"

"No, I'm serious, very rock and roll. Don't apologize."

"But I'm embarrassed though. That's not rock and roll. I didn't know you were watching. I just— I wanted to be professional."

"Why? This isn't business school, you know."

"Yeah, I know that."

"Good. Then don't stop being yourself, Reagan Wilde, Boss Lady extraordinaire. My friend Keith will call you. I sent him your info. He books at a few venues throughout the Southwest." He rubs his thumb, pointer, and middle fingers together, signaling there will be money involved.

"Thanks, Nick. I owe you."

"Nah, this was all you and your guys." This time, he winks, and then hands me an envelope. I open it to see a stack of green bills. It's mostly ones and fives, but it's still a paid gig. He gives me a hug, and then whispers that Asher's looking this way. He's been paying attention, but I'm not sure what he thinks is going on. As Nick leans away, I feel another buzz in my pocket, and I'm reminded of my other problem. I hold off the urge to check it until Nick and I finish talking. He tightly squeezes my arm and walks away.

I remind myself that no matter the root cause of the buzz, I shouldn't get excited or anxious, and quickly disregarded that thought as I dig furiously in my pocket. For the first time in a while, it is exactly who I expect: Oliver.

Good night, Reagan. I can't wait to talk to you tomorrow.

He isn't going to forget our conversation, and tomorrow, I will have proof it isn't a dream. I remind myself again that this is future Reagan's problem. Tonight is about the band.

I search the room for the guys, and I see they're still talking to a few lingering folks. I skip over and plan to tell them the show rocked, and then I'll tell them about the cash, which we will obviously invest in recording or more touring. It's just the start of our success. I'm a good manager, and they need me. I'm proving it to myself and to them.

"Well, hey there, My Guys. Great show tonight."

I can tell they sense something is off, but they probably attribute it to whatever happened between Asher and I earlier. They don't expect for me to be in such good spirits, but the mixture of alcohol and good music has surprisingly forced me to have fun. That, mixed with my plans to ignore my emotions, makes for a good combination.

"Okay well, clearly I've left you speechless with my positivity, which shows me, as your manager, that you may need some more encouragement."

Phil chuckles and rubs his beard, and Marty rolls his eyes in a loving way while beginning to pack up his stuff. Asher is finishing up a conversation with a fan who is too pretty for my liking.

"You know what I find to really motivate people—money. And guess who is collectively $176 richer? My Guys."

Marty stops packing, and all three guys turn towards me. Marty squeals. "Are you serious?"

I nod, but before I can say any more, Asher does.

"It's our first paying gig in quite some time, all thanks to you, Reag."

And suddenly, I feel close to him again. The room drifts away and it's just the two of us. I think to myself, *You can't deny that there is a connection here.*

"I think we should use the cash to save up for recording time," I say.

"That's exactly what I was thinking. Completely agreed," he says. I wonder if the room has drifted away for him because he's just staring at me.

"Okay. Yeah, well, this is weird." Phil gestures to the two of us.

"It's beautiful." Marty puts his arms around the two of us and pulls us together in a hug. Phil must think we're crazy, but he's missed all the moments before this one. He won't be on the outside forever, but for right now, the three of us know there's something going on.

"The money, I mean. *That's* beautiful," Marty quickly corrects himself, then pulls Phil back towards the gear to keep packing.

"They're funny, those two." Asher says through a smile, and I know he knows it was a good set.

"Would it be better to be a full band though?"

"Reagan, please, can we just drop all of this for tonight?"

I change the subject, sort of. "Did you used to get paid for shows?"

"We did sometimes, but not consistently enough that it mattered. That's why we need someone like you."

"Hm, someone *like* me?" *But not actually me,* I think to myself.

"Well, I'm just saying someone to keep us focused on growing the band while we focus on writing good music. I hope that someone will be you."

I feel an uncontrollable smile spread across my face.

"Sooo, drinks to celebrate?" I sing in a harmless yet flirtatiously way, showing off the latest trick I learned from Nick.

We meet up with Phil and Marty at the bar, where we all take a tequila shot and retell the story of how we all met to Phil.

"You really thought he was a serial killer, and you could kill him with a picture frame?"

"I mean, now that I know him, I know I could seriously wound him with the frame. Look at his delicate body."

"Delicate? I think you mean godly." Asher flexes his arm muscles.

"Please. Do not get carried away—you're hardly statuesque."

It feels good to be this way with them. I try to put Jerome, Oliver, Kitty and any other problems out of my mind and instead focus on the success of tonight. We stay at the bar until Cyrus kicks us out. I kiss him on the cheek on my way out, and Phil follows suit.

"Okay, not to be the dad of the group, but Reagan clearly doesn't want to be responsible today, so I'll just say we need to take this party home to Phil's mom," Marty says, far too pleased to get to play the role of responsible adult.

I give him a dirty look before nodding in agreement. I don't want to be responsible.

"She's going to kill us if you wake her up," Phil says plainly. I believe him.

"She'll kill *you*, Phil. She's pleased as pie to see my smug mug." Marty pinches his own grinning cheeks.

"Marty is probably right; we should go home. We've got another show tomorrow." I bump my hip against Marty and link my arm between his. I'm grateful to have his friendship. It's one of the only I've had where I don't have to think about my place in his world.

"Let's walk." Asher suggests before starting down the sidewalk without our response.

"Can we even walk from here?" Marty questions responsibly, but Asher's too far down the street, wobbling side to side like he's leaning off a tight rope. Marty looks at me as if to say, *Here's your chance, please take it.*

"It doesn't look like he's stopping. I'll catch up with him. If we can't walk, I'll call a Lyft. Which you should do too." I say. I don't take my eyes off Asher.

"Ugh fine, I'll call my mom." Phil groans to our surprise. He must have finally caught on that something was happening with Asher and me. "If you need us to get you on the way home, just call me. She can scoop you two up too."

Marty beams. "God, I really missed your mom."

"Leave it alone, Marty. You've got Jess," Phil jokes while digging his elbow into Marty's side.

"It's just been so long..."

"This is disgusting," I say. "Marty, call your girlfriend. Phil, thank you. I'm going to catch up to our drunk lead singer and we'll call you if we need a ride."

I rush to catch up with Asher and find him trying to grab a cigarette from a stranger just outside of a different bar. "Excuse him, sir, he doesn't even smoke. Let me get him out of your way."

"I smoke sometimes, Reagan. You don't know me." Asher shouts back, and I realize he is way more drunk than I expected.

The stranger throws his cigarette down and moves back into the bar.

"Wow, Asher, making all kind of friends tonight."

"Yeah, it's nothing compared to you and that new friend of yours."

He's struggling for words, but gesturing to show height and length, while pointing to his muscles.

"A heavy box?"

"Nick. That guy, Nick, in there." He points towards the bar we came from.

"Oh, so you *do* know his name?"

"Unfortunately."

"Nick is band business, that's all. Business that got us paid, and if you check your Instagram account, even more followers. Which leads to more bookings and more followers. A healthy, self-fulfilling cycle that enables all of us to keep doing this thing."

"You talk about this like this is more official than a band."

"It is both official *and* a band, and we're just getting started."

"I like that you think that about us. I want that for us. For the band, I mean."

"Me too. My eggs are all in your basket, remember that. Even my *mom* has warmed up to the idea."

"Moms love me."

"Ha. No, they don't."

"Yeah, they don't..." He trails off, and I wonder if he's ready for me to call a car.

"Should we walk? At least partway?" I offer. I know we can't walk all the way home, but we can go part way, sober up, and call a car. I can't stop myself from thinking that if we're talking, then he's not talking to Kitty.

He nods and heads off decidedly in the wrong direction.

"Asher let's go to where we have a bed. This way." I point and start heading off the opposite way from him. He sprints quickly to meet up with me and then slows to my pace. We're both quiet, and I'm remember the last conversation we had alone. I feel nervous, but I know we need to say something. Before I work up the courage, he does. He stops walking and throws his gaze in my direction. I can tell by the way he's looking at me that he's spinning in his own head.

"I'm sorry I didn't tell you about Jerome. It was just hard to talk about. I don't like how that happened. I was the bad guy in that situation. I should've been happy for my friend; he is the better musician. I don't like that part of me; the jealous part. And I didn't want you to know that part of me."

"It's okay that you didn't tell me. I have a hard time believing he is a better musician though."

He smiles wide and stops directly in place. "Reagan, can we just, can we just talk?"

"Yeah, sure, of course we can."

"How about over there?" He points to a bench along the sidewalk, and we stroll over. He gets to the bench first and sits directly in the middle. I sit down towards the end, some distance away because I'm not sure what kind of conversation we're about to have. He slides his body closer to mine, and I'm glad to have the heat, and the tiny shock of electricity. I don't know what I want to hear from him, but I know I don't want it to hurt. I'm tired from the day, and the prior explosive conversations I've already had. Topics surrounding Asher, Jerome and Oliver flood my mind. I just want this conversation to center on something positive. I want to leave it better than we arrived.

"I'm sorry about Kitty. About talking to her, and about not telling you. I didn't know how you felt about me."

I didn't have Kitty on my emotional topics bingo card, and now realize I should've.

"You don't have to be sorry for talking to her. You didn't do anything wrong. I was just hurt because I told you about Oliver and then you didn't tell me what was going on with you. I thought we were more connected than we really are, and that's why I was upset. But we can just move on."

"I don't want you to be mad at me though."

"You're apologizing for *talking* to someone. You can talk to people; I can talk to people. We can't get mad at each other for talking. We just need to figure out what that means for our relationship. If we're putting the band first, we can't let feelings get in the way. We just have to decide how we're going to be with one another."

"How *are* we going to be?"

"How do you want to be?" I want him to take the lead, but he doesn't.

"Well, you said you're falling for me," he says easily, without giving an indication of what that means to him.

"Yeah, I guess I thought I was, but I was wrong. It was a stupid moment, and I said something stupid."

"Oh, so what you thought you could love me for what? Like four seconds? Come on, Reagan, be real with me."

"How can I be real with someone who literally doesn't tell me anything? You don't tell me how you feel about me, or why I'm here or why you're talking to some shitty ex."

"I thought we weren't going to get mad at each other for talking to people."

I give him a dirty look in response.

"And you're no different, Reagan. You're still so hung up on your ex, you'd do anything for him."

"Yeah well, maybe I should just go back to him then." It falls out of my mouth before I realize I'm trying to hurt him.

Asher shifts away from me, taking the heat and electricity with him. We're hurting each other. Someone needs to stop it from going any further. I need it to be him because I don't have it in me to heal us both. I'm hurting, and I need him to tell me what I mean to him. He could tell me he doesn't want me to go, and that would be enough. He could tell me he wants me to stay, but only as his friend and his manager, not his girlfriend. He could say I'm important to his dream, that we have a connection, but it isn't romantic. He could say he wants me on this journey, but he doesn't want to risk the band, and because I'm a part of that now, I'm part of him in that way. It doesn't have to be that he feels the same way as I do, that he loves me, but he's too afraid to say it. I would stay under any condition that makes me feel that the connection is real. But instead, he finds a way to hurt me and make it count.

"Reagan, you can't do that."

I breathe in deeply, holding on to all the air my lungs can gather.

"He doesn't want you anymore."

And just like that, the air is knocked out of me.

"I'm sorry, but he doesn't. I know that's hard to hear. I've tried to be patient with this, but you need to move on. He sucks if he can't see how great you are, so stop wanting someone who sucks so much. It sounds easy, and I know it isn't, but a lot of time has passed, and you've hardly moved on. You want to know why that is? I think it's because you're so lost. You're clinging on to him because you want someone else to pick what comes next in your life. But no one is going to make you happy because you don't even know what you're looking for. I can't just figure that out for you. You can't put that on me. You said you love me; well, I think you love the idea of being *with* someone. You can't stand the idea of being alone."

In this moment, it all feels crystal clear. I have allowed myself to fall in love with assholes. I deserve better than this. I love parts of Asher Blair, but not this righteous creative who thinks he knows the answers to all life's questions. So, I tell him exactly that.

"Asher, I *thought* I could love you. Maybe I had my wires crossed, trying to find love in someone, anyone, and I found you. There are marvelous things about you, but you are also just the worst. That's why you're allowing yourself to go back to Kitty. You don't want that part of you, that worst part of you, to go. I don't get it. I don't like that part of you, but whatever. That's your problem. If you think I'm holding on to the past, the same could be said of you.

"So no, I won't love the man who allows himself to go back to his ex because she's familiar and allows him to self-destruct. Meanwhile, you're chastising me for doing the same thing as you! I deserve better than this and better than you. And maybe it isn't even Oliver, but don't tell me I'm delusional, because he called me tonight and he wants to get back together. He begged for me. He wants to talk to me tomorrow, and you know what? I might as well let him."

His eyes narrow in on me like he's shaping me up. "What are you talking about?"

"Tonight, he called me and told me he wants me back. So if you don't think I'm worth it, at least he does."

He gets quiet again and puts his head into his lap. I realize he is very drunk and may not even remember this conversation tomorrow. I can't stop the conversation from happening now. I need him to hear what I have to say, but more than that, I need to hear what he has to say to me.

"So are you going back to him? If so, I'll need you to let me know so I can get the show details figured out, find someone else to help."

"Seriously? *That's* what you care about right now?"

"Of course, it is. Why are you upset? You're getting what you wanted. It's just like I said, you only care about being in love. You don't care about what we're building. You're going to sacrifice our tour and our showcase just so you can go back to him."

"Asher, that is *not* what I want. You know that. Why are you being like this?"

He leans back in his seat, extending his legs long across the sidewalk. He doesn't respond. He rubs his temples like he's annoyed. I want to cry, but I don't let myself. He seems like he couldn't care if I tore my heart out and gave it to him on a platter.

"I don't *want* to go back to him, that's not what I'm saying. I'm just saying you don't know what you're talking about, so please don't talk to me like that."

"Like what, Reagan?"

"Like I'm stupid. Like I'm an idiot, like you don't care about me. You *do* care about me. You don't care about Kitty. I don't want to go back to him—that much was clear tonight when I didn't go running. Right after he told me that, do you know what I did? I went back in the bar, and I danced by myself. And now, I'm here with you. I'm figuring out what I want, and who I want to be."

He shakes his head. "Listen, you don't have to prove that to me." It isn't what I want to hear.

"Asher, I thought we were going to talk, so let's talk. What do you feel for me? Don't just tell me all the ways you've analyzed me and determined I'm broken. I get that you think I'm not my own person, but I also think that you can tell I'm trying to grow. I'm trying to figure out my dream, and I think you are too. That's what binds us. You must feel something more for me than just feeling sorry. I know I feel something more for you. I care about you more than I've cared for anyone in my world. I'm not saying it's romance. I *do* care about you, so much, but I'm not the kind of person who just needs romantic love. I'm saying there's a bond between us that runs deep. We're different, and our connection is different. You're rooted deep inside my being."

It feels like I'm cutting the words out of myself. He doesn't even try to stop the bleeding.

"Please, just say something. I thought we were going to talk."

"So are you going back to him?"

I scoff. I can't believe that's what matters to him right now. If I mattered to him, then that would not be the first thing on his lips.

"Asher, I'm saying that part doesn't matter right now. What matters to me is this conversation. You just said a lot of hurtful things, and I'm trying to help you see how I'm feeling."

He stands up. I don't want him to walk away, but more than anything, I don't want him to see that this is tearing me apart. I continue, determined to hurt him, and get us both home. Tomorrow, it will be easier to talk.

"Well, you really *are* making it an easy choice for me. I think we should call a car."

"I want to walk."

"You're being a child. It will take you hours, and you need to be alive for the show tomorrow."

"Fine, I'm being a child. I'm going to walk."

It spills out of me again, and while I'm saying it, I don't regret it. "I wish I wouldn't have told you how I felt. You didn't deserve that."

I stand and walk decidedly in the opposite direction. He doesn't protest or call after me, and that says everything. Any decision I make will need to be my own. It can't be at the expense of someone else, no matter how strong of a connection it seems to be. I turn a corner and find a spot on the curb. We had wandered into a neighborhood, and I hope the neighbors haven't heard me raise my voice. I dial Marty's number and decide he can be the adult tonight. He rooted for us, but he was wrong to.

He answers the phone, and I can tell he didn't expect it to be bad news.

"Hi. I need you to go get Asher."

"Okay. Are you okay?"

"No, I'm not. But right now, I just need you to go get him. I can't deal with him right now."

"Reagan, I'm sorry. He's a good guy, but when he's not okay, he's not good. I think he just— he was surprised by how much he cares about you. He's afraid you don't feel the same. He's just being dumb."

"I can't do dumb anymore, Marty. I don't deserve that. He won't even tell me how he feels about me."

He's quiet, but I know he agrees.

"I'll see you at home." I hang up and realize I'm alone. I don't know where Asher is, but that's not my problem right now. I'm ready to go home.

I call a car and wait. I check the time, and see that it's three a.m. I can't even remember the last time I was out at three a.m. I decide it's the quietest hour of the day and use the quiet to think for myself. Asher is right about some of what he said. I need to figure out where I'm going on my own. I can't be influenced by how I feel for someone else. I'm tired of making my world revolve around another person, only for them to leave me feeling lonelier than I've ever been in my life.

My phone starts to ring, and I assume it must be the driver.

"Hello?"

"Uh, hi. Wow, I didn't expect you to answer."

The voice is familiar. I wonder if I've died and gone to hell after the day I've had.

"Jocelyn?"

"Reagan, there's been an accident. Oliver was in an accident. He's not okay."

I hold my breath.

"I think you need to come home."

I've run out of air.

Sixteen

Tragedy is an unexpected visitor who doesn't care about what you were planning, putting off, or hoping to do. It's a careless taker who doesn't consider that not only had I *just* spoken with Oliver, but I'd also once loved him fiercely. Tragedy had no care for the fact I had a hard day, and a newly re-broken heart. The only blessing tragedy brought with it was a heavy, dull coat that I used to mask the pain of speaking with Jocelyn. She could've told me all the intimate, juicy details of how her affair started with Oliver, and I'm not sure I would have felt a thing.

Jocelyn doesn't wait for me to ask about what happened, instead she proceeds to tell me that Oliver had been out that night. They had broken up, just like he said. I don't bother to gloat, even though she expects it. We're both feeling worse than we ever knew we could feel. She explains that he left the apartment to go do whatever it is someone does after a breakup. She expected him to return after a few hours, but by one a.m., he still wasn't home. She called him repeatedly, until he picked up. He eventually answered, said horrible things to her, and so she told him not to bother coming home.

"I could tell he'd been drinking. I probably should've let him come back, asked him to, even, or picked him up. I had been drinking, and I was emotional. Of course, now I feel bad." Her voice sounds tired. I feel sorry for her, but I don't plan to reveal that fact. She wants me to console her, but

I won't. We both care for him. We both deserve consolation, and neither of us will get it from the other.

"I tried to go to sleep, but of course I couldn't, so I was up late watching the *Real Housewives of New Jersey* when I got the call. What a stupid thing to remember, but I'll never be able to forget that's what I was doing when she called. His mom. I guess they called her first, but she's out of the state, so she called me so someone could go be with him."

The hurt happens instantly. We were together for years, but that didn't matter. Oliver's mom knew to call Jocelyn. That made whatever it was they had real. I don't fixate on the fact for too long because she continues.

"It isn't good. He doesn't look good..." She trails off.

"What exactly happened?"

"We think what happened—or, what the police told me from what they can piece together—is that he was out drinking, and I guess he thought he could bike home. He was in downtown. They said his blood alcohol level was .2. I didn't really know what that meant, I just knew that was high. I Googled it, and it said something about a possible blackout. Which makes sense."

She hesitates to get to the point. I don't want to rush her. I'm not sure I want to know what's coming next.

"They think he was going like thirty miles per hour down one of the hills before he turned on 1st Ave. Maybe he thought he'd be the only one on the street, but of course, he wasn't." Her voice cracks. "It wasn't the car's fault. It stopped to make a turn, and he probably didn't see it. So that's how he went through the back window."

I gasp; I can't help it. I picture 1st Avenue. It's a street we walked down on our way towards Pike Place Market on weekends we stayed together in the city. We had wine at the corner shop in Pioneer Square. We stood in the main square, and he told me he loved me, not once but many times. So much happened for us on that one street.

"I only got to see him for a minute, and since they told me what happened, no one's come back to talk to me. They called his mom to find out his blood type when I didn't know. I don't know what she said." She breaks out into loud tears.

"How would you know that, Jocelyn? That's not your fault." My kindness surprises me.

"He saw me when he was coming in. He was conscious."

"Conscious is good."

She ignores my comment and instead says, "I think he thought I was you."

I don't know what to say to that or why she would even think that about him unless she is feeling insecure. Maybe she's trying to manipulate me, but she seems so sad, I can't imagine her using this moment to do something so painful. I think about telling her that maybe he thought that because we spoke a few hours earlier, but I know she'll take that personally, like I'm trying to hurt her.

My driver abruptly stops in front of Phil's mom's house, and loudly barks, "Thank you," in a way that almost sounds like he'd rather be saying, "Get the hell out of my car." I assume he's annoyed about my being on the phone for the whole ride. I want to shout back at him that I'm just trying to find out if my boyf – my ex-boyfriend is going to make it through the night. Instead, I manage to mumble, "Thanks," and jump out of the car.

"Reagan, I think you should know that he said he still loves you. He even told me so before the accident. And then he said it again when he got to the hospital in his drunken, smashed up stupor, obviously thinking I was you."

I don't respond. I don't know what to say. I'm sure she thinks this is the first time I'm hearing this. She probably half expects, half wants me to fall into pieces. Maybe she thinks she's making up for everything she's done by sharing this news with me. Whatever her reasoning for sharing, it doesn't matter. This isn't how I wanted any of this to happen.

Then it hits me, heavy and all at once. Could this be my fault? If I'd responded the way everyone thought I would when he called, then maybe he wouldn't have gotten on his bike tonight. If I was home in Seattle when he called, maybe I would've gone to him, and we would have had the chance to restart our life. Instead, he may be fighting for his. It feels like I've been punched in the stomach. This isn't anything like I wanted it to be. So I say something, anything, to move on from this moment.

"How long have you been there? At the hospital?"

"Just a few hours. I had to call his mom back first. I was trying to get more information. I'm sorry I didn't call you sooner."

"You don't have to be sorry about that. You really didn't need to call me. Not that I didn't want to know, or that I shouldn't know. It's just— I'm glad you did at all."

"He's always been more yours than mine, Reagan. Even though we hurt you, he still loves you, and I shouldn't have taken him." She is crying, quietly now.

"You can't take people, Jocelyn. They make their choices."

I look over at Phil's driveway and notice that the van still isn't home. I don't want to be the first person to get home. I've sobered up, and there's no way the guys have. So instead of walking inside, I decide to take a walk through the neighborhood. Briefly, I think of Asher, and hope he's safe. I'm sure they found him, and Phil's mom is cursing him even more than she was before. It feels wrong to think about the guys. Everything that happened tonight seems small by comparison.

"Jocelyn, what do you need from me?"

She continues to cry, and I understand that's all she can do. I stay on the phone and keep walking. She just needs to know someone is here for her right now. I just need to do something for someone, anyone, other than myself. Emotional procrastination of another form. So I'll do that. I'll be there for *her*, right now.

As I walk the neighborhood, I can hear the faintest chirp of birds beginning to welcome the day. It seems too cold to be morning, but the increasing and gradual brightness of early morning is proving me wrong. I shiver and wish I would've brought a jacket with me after all. When this whole adventure started, I hadn't thought about changing seasons or falling temperatures. We were planning to go to Los Angeles next. It'd be warmer there. Maybe we'd even drive through Phoenix. It crosses my mind that maybe we could visit Jerome. We *should* visit Jerome. The thought feels like one I've already had, and I wonder if that was Karol's plan all along—plant the seed and let me execute the reunion.

I reach the end of the block and turn back to walk towards the house. The lack of awkwardness in the silence between Jocelyn and me is surprising. I let it carry me through the rest of the walk home. I can see Phil's house now, and stop short to watch the van pull in. Karol pops out of the car in a fluffy blue bathrobe and scurries inside. I catch one yawn from her and what looks like side eye as the guys jump out of the car. Asher climbs out last. He doesn't look upset, and that part hurts my heart. I wanted him to jump out, and rush inside to find me. But if he couldn't do that, he at least should've looked sad. He's staring at his phone, and I'm sure he's talking to her. I want to scream *that's not acceptable! Part of the deal is that when one of us is breaking, we both are, and we must work on putting each other back together*. But of course I don't. These are the unwritten rules I assumed he knew.

Jocelyn's quiet now, and I'm getting tired.

"Jocelyn, what do you need?"

"Please, can you come to the hospital. I can't do this. We need you."

It's been a hard day, but I never thought about going home until now. Even with Oliver calling, and Asher being difficult, I didn't consider that maybe it was time to call it quits. I thought Asher and I could patch this up. We'd keep going on the trip. We'd win the showcase, and then whatever came next, we'd be able to handle together.

"I'm in Colorado," I exhale knowing the excuse isn't good enough.

"Okay, maybe not right now, but I could book you a flight home for later today?"

I look up at the house once again and close my eyes tight. I'm hoping that maybe Asher saw me outside and is waiting to talk to me, like at the truck stop or earlier yesterday when he found me in the bathroom. I open my eyes already knowing the answer. The front door is shut, and I'm the only one outside. The truth becomes increasingly clear like someone's used bright yellow highlighter to make a point. There are people at home who need me now, and Asher isn't one of them. I've planned enough to get them to LA. It's enough to give him a second shot at his dream. He can go on building the band and rekindle things with Kitty. I can go back to Oliver. Maybe this whole situation is big enough that Oliver, Jocelyn, and

I can slot back into our original roles. We can all end up with what we once wanted. I just can't help but notice the thought stings.

"Okay, buy the flight and send me the details."

She at least owes me the flight, and I have no extra money.

"Thank you, Reagan," she says sweetly, almost as if she's asking for forgiveness.

After we've hung up, I slink back into Phil's house like someone who does not belong. My heartbeat vibrates throughout my body, either from fear or exhaustion. I need to keep busying myself, or I may fall apart. I take out my phone and start writing a to do list: pack a bag, find a ride, thank Karol, say goodbye to the guys, send them the trip details, tell them to go see Jerome, call my parents, fix things with Asher. *Fix things with Asher.*

I can do everything on the list, except for maybe the last one. To fix things, we need to talk, and that likely isn't going to happen early this morning. I can't swallow the thought of leaving without explaining why. I just need him to know that we don't have to break because of this. I can convince him, and myself, that my going home is more about my character and less about the power *they* hold over me. He must understand that. And when he does, then we can keep the band going, and we'll both be better for going through this. We don't have to say goodbye.

As I pace throughout the kitchen, deep in thought, footsteps sneak up behind me. "Good to see you bright and early this morning. Where did you disappear off to?" Marty jokes, rubbing his eyes like a child. I almost feel bad that I need to break the news to him first. From Marty's point of view, he probably had a pretty good day. He got to play a show with his best friends that they collectively killed. In a few weeks, they'll win the showcase. I don't even doubt it, and after tonight, I can tell he doesn't either. I think about how insecure he felt a few days ago when we played the last show. He thought that this could all be for nothing. How quickly time changes your perspective.

I string words together to say out loud. "Is it morning already?"

His face changes quickly and I realize I must sound as bad as I feel. "What's wrong? Is it Asher? Did something happen with Asher? I mean, of course it did, because we picked him up, but he made it seem like it was just a fight, and you were tired." He puts his hands on my shoulders. "It'll be okay. He's gonna figure it out."

I scoff at the thought that he thinks this is just a *fight*, and not the end of everything we hoped for. I try to knock the negative thoughts out of my head and remember my positive talk track. We can all be better for this. Or maybe I should just leave now with no plans to return. As I debate the pros and cons of disappearing into thin air, Marty presses me.

"Reagan, we've known each other long enough to know that you aren't good at hiding emotion, try as you might. What's going on?"

"I don't know where to begin."

"Come on. Let's sit down and talk." He guides me over to the kitchen table, then he rummages through the cabinets to get two glasses before filling them with water. "Asher's still awake, so we should be quiet unless you want to talk to him. It may be better to wait until the morning though. He's still drunk." Marty sounds disappointed, and suddenly I picture him as someone's dad. I want to hug him because he's taking care of me. I hope we can still be friends when this is over. That thought is the thing that breaks the dam, and tears fall all at once. I take a sip of water and he pats me gently on the back.

"I *will* need to talk to him at some point tonight. Maybe you can help me figure out how."

"Well, he's in one of those classic nasty Asher moods. That's partially how I figured out there's something wrong between you two. Well, that and you left him in a random neighborhood to fend for himself and fight off raccoons."

I can hear faint chatter in the back room. "Is he talking to himself?"

"May as well be, not like she'll actually listen to him."

"She?" I know it before he can answer. "Ah, Kitty. What a stupid name."

He nods but doesn't say anything. I want him to agree with me so desperately. I want him to say she's awful and they will never work.

"Do you like her?" I ask trying to push him in the direction of saying something mean.

"Not particularly, but I don't know her very well. Asher and I basically stopped talking right around when they got together because of the band stuff..." He trails off.

"Karol told me a little about the demise of the band."

"Oh, lovely. She's great, I love Karol, and that doesn't surprise me one bit. She loves to share things she really shouldn't. You wouldn't believe what she told Jess about me and who I used to date." He laughs, but I don't. I'm too tired. He says the thing on both of our minds. "So you know about Jerome then?"

"I know what Karol told me about Jerome. She said I'm basically the new Jerome."

This time, he's shaking his head. My body feels tense, and I look down to find my hand is balled up in a fist.

"That couldn't be farther from the truth, Reagan. Asher and Jerome were close, they were best friends, and you and Asher—well, you're as close as best friends in my opinion, but you'll never be like them."

"What does that mean?"

"They really loved each other, and they really hurt each other. Yes, Asher thought Jerome was taking the audition from him because he was being an insecure, self-centered douche. He never should've treated Jerome that way. He iced him out, and he pushed us all away as punishment. But that was all about Asher. Jerome falling apart was all about Jerome. Yes, I wish we could've done more to help him, but I can't blame myself for him falling apart, and Asher can't be blamed either. Before any of that happened, Jerome was already going through his own stuff. Asher was doing his best to help him. We always could've done more, but when people break and break and break, eventually they need to be the ones figuring out how to stop themselves from getting to that point."

I think about what he's saying. People need each other, but not too much. They need to focus on themselves, but not overdo it. They need help healing, but they also need to heal themselves. They must know when they're giving too much, or not enough. There's no equation for knowing how much to ask of someone else or how much to give away, so we all give and take and give, and still, we break apart or become codependent, or entirely too independent.

"I still don't understand what's going on with Asher and me. Isn't that pathetic? I told him I was falling in love with him earlier tonight."

"You did? Wow. What did he say?"

I stare at him blankly. I want to yell, scream, and shout, "Clearly, not well." but the look gets the message across.

He responds, "That was a stupid question. I'm sorry."

"Why is he talking to her? Does he care that he's hurting me?"

"I think he does, but he's also hurting."

I roll my eyes.

"I get it, Reagan; I know that's stupid. He has a lot of growing to do, but he's doing it. He's getting better. I know this is a major setback, but he's going to wake up tomorrow and see how stupid he's being. That's why I just think you hold off on tonight and try not to give up your hope in him entirely. He's never had someone like you in his life. He talks about you all the time, even when you're not around. I know he would be broken if he knew he could lose you. And I know he should be the one telling you this, not me, but I can't let you think you don't matter to him because he's too scared to say something." Marty's almost out of breath when he finishes talking. He seems desperate. All I can think is that this is what Asher should be doing.

"Don't you think I've given him chances?"

"You have, but hasn't he given you some too? He's trying to push you out of this funk you're in, and towards something you *want* to do. I see how you are with the band, and how it pushes you out of your comfort zone. He's helping you move into this new version of yourself. You're growing together. That's something amazing."

"Yeah, that's something." I smile, but it quickly disappears. Relationships are about grace. I get where he's coming from, but I already promised to leave. Decidedly, I say what comes next. "When it comes to giving and taking, I think I've given all I can right now, and I need something more from him."

"I understand that. I do. Just try to give him tonight if you can."

"I can't. I'm going home."

"Woah, what? Please don't do that—" he starts in, but I cut him off.

"I have to go home, Marty. Something happened with an old friend. He's in the hospital. I'm not sure if he— I'm not sure he'll be okay." I don't have it in my heart to tell him that friend is Oliver. The two of us have never discussed Oliver, but he must know something. I see concern spread across his face, and I almost feel bad for not saying more.

"I'm so sorry... What happened?"

I proceed to tell him, and when I finish, I end up back at square one. Asher. "I don't want him to think I'm leaving because of this fight, or that I don't care about him or the band. But I think that's what he'll think. He won't understand, but they need me, and tonight he showed me that he doesn't."

"Reagan, this has never been about needing you. We could've done this without you, Reagan. That's not a way to measure how much you're loved. We love you, and we want you here. All of us. Not needing you shouldn't be the reason you leave."

He and I both know that hearing this from him isn't enough reason to stay.

"I need to go see Oliver. If he doesn't..." I can't get the words out.

Marty rubs his hand up and down my arm and whispers, "I know, I know," until I'm ready to speak again.

"I just know I couldn't forgive myself if I didn't at least go see him."

He surprises me and doesn't protest. I loosen the grip on my balled-up fist. At least I won't have to fight this battle.

"What can I do?"

"Could you take me to the airport in a few hours? I need to pack up. And can I give you the details for the next few shows? I can send more once I've talked to Nick's booker friends."

"Yeah, of course. But don't you think you'll come back? At least for LA?"

I look towards Asher's room and the light is still on, his voice still mumbling. "I don't know. I guess we'll see how it all goes."

"Okay." He looks at me unhappily, knowing there's nothing left to say. I want to ask him if he thinks this will be enough to push Asher towards me, or if he'll move farther away. No matter the answer, it's just speculation. So instead, I ask him about Jerome.

"Karol said Jerome is in Phoenix. If I plan a show there, do you think you could go see him?"

"Reagan, I don't know if that's a good idea."

"Don't you think that if you don't go, you won't be able to forgive yourself?"

He looks at me with disbelief in his eyes. "Some pretty bad things could go down. But you're right, I may not be able to forgive myself."

"Is that a, *yes*?"

"It's an *I'll try*."

"One more thing."

This time, he rolls his eyes.

"Can you please say hi to Jess for me? I miss her."

He smirks. "Of course. I do too. She's coming to LA though. You could see her then."

"It's an *I'll try* for me too." I pat him on the shoulder and start to stand.

"I changed my mind. You should talk to Asher tonight. He'll be devastated if you leave without a goodbye."

I nod, and we both know it's what I want.

"You should get a bit of sleep. I'll wake you up in a few hours."

Marty stands and gives me a full-body embrace before zombie-walking to the couch and passing out. I shuffle down the hallway toward Asher's room.

He's still on the phone. The door is slightly ajar, and I peek inside to see him sprawled on the hard wood floor, staring straight up at the ceiling. He's wearing a KORN T-shirt that must belong to someone else, and brushing his hand through his hair. He must've been doing it for a while now because his hair is standing straight up in a way that can only be accomplished through repetitive motion. He's still on the phone with her. I wonder what they're talking about and imagine it can't be like the things we talk about. Biggest fears, or memories of childhood.

I want to walk inside the room and lay on the floor next to Asher so we can talk, just the two of us again. I'd put on a song we both love and can half listen to while we talk about nothing and everything. I want to go back to Mrs. Blair's and start all over again. I'd be careful to be true to myself, and careful to show him how he makes me feel. I'd ask more of him, and he'd be able to give it.

My weight shifts and wakes up the creaky floorboard below me. We make eye contact, and my heart drops in my chest.

"One second," he whispers to the person on the other side of the phone.

I want him to tell that person he can't talk anymore. I want him to say something witty or comforting, and for the two of us to spend the hours we have left being with each other. Instead, he says something devastating.

"Good night, Reagan."

And with that, he flips his body over to face away from me and uses his foot to close the door. I spend a few extra moments lingering in the silence. I wonder if this is how I'll remember him.

I look down at my phone hoping it can save me from this moment. Instead it says 4:34 a.m. and I decide to use the time as a sign to keep moving instead of crying. I rush upstairs and spend the remaining hour packing, writing notes for the shows, and drafting a thank you note to Karol. I spend the remaining twenty-six minutes writing a goodbye letter to Asher. Then I wake up Marty, give him the notes, and ask him to take me home.

Seventeen

The early morning light beams in through the plane window, waking me up as we begin our descent into Seattle. Peeking past my neighbor in the window seat, I catch a glimpse of Mount Rainier shimmering in the rare show of sunlight. It is a mighty way to be welcomed home, and almost helps me forget what I've just done. The relief lasts only a few minutes before I'm back in reality.

Before we pulled out of the driveway on our way to the airport, Marty pressed me to say goodbye. It didn't take much convincing for me to explain that I couldn't do it, and so we left both knowing I was making a mistake. By now, Asher's probably waking up and Marty will be the one to tell him that I've left. I hope he understands. I tried to explain it all in the letter.

Oh no, the letter.

In the light of day, I'm wondering if that was the biggest mistake of all. I couldn't recite everything I wrote in stream of consciousness note, but full pieces are coming back to me now.

I know you'll be surprised that I left, but I'm trying to do the right thing. This doesn't mean I don't want your dreams to come true too.

Yes, he's that right thing, but that doesn't mean he's my right thing. It's not because I have feelings for him. I think those are over. I realized that last night, dancing in the bar, by myself. I don't need him, or anyone else, to complete the life I'm building. But they needed me and not going would say more about me than about them.

And just so you know, when I say I don't need anyone to complete my life, I mean it. That doesn't mean I didn't mean it when I told you I was falling in love with you. It happened quickly, but you understood me instantly. I've never felt seen by someone the way you saw me. The light between us is what keeps me coming back to you.

But that's not all. You've also helped me move on from something hard and have shown me that I deserve this life I'm building. And I like building it with you...

I want to bang my head against the airplane seat, but don't want to wake up either sleepy passenger beside me. I told him he was a good musician. I said that I was proud of him. I asked him about where he was headed with Kitty and reminded him that he shouldn't settle for some girl who abandoned and broke him before. Then I remember I also said he should go see Jerome. And I bet that will be the thing that hurts him the most.

I'm nervous for him to read it, but there's also a side of me that's ready. It's cringey, sure, but if I hadn't written it, then I may never have gotten to say to him all the things I needed to. I wish I could've spit it out when we were in the bathroom, or on the walk home last night, or even when we stopped at that rest stop all those days ago. I wish I would've said those things from the start, from the floor of Mrs. Blair's house. I don't know if it would've made a difference, but at least I wouldn't feel this way right now—awkward, lonely, trying to do the right thing, while wondering what the right thing is.

"Welcome to Seattle-Tacoma Airport. The local weather outside is forty-three degrees, but we've got a little sunshine. Thanks for flying with us, folks."

The voice on the speaker trails off, and I accept the fact that it's time to see Mom and Dad. After living with them for months, I'm surprised we haven't talked more, but I'm also grateful for the space they've given me. It almost makes me excited to see them. I haven't told them exactly why I'm coming home. I tried to keep it vague because I didn't know how to explain what had happened to Oliver. I hardly knew myself. But of course, they must know something is wrong because I texted them that I was coming back at 4 a.m and here I am now.

I find them just past the security gate, each waving back and forth with one hand while holding a welcome home banner between them. They take turns to hug me as soon as I finally reach them. I notice mom hangs on a little longer, but dad ruffles my hair like I'm a kid. As we start out of the airport to find the car, Mom immediately jumps into her personal list of offenses that occurred *just* at the airport today. "Then this guy just cuts off your dad. Like hello, we were signaling." The sweet moment focused on my return has already passed.

As we jump into the car, she brings up the My Guys Instagram, and tells me that she asked the other moms in her book club to follow the account. I chuckle, surprised to find I'm not annoyed by her right now.

"I am so proud of you. You seemed happy in your video last night."

I try not to pay attention to the words "seemed" or "last night". She reaches around the seat, grabbing my calf with her hand and squeezing hard. It feels like love, but I catch her eyes in the rearview mirror, and I see concern starting to spread across her face.

"So how long are you home from your rockstar life, Reggie?" Dad chimes in, using a sweet nickname I haven't heard him try on since I was nine or ten. He is wearing new aviator sunglasses and his cheeks dimple when he smiles at me in the rearview mirror. I had no idea how much I missed them.

"I'm not sure." And I'm not. I offer him a smile in return.

We're entering Seattle city limits now, and I hold my breath, hoping it doesn't hurt too much to be back. The thought crosses my mind that there was once a time when it pained me to walk through the city because of the memories Oliver and I held here. I entertain the thought that this time, if I feel any pain, it could be because of either boy.

Dad doesn't know that so he pulls off the highway to take a detour through downtown. He knows I love the way the city streets frame the Sound. As we turn onto 1st Ave, I try not to think about Oliver's accident but can't help myself from wondering if it happened here or over there.

I allow myself to say hello to Smith Tower as we pass it, and wave at my favorite book shop situated on the corner. We head up 1st Avenue, and the road fills with traffic as we pass by the market. Dad asks if I want to stop, and Mom loudly whispers that we should just go home. Call it mother's intuition or whatever, but she can sense I'm not okay, and it helps me realize I'm *not* okay.

"Nonsense. She loves the market, right, sweetie?" Each loving pet name shows me that he missed me too.

"I do..."

I can see him smirking, a small victory demonstrating that he too knows his daughter.

"But I am feeling very tired. Maybe we could go later?" I hope the concession doesn't hurt his feelings.

"Fair enough. I bet you had to wake up early." He shakes off the rejection for my sake. "So, do you have the dates for the big concert? It's in LA, right? How many concerts between now and then? Do I call them concerts?" The light turns green, and he speeds off, away from the market.

"You can call it a show."

"How about a gig?" Mom asks seriously.

"Sure, you can call it a gig. The guys are in Denver. They could stay there for a little while, play some regular places, or hit the road if they wanted to try out some new venues. They have options."

I texted Nick when I left town to let him know I had to go away for a few weeks. Family emergency, I told him. I asked if the guys could play some more shows in Denver. I didn't expect a reply, but I got one, just before I took off. Between his contacts and the venue in Denver, the guys really did have options.

"All thanks to you, I imagine." Dad chimes in.

"But you're still going to LA, right?" Mom asks with a tone of concern.

I stare out the window, and realize I feel sad as we pass through the city streets, but not defeated. It isn't like before, when I barricaded myself in my room for weeks. I won't do that now. No matter what happens, I'll recover and rebuild. Yes, this fabulous adventure was done with Asher, but it wasn't *because* of Asher. With or without him, I will be okay.

"I haven't decided if I'm going to keep doing the band stuff."

Mom spins her head around, eyes are wide, but she says nothing. I remember a time when I expected her to hate the idea of me working with the band. She wanted me to work on Wall Street or be the next CEO of some huge company. I think about telling her the truth about why I'm here, but I'm not ready.

"Yeah, I just— I'm here to see a friend, and I don't know how long that will take."

I don't wait for a response; I can tell she's concerned and trying to figure out her next move. I check my phone. It's almost ten in Seattle, which means it's nearly eleven in Colorado. Marty texted me when he got back to Phil's, wishing me a safe journey and letting me know he'd review the notes I left about the gigs, and hoped I'd think about coming back before LA. There have been no other messages. As unsurprised as I feel, I also hoped to hear from Asher. I wonder if he's read my note yet.

I text Marty: *Thanks for being a good friend. I'll think about LA. I hope you got some sleep. Can you let me know when you give it to him?*

After a few minutes of silence, it's clear Mom can't help herself. She watches me from the mirror as I type, and then put away my phone. Once I finish, the inquisition begins.

"So, a friend? I thought most of your friends had moved away."

"Yeah, they had. They came back."

"Do we know this friend?"

"Charlene, you are giving this girl the third degree. I thought you said we should let her rest." Dad for the rescue.

"Yes, I did... You're right, I did." She sits there, nodding her head, and I imagine her repeating those words to herself over and over again in an attempt to stay quiet. But she'll figure it out eventually, one way or another.

"You *do* know the friend. It's Oliver. And Jocelyn, too, I guess."

"Oh wow. I had no idea they were friends," my father says obliviously.

We're a few blocks away from our house now. I wonder if it'll hurt when I see Mrs. Blair's. I feel ready though. I'm preparing myself not to fall apart.

"Yeah, we don't really," I utter.

Mom keeps her eyes on me, waiting to learn more. We're on our street now. When I see Mrs. Blair's, I can't stop the memories. I don't even try to. I think about stumbling home, drunk in the afternoon after a day with Asher. My body fills up with bright, light joy. It's a wonderful memory. I want to laugh when I think about trying to defend myself with a picture frame. If the good memories keep coming, I don't have space to address the bad ones.

We pull into the driveway, and I pop out of the car before Mom can ask me anything else. Baby steps—I'm taking baby steps as long as I'm sharing with her.

My dad grabs my bag from the trunk. As he pulls the luggage inside, he adds, "Well, I'm sure you'll need your rest before you see them. Maybe we can talk more after lunch. I'll make you a sandwich or some eggs when you wake up."

Once he's inside, Mom and I have a moment alone in the garage. She chooses then to tell me she's happy that I'm home, and embraces me again, holding on for that extra few seconds. We head inside, and I drag my body upstairs. I feel woozy because I'm so tired, and maybe a little hungover. Inside my room, I take inventory of the space: bed, dresser, lamp all in the same place. I fling open my closet door and sift through all the clothes I used to wear. It's strange to find everything exactly as I left it. This time though, I'm different.

Eventually, I wake up to a *ding* from my phone. It's Jocelyn, asking if I landed already. I text her back: *Yes. I'm resting. Will come to the hospital soon.*

She likes the message. We're cordial, that's good enough.

I think about all that's changed in the time since I've last seen Jocelyn. She's fallen in love with my first love. My first love is fighting for his life. They were my whole world at one point, and now my world is bigger. I have met so many new people. I have friends. Marty is my friend, Nick is basically a friend, and in time, Asher and I will be friends again. When you have a connection like that with someone in your life, I think you're always tied to them. I don't have evidence to prove that, but it's something I feel so strongly that I know it must be true.

After a brief rest, I hop out of bed and steer myself towards the shower. I may be going to see Oliver and the girl who broke my heart, but there is no reason why I can't look good. I turn the shower on and let the warm water rush over me. I realize I still don't have a text from Asher or Marty. I wonder how Asher's responded to my disappearance. I want to know if he still plans to see Kitty. I mean, of course he does—he'd already made up his mind before, I don't know why he would change it now. I want to know if he's decided to go to Arizona. In my notes to Marty, I offered suggestions of venues they can play at, if they only call ahead. I hope they go, in part because I want that for Jerome, but also because if Asher goes, it proves he read my note. It proves I mean something to him.

I turn off the warm water, then find myself a hair dryer, a curling iron, a light shade of pink lipstick, and an outfit that kills. I give myself a wink as I walk out of the room and try to put out of mind that I'm going to the hospital. Crossing the threshold into the hallway, I startle my mother, who jumps back two feet from my door. She immediately opens a magazine and pretends to be reading it. I'm guessing she was just waiting for me to come out. Not a lot of people read magazines standing up in the hallway. Even fewer read the *Puget Sound Business Journal* standing up in the hallway.

"Well, hello, mother dearest. What are you up to?"

"Oh, just heading to my room going to lie down for a little while." She delays looking up from the magazine. When she finally does, she says, "You look nice."

"Thanks, I'm going to the hospital," I say matter-of-factly, and I can tell she thinks I'm joking. "No really, I am."

"Wait, what. Why? Oh my God, is she having a baby?." She looks like she's going to go down to that hospital and slap Oliver across the face.

"No. No. There was an accident. Oliver was in a bad accident."

Her face softens, and she brings me in for a hug. I want to pretend I don't need it, but I do. No matter what has happened or will happen, I'm scared for him. I proceed to tell her everything from the moment I found them on the couch to last night's call. I tell her a little bit about my fight with Asher, and not knowing where we've left things. She needs to know it all, or I'm afraid she'll push me back towards the band.

"Well, I'm very proud of you, my kind, sweet, smart girl." She hugs me again, and then says, "Please just don't push yourself too hard. Make sure you can handle it—I know you can—it's just this may be a hard day for you, depending on what shape he's in. Remember, you don't need to sacrifice yourself for anyone else, so take the space you need to."

"I know, thank you. I think I'm okay to do this—to see him and her, together, I mean. Although they aren't together."

"Just be careful. I don't know what Jocelyn is going to do to you, but it'll be something. She hates to lose." Mom's face spreads with disgust.

"Mom. She won't do anything. They're at the hospital..." I trail off because my mom is right. Jocelyn may lash out and try to throw hospital Jell-O in my face.

"And I know you said you've moved on, but I can't help but feel a little weary of you seeing Oliver again. After the state he left you in..."

"I know, Mom. You don't have to be worried though. It's different now. I'm different now." A smile spreads across my face, and it's infectious. She's smiling too.

Eighteen

I'm thrust into the hospital as soon as I arrive. People rush past me with their faces frozen in fear but their bodies moving quickly towards whatever fate awaits their loved ones. I think about Jocelyn, rushing around less than twelve hours ago, worry decorating her perfect face. She texted me on the way here that Oliver is in stable condition. He is awake, and the doctors think he'll be okay. No doubt, it will be a long journey ahead, but *okay* is better than when I talked to her last. I assume okay is better than most of the other people here, hurrying around with concern staining their faces. So, I get of their way and let them rush past me. I move deliberately toward the hospital map, trying to figure out what comes next. My eyes are drawn to the reception desk on the fourth floor, and that seems like the place to start.

I call an elevator, which takes a few minutes to arrive. The doors drag open, and I twist my face into a smile to greet the others inside. There's only three of them, but it feels crowded. There is a man who looks like he's only a few years older than me. His foot is tapping, and his forehead is rolled in wrinkles. Next to him stands an older couple with their hands intwined. They don't let go when I get in. They don't flinch. They're unmovable. I want to assume that their reason for being here is benign, but the silence in the elevator is tense. It grows as we move up the floors until finally the doors open and everyone bursts out. The feeling is palpable, and it spreads. I'm tense, anxious, and sick to my stomach, and then I see Jocelyn.

"Reagan." She waves in my direction, and I take her in.

She's beautiful. Her hair is done in tight curls, and she's dressed in a form-fitting Maude dress like she is going to brunch after this. I'm grateful I showered, and I'm trying to remember this isn't a competition. She strolls over slowly. She isn't panicky or rushed like anyone else I've seen here today. When she finally gets to me, she extends both arms and waits for me to embrace her. And to the surprise of both of us, I do.

"Look at you checking in. I thought for sure you'd call me when you showed up."

I try to remember if her voice always sounded this annoying. She flits her hand about like she's a Valley girl, and not someone who grew up on top of a lush, green hill in the Pacific Northwest.

"I'm so glad you could finally make it. I'll go see if he's awake and if you should come in or wait a little while. You may as well get one of those little visitor badges from reception."

Before I utter a word, she disappears, but that doesn't stop me from muttering under my breath, "I guess I *would've needed a visitors badge*, even if I had called you."

I try to shake her off, and chalk this up to Jocelyn being Jocelyn. Once upon a time, this was a version of Jocelyn I loved very much. Now this is a version of Jocelyn that needs me. I remind myself of that a few times over. Nevertheless, it would have been wonderful of her to tell me which room Oliver is in, but that would have been far too easy, and she is far too petty. She begged me to come home, and now that I'm here, Jocelyn is treating me like I'm late to a dinner party, and she's annoyed I even had the guts to show up.

"Hi, how can I help you?" the front desk clerk barks at me without looking up from his computer screen.

"Hi, I'm here to see Oliver Winkle. I'm not sure which floor he's on, I don't know the unit or whatever either." Another thing that would've been nice for Jocelyn to share.

"Family member or friend?"

"What?"

"Are you friend or family? Can I get an ID and can you fill out this form too?" He flips it across the counter, but still doesn't look up from the computer screen.

"Oh, friend, I guess."

"Okay," he says while marking something down. "Visiting hours are from now until five tonight. You can take the stairs or the elevator to the fifth floor." He looks up from the computer, flips me back my ID and waits for me to finish my paperwork. I check boxes and sign lines without reading. When I'm done, he rips it away from me, and tells me to head to room 514, and returns to staring at me blankly as if he'd rather be saying, *Okay, shoo. Go away now.*

"Do I need a badge or something?"

"Not unless you brought your own. We don't do that here. Anything else?" His eyes are back to the computer.

"Nope. Thank you."

I take the stairs because I don't want to slow anyone else down, and because I need to burn off my anger before I see Jocelyn again.

When I pop out of the stairwell, room 514 is directly across from me. I can see through the window before they can see me coming, and I realize she wanted me to find them here. She's sitting at the side of his bed, stroking his arm. From this side of the window, where I don't know them, she looks like she cares about him. I've never seen her care for anyone else other than herself. Oliver looks neither grateful nor amused. He's awake—I can tell that because his puffy lips move up and down ever so slightly. Both of his legs are in casts lifted above his body. His left arm is in a brace. He doesn't look like the person I once loved with my whole being, but I know, somewhere, he is in there.

"Reagan. You came," he shouts as I reach the door. He adjusts himself and pushes Jocelyn's arm away from his own. It pains me to hear him call my name like that. Obviously, it hurts to see him hurting, but it hurts more to hear how excited he is to see me because he never used to get excited. When we were together, he expected me to be there where and when he needed me. But his expectation washed away any excitement.

Jocelyn presses her lips together like she's going to cry, and then she exhales heavily. I wonder if that is how I looked when I was losing him. Pulling down her tight dress, she shimmies up and shoots me a smile. I want to say to her that I understand what she's going through, but I can't, obviously.

"Of course, I did. You're looking... well—"

"Hilarious." He's doing his best to smile through his swollen face.

"You didn't let me finish. You're looking well, like a pile of shit. What happened to you?" I move over towards the bed and stand awkwardly by his side, close to Jocelyn, and close to Oliver. Uncomfortable for the three of us.

"At least I know you still have your sense of humor, even in your rock star stage," he says flirtatiously, not even embarrassed by the fact that he looks like a smashed prune.

I catch Jocelyn rolling her eyes and give her a look that says, *I'm not amused by you*. I've never felt more like my mother.

"I'll give you two a moment to catch up. I'll go get you some more water with ice, Oliver. And call your mom to give her an update," she hisses.

"Sure, great, thanks." He dismisses her quickly and then turns to me. "Can I get a hug?"

I wonder what his motive is. I look at him hesitantly.

"I know, it's weird to ask, but I had a near death experience, so I'm hoping you'll forgive the weirdness. If not, maybe chalk it up to brain damage." He laughs because he's trying to play it cool, but that's hard to do while trapped in a hospital bed with both of your ex-girlfriends.

I bend down and give him hug. He's warm and swollen. I don't want to hurt him, so I do it all delicately. It surprises me when I begin to cry.

"Hey, hey, I can't feel a lot, but that feels like a tear. Are you okay?"

"I should be asking *you* that. I'm sorry, I just— It's hard to see you like this."

"Yeah, I still haven't looked in a mirror, but at least I'm breathing."

"Seriously. I was worried after I heard from Jocelyn that things weren't going to be okay, but you seem to be doing better." I smile, still feeling uneasy. I squeeze his one good appendage tight, happy that I can even be doing that.

"Jocelyn sure has a way to make a situation seem worse than it is." He chuckles, and it almost seems cruel. "It's good to see you. I'm so glad you came. You look... good."

We're quiet for a minute before we realize Jocelyn has been standing at the end of the room. I wonder how much she heard, and I try not to think about how badly it would hurt to be her.

"Babe, your mom says hi, and she's glad you're feeling better. I need to run back to *our* apartment."

Hearing her lean on the word *our* makes me feel less bad about anything she may have heard. I try not to give anything away.

"So, I'll go do that and then I'll be back to say good night. Oh, and don't forget the nurses are coming in at five today, Reagan, so you'll need to leave before then."

I check the time and see it's 3:04 p.m. I'm surprised she's leaving us with any time at all. She lingers, awaiting a response, but when one doesn't come, she strolls over to Oliver, kisses him on the cheek, pats me on the back, and hollers "Ta-ta," on her way out. I want to remind her that it's *her* phone call that brought me back here to begin with. If she doesn't like it, she shouldn't have asked me to come home. Maybe she expected Oliver to see me and realize that it wasn't me he wanted after all, or perhaps it was guilt. When she's finally gone, Oliver and I each take a deep breath, and then he continues.

"So, how is the tour? What are they doing without you?"

At first, I'm surprised to hear him asking about the tour, but then I remember social media keeps you caught up on everyone, whether you like it or not. And we both know that he knows there's another guy involved. I think about telling him what happened with Asher and my terms of departure, but that won't help anyone, so I lie and tell him they're doing fine. "In a few weeks they'll be playing the last show of the tour in LA, and then I guess we'll have to figure out what's next."

"*We'll*? So that's like a *thing* now?" he asks, hopeful the response will be in his favor.

"Hm, yeah, I guess I don't know."

His eyes light up when it's clear I'm having my doubts. One man's uncertainty is another's joy. "Well, I can totally see you in music. You used to listen to more music than anyone I've ever met. Plus, you're good at everything you do."

"Have you listened to them? My Guys?"

"Oh, uh a little."

"So how would you know if I'm any good at it?" I say, half-jokingly, half wanting to know what he really thinks. He never listened to the music I liked.

"Well, I know you. And I've seen some of the stuff on Instagram. I didn't hate it. But hey, I'm no music junky like you. If you're doing it, it's got to be cool. You always were cool."

"I'm glad you think I'm cool. Means the world," I tease.

"I always have Reagan, even when I've been dumb." His voice gets quieter. Serious. "I'm glad you came. After we talked, I was so afraid we wouldn't speak again. I really meant what I said. I miss you."

"Yeah, I guess I don't really get why you miss me. I mean, you're with her now. You *chose* her. You could've always been with me."

"I was dumb. I was blind, and I took our relationship for granted. I was unhappy with my own life, and I blamed you for it. Then I made the worst mistake I could... I thought someone else could fix the way I felt, but I was dead wrong, Reagan."

"So, what's going on with all... that?" I use my pointer finger to twirl around him and the door frame where Jocelyn walked out.

"Well, we broke up. And then the accident happened. And now we're all here. So as far as I know, I'm still broken up. And you promised me we'd talk today."

"Ha." I shriek, surprised by the sound of my own voice. "You remember?"

"Of course, I remember. I kept repeating it over and over to myself, *I need to talk to Reagan*, and when I finally woke up in this hospital, I was still saying it."

I think back to Jocelyn saying he called out my name.

"Why did you break up with Jocelyn?" The words spill out of me, and when they do, I'm glad I said them.

"Well, it didn't take us long to see we don't work. We had two things in common. First, we both loved you, and second, we're idiots who wanted to have a good time and didn't care who we hurt. After we hurt *you*, we moved on with our lives, determined to forget you.

"Of course I couldn't, and then your life kept going, because that's who you are and what you do. Ours stood still and we were forced to see each other for what we were: boring, unhappy people who just ruined the life of the one person who truly loved us, faults, and all. We tried to pretend we were happy for a while. We came back here, thinking maybe that would maybe make us happy.

"But when we came back here, you were gone, and of course, you wouldn't have wanted to see us, I get that now, but at the time, it crushed me because all I wanted to do was see you. The thought of never seeing you, never running into you? I couldn't bear it. I wanted you back. I still do. And then I couldn't take it anymore, and I broke up with her. She knows I want you back and she's not ready to let it go. I guess if there is an us, I'm not saying there's going to *be* an us, but if there is, then there's no place for her."

As he spills out everything I ever hoped and prayed to hear, an overwhelming sadness envelops me. We could pretend to be okay in each other's presence right now, for the sake of Oliver, but there was no future where the three of us could go back to the way things were. At least one of us would be hurt at the end of this. At least one of us would be alone.

"Wow, well, screw you, Oliver, and screw you, too, Reagan," Jocelyn shrieks in a distinct, non-Valley girl accent. She throws two pillows in our direction and rushes out of the room. She either had a change of heart and regretted leaving us alone, or wanted to do one last nice thing for Oliver before she left him with me.

"I'm sorry, Reagan. She's just so... crazy," Oliver says casually, like what just happened isn't worth discussing further.

Unexpectedly, I feel a volcanic-like anger starting to erupt. "Oliver, you could see her behind me, couldn't you? You *knew* she was there, and you decided to say that anyway. You can be such a dick." And before I know it, I'm rushing out of the room after my ex-best friend. I catch up with her before she gets on the elevator. "Jocelyn, please wait. What is going on?"

"I think you know damn well what's going on, you, you *man stealer*," she howls, hoping to draw attention to me.

People crane their heads in our direction.

"Jocelyn, get out of the elevator," I whisper firmly. "Let's go talk."

It doesn't take much convincing. She nods her head, and we walk over to two chairs in the hallway.

"Before I say what I'm going to say, you need to know I'm not saying it to be mean. I'm confused about what's going on. It sounds like your relationship is over. Why are you throwing yourself at him? That's not you."

"I'm trying to save something good."

"Well, that can't be it, because the way he talks about you doesn't seem so good."

"Don't be a bitch. You already won him back; you don't need to rub it in."

"You know that's not what I'm trying to do. I came back here because *you* called me."

She gives me a disapproving look. I'm sure she regrets asking me to come back, but her silence allows me to continue.

"You aren't going to win him over tonight, so just go home. He's being a jerk, and he doesn't deserve you waiting on him. I will stay here until five in case anything changes with him. You can come back tomorrow if you want, and only if you want. You don't have to take care of him."

"Yeah, so you can steal him. Great idea, Reagan." She looks at me with hatred in her heart. I'm not trying to be unkind. I know what it feels like to waste your time wanting someone to love you when their head is turned in another direction.

"I don't *need* to steal him. It seems clear to me that he already wants me back. He called me last night and made that much clear."

I see the pain flash across her face. Drunken ramblings from the night of his accident were one thing, but a phone call before is another.

"You can't force him into wanting you. Trust me, I tried. It will only push him away."

"I know." She sighs quietly.

"Go home, Jocelyn, and come back tomorrow."

She looks me directly in the eyes, and I recoil, expecting her next blow to hit the hardest.

"You were always smart. I'll see you tomorrow." She stands up, doesn't ask for a hug, and still manages to strut to the elevators.

I breathe in and out, now unimpeded by her presence. Releasing the tension is a relief that I can't enjoy for too long. With Jocelyn gone, Oliver and I will have to talk about what he said to me when we spoke on the phone.

For months, I begged the universe, bartered with the powers that be, and prayed to anyone that would listen that he would want me back. Then suddenly, when I didn't need him anymore, he appeared in the worst possible way. Under the dim light of hospital bulbs, I'm not sure if I love him anymore. I decide to buy myself some time and seek out a cup of coffee. I settle into a table in the corner of the cafeteria, facing an outside window. The clouds are moving quickly, but as they blow away, another gray cloud replaces the one that came before it.

In the back of my mind, I can't stop myself from thinking about Asher and the band. It has only been a day, but I still haven't heard from him, and it's been a few hours since I last heard from Marty. I'm desperate to know if Asher read the letter. I know it will hurt if he has and hasn't reached out, or if he hasn't and has no intention of speaking to me again. I'm tired of holding everything in.

"Screw it," I mumble to myself while dialing Marty.

It rings three times.

"Reagan, hi hey hello?" He's breathless, and I hear shouting in the background.

"Alive and in the flesh. What's going on, Marty?"

"Oh, Reagan. You'd be so proud—we're going to *Arizona*," he whispers. The shouting grows quiet. "That's not even the best part. I called Nick's friend, and he got us a few gigs while we're there."

"That's amazing, Marty. Do you know if you'll see... you know who?"

"We're working on it. But Phoenix ended up being his idea, so I think he wants to go. If nothing else, *I* want to see Jerome."

I'm beaming. This is proof Asher had to have read my note. He wouldn't have chosen to go to Phoenix on his own. I had some influence in this decision, which means that our connection is real.

"Well look at you, Marty. You're doing just fine without me."

"That is far from the truth, Reagan Wilde. We miss you dearly. We all do."

"Do we?"

"You haven't heard from him yet?"

"Nope."

"It hasn't even been a day, give it some time."

I know Marty is on Asher's side, but I also know Marty is rooting for us, and at the bare minimum, be friends. He wouldn't want that if Asher didn't want that either.

"Did you give him my letter?"

"I did, yeah. Right after I got back. He had sobered up a little and I was crawling back into bed. He asked me about you when I got home. I didn't tell him everything but told him you had to go home. He asked if it was for him, and I told him it was, but not in the way he was thinking. I told him he should reach out to you, but I think he's still processing everything."

"I put it all in the letter... about why I'm here. And I would like to come back. I said that too."

"I am sure you did, Reag. He can be delicate, quick to anger and doubt. But he'll come around. You mean too much to him."

"I don't know... What about Kitty?"

"What does she matter?"

"She matters to him."

"You can still be friends if she's in the picture."

I stay silent. I'm contemplating.

"Do you have to be more than friends?" he asks nervously.

I wonder if Asher told him something he isn't telling me. I can't handle that today.

"Where are you?"

"We're still in Denver. We're practicing. We'll be at Karol's for at least a few weeks before going to Arizona. Just to have a homebase. We're a little lost without you. Even Karol misses you, by the way, but she appreciated the note."

Before I can respond, I hear someone on the other side mumbling. I make out a few words. "Is that Jess?"

It's Asher's voice. His presence is proof that he can call me if he wants to.

"No, Jess is at work. I'll call her later," Marty chirps back.

"Let's go practice then."

"Yeah, just a few minutes."

"Is it about the band?"

"Yes," Marty lies.

My body goes stiff, and I find myself digging my nails into the Styrofoam coffee cup.

"Asher, please," Marty mumbles before he says something I can't hear. Then Marty returns to our conversation. "Hey, sorry about that." He's quieter now.

"Yeah, it's fine." My chest feels heavy. "I should probably get going."

"Don't worry about it, Reagan. He's being an idiot, but he's working on it. This isn't like last time. He's going to figure it out, and you'll be back on the road with us in no time."

I almost want to tell him that while I want to be back on the road, I also want to clearly understand the terms in which we'll be operating from. I need Asher to tell me what I mean to him, because I can't keep guessing and getting it wrong.

"Yeah, we'll see. Well, good luck with the show tonight. Nick should be able to help with a few more gigs. He texted me this morning, and I let him know you'd reach out."

"Reagan, wait. Don't you want to come back?"

I want to say to him that sometimes good things run their course quicker than we'd like, but it hurts too much to say out loud. Instead, I'm silent.

"Please, Reagan, just think about coming back. Please. Don't let his silence be the end of this for you. Plus, he knows he's wrong."

"Hilarious. He can't imagine a world in which he's wrong." I'm trying not to get emotional. "Can you let me know if you end up seeing him? Jerome?"

"Of course. Of course we will, because we *will* talk soon. Jess is coming to LA; you know you could too."

"I know. And Marty?"

"Yes?"

"Can you let me know if you think he reads the letter?"

"I'm sure he will. In time. He's just taking his time."

"I hope he doesn't take too much time."

It slips out, and we both know that I'm thinking about what happens next with Oliver.

"We'll talk soon." He says goodbye, and I hope he doesn't feel like I'm abandoning him too.

My cup of coffee is cold, and I decide it's time to head back to Oliver. It's 4:34, and the nurses will be coming to check on him soon. I get an extra cup and fill it with ice water. When I get back to the room, he's staring out the window, and I can see his chest move up and down with each breath. When we used to sleep together, he always found himself laying on his side. At first, he was always spooning me, allowing me to live in the comfort of a smaller, more cuddled spoon. But over time, he stopped cuddling, and would sleep with his back turned to mine. At first, I wondered what it meant. Had our relationship been breaking into tiny little pieces starting with our sleeping routine?

But over time, when I woke up before him, I began to relish that his back was to me. I could spend my early waking moments listening to the soothing sound of his breath. I'd grab the book by my bedside table and read a few chapters until I was good and tired again. Then I'd roll over and let him be the small spoon. He'd curl in tightly to the comfort and I would feel love in that small expression. He may not have loved me in all the big, loud ways I wanted, but there were dozens of small ones that showed me love was there.

"Hey, I got you some more ice water."

Even with puffy eyes and a banged-up face, making eye contact with Oliver allows me to feel that old connection. Things with Asher are ending, and I have to accept that. This time, things with Oliver could be different. I could use what I've learned with Asher to be the person I always dreamed of being. I have grown, I have desires and interests for myself.

"You came back?" He shifts his body until he's positioned in my direction. "I'm sorry I called her that. I just feel like I need to be mean to her to have you back."

I shake my head like that's the most ridiculous thing I've ever heard. But I don't say it. I stroll to his side, taking hold of his right arm, hoping to shift him up higher against the pillows. "Is this better? How can I help you?"

"You came back, that's all that matters. I was so afraid you'd go after her and never come back for me. It sounds stupid, and that's okay if that's what you choose. I know I screwed up, so you get to pick whatever you want. You always did. That's what I realize. You always get to pick what you want, and I took you for granted because you just kept picking me. Being picked by you is just about the best feeling in the world, and I just want to feel that again."

"So you think you'll get that chance again?"

He looks into my eyes, contemplating an answer. "I don't know. All I can do is hope. But I'm here now, and so are you. I'll just keep hoping."

I don't know what to say to that. Betrayal breaks a part of you, but maybe if you love someone enough, you can heal. I could hope for that too.

"I know this is a lot, Reagan, I'm not expecting anything. Honestly, you just being here is more than I ever thought I would get. Certainly, it's more than I deserve." He reaches for my hand, and I let it land on me like a delicate butterfly.

"Do you remember what happened last night?"

"I remember calling you. I know we talked. It wasn't exactly how I wanted it to go, but I felt hopeful. I had a little more to drink and decided to ride home. No surprise, that was an idiotic idea. I put everything at risk, including us." He squeezes my hand. "I was riding down the streets, fast. Didn't use my brakes once. Stupid."

"Very stupid, Oliver."

"I'm sorry, Reagan," he says without missing a beat.

"You don't have to apologize to me. Apologize to whoever's car window you went through."

"No, I'm sorry about her. I'm sorry about the detour I took outside of us. You are the love of my life. I was in love with you while we weren't together, and I still am."

This is what I dreamed about hearing. No, this wasn't how I wanted it to happen, but here it is, happening. Here is someone telling me how they feel, being honest, and fighting for me.

He ignores that I haven't responded to his proclamation.

"Do you think you could stay here awhile?"

I check the clock and notice it is fifteen minutes until five p.m.

"I think they'll kick me out in a moment here."

"That's not what I mean. Can you stay in Seattle for a little while? I really miss you, Reagan. I want there to be an us again. I can't win you back from this bed. I want to have a fair shot."

In every other scenario I played out in my head, I found myself jumping up and down shouting yes. But now, I feel uncertain. He's forcing me into a corner, and I can't give myself to him. Not yet.

"I think your nurse is going to show up any minute now, and if I'm not out of here, Jocelyn is going to find out and pillows won't be the only thing she's throwing."

Hope fades from his face, and I try quickly to restore it.

"Hey, really, there's no point in rushing into it. I have no plans to go anywhere any time soon. And judging by the looks of it, neither do you." I squeeze his hand tight this time and lean in to kiss his cheek. I still care about his happiness. I shuffle out of the room while the nurses start in. His eyes follow me as I leave. I spin around to wave goodbye. Oliver is picking me, and now the choice is mine.

***

The nights and days that follow the accident breed a new kind of normal. Each day, I wake up and have breakfast with my parents. We go on walks in the early morning and then I slip off to take care of my patient. Oliver gets stronger, and by the end of the first week, he can go home. He rents an Airbnb close to the hospital. I drive him to and from physical therapy a few times a week. On the days that I can't, Jocelyn drives him, and the three of us pretend that isn't strange. Every day when I come home, my mom reminds me she is happy I am here. I try not to obsess over the fact that she never shared that sentiment with me after the first breakup. Every few days, Marty sends me a text before a show. He asks if I'm coming back, and I ask if Asher has read my letter. Then night comes, and before I fall asleep, I replay moments of my time with Asher and the band. Then I start the day all over again.

Four weeks pass, just like that.

Nineteen

"So, you aren't with Oliver?" my father questions me over weekend breakfast.

This meal is a luxury we both enjoy. It isn't simple like oatmeal or yogurt, but rather, a feast complete with coffee, eggs, toast, and bacon. I've just told my parents that I got an internship in town. I'm not entirely unsurprised that they are surprised. I hadn't told anyone I was interviewing, not even Oliver.

"No, we aren't back together," I say proudly while shoveling a piece of bacon in my mouth.

It isn't like he hasn't tried to get me to recommit, but it doesn't feel right. He's still healing, and Jocelyn is in our orbit. I think back to what he said in the hospital, about how there's no place for her if we are to get back together. I may not like her, but I'm not ready to take away her whole world.

"But you're staying in Seattle? And not going back to the band?" He eyes me while sipping his coffee.

My mother is silent and doesn't look up from the piece of toast she is buttering and re-buttering.

"I don't think so."

I try not to let the pain show as I let the words out. All it would take is a phone call from a certain lead singer to send me back, but the phone call still hasn't come. We all take a sip of our coffee, and I tell them about the new job.

"I'm working at the indie radio station, KEXP, as a production and program intern. The program manager picks which bands we put on the air."

It seems too good to be true. It wasn't something I ever considered doing before all of this, but slowly, I am finding my way to the person I'm becoming. Once, when I was younger, I heard my mom say to a friend that people are with you for a reason, a season, or a lifetime. The thought crosses my mind that Asher could have been a reason—a very good reason that led me to this part of my life.

"That sounds perfect." My mother pats me on the back and stands up to collect our plates.

"I can't wait to hear what you put on the station. It'll be my exclusive station for listening to music. I'll cancel my Spotify subscription," Dad chimes in while picking up his coffee cup so my mother can't take it away with the others.

"Maybe don't cancel your subscriptions. I'm not picking all the bands just yet," I say, while forcing a smile on my face.

I know this decision will only lead to more questions about Oliver and my departure from the band, but I'm still not clear on what it means for me or for My Guys. I take my cup to the sink and slip out of the room before we can discuss it further. They know it's time for me to go to Oliver's, so they don't bother to ask where I'm off to.

It's not raining, so I take my bike. I bundle up in a Patagonia fleece, a beanie, and warm gloves. I put on a new playlist I made while wishing for warmth, entitled It Felt like Summer. The bike ride to where Oliver is staying is about thirty minutes, but it's the closest I'll get to alone time today, so I don't mind.

When I arrive, Jocelyn's car is still in the driveway. I wonder if that should bother me, but it doesn't. I use the keypad to enter the house without disturbing them. Once inside, I stop the playlist and begin disrobing all the layers of jackets and winterwear. They still can't tell I entered the house, but I can hear them in the back. There's some light laughter. I sneak back quietly, hoping they won't catch me. I want to know what they say to each other when no one is around. She's laughing, and it sounds sincere.

"No, stop, no, you didn't. Stop. I can't. My stomach, it hurts." She's laughing. Hard. And I can't imagine anything being *that* funny.

"Reagan. Hey, babe." Oliver catches me entering the room, and her laughter stops instantly. I want to say, *Don't stop on my account*, but nothing comes out. He tries to get up to welcome me.

Jocelyn and I both say in unison, "Oh, don't bother," then we glance quickly at one another with the acknowledgment that we mean the words in very different lights. She steadies her breathing and stands to leave.

"Oh, don't go. It looks like you two were having fun," I say, not meaning to sound hateful, but of course, it comes out that way.

"We were just talking about this one time when I was at camp and I was working the rock wall..." he starts to explain, but she can't help herself. She's laughing again, and so is he. This is when I realize that what they had once is real, and I feel bad for entering the room.

"I should go, I need to get to work, plus I can't hear that story again. It'll kill me." She gives him a kind smile, but her eyes say she's sad to go.

"You're working?" Again, I say it not meaning to be nasty, but it slips out.

"Yes, I am. I'm working at Nordstroms as a sales manager. Downtown. Come see me in the shoe department."

She winks at Oliver, and a smile spreads across his face. She's sticking around on his account. I want to ask why they aren't together anymore. Sure, he may think he has feelings for me, but I can tell he hasn't stopped caring for her.

She squeezes his arm and then leaves the room without saying goodbye to me. It's like she forgets she broke my heart first, and somehow this is all my fault. Once she's gone, the silence feels awkward.

"I'm sorry if it's weird that she's here. I can ask her to stop coming around if you'd like."

I know he's trying to show that he's picking me, but if he were, I know he wouldn't have added *if you like*. It would just be done.

"But what would *you* like?" I press him, hoping we can have the conversation I know we've been needing to.

"You know what I would like. This." He stretches out his hand so it's on top of mine. He feels warm, and familiar. I'm surprised at how quickly my body accepts his. We haven't been close in all the weeks that I've taken care of him. When I don't reject him, he slides his fingers underneath my own. I become very aware of my sweaty palms, but he doesn't stop there. He slips his other hand around my thigh, then squeezes tightly. I still don't pull away. He traces the hand formerly on my thigh up to the back of my head, pulls me close, and lingers for a moment before pulling my face towards his. Our lips touch, I close my eyes and at first it feels like everything I've ever wanted, but then I realize it's completely lacking the magic of love. Slowly, he moves away and brings his eyes to meet mine.

I'm searching for something in his eyes, but I don't find it. It is then that I pull away. "Oliver."

He shakes his head. "Reagan, she doesn't matter to me."

I think of how much she cares about him. About how much he makes her laugh. If you can do that for a person, that isn't nothing. That's very clearly something. But it isn't even that. Even if that connection, that spark, between them wasn't there, it wouldn't matter because I know now that spark isn't there between us.

He must know that this is where it ends because he doesn't fight me when I tell him I think we should stop seeing each other. He's better now. He doesn't need me anymore. It's something we knew was coming for a while.

The end of our season.

Twenty

I put on the playlist again and start the bike ride home. The air is cold, and the sky is dark like it plans to rain but wants to tease us first. As the songs flip from one to the next, I decide to take a detour. I pass the library, the neighborhood bar, and climb the hill to the park that overlooks the city.

When I get there, I set the bike down, and find a picnic table to lay on top of, planning to stick around until it rains. Three songs play and then my phone chimes. It's a text from Marty. I click on the image to find a smiling Asher Blair. He looks tanned, and still hasn't cut his long, dark hair. His arms are around some guy I don't recognize with piercing blue eyes and short blond hair. They're sitting at a table outside at sunset. Behind them I can see the desert. Is this the Jerome I'd heard so much about?

Marty sends another text: *We made it Arizona.*

He read the letter. If nothing else, he read my letter.

Another buzz: *You could meet us in Arizona. Or Los Angeles. Jess is coming, and I think Jerome will too. We're all happy we got to see him, and we all know it's because of you.*

I pull my fingers out of the gloves. It's freezing, but I'm not ready to go home.

I respond, *I bet Phil's mom is thrilled. She should be the one to thank.*

Then he sends: *He misses you.*

And I say: *Then he should tell me that.*

He says: *I agree. How are you?*

I say: *I'm good.* I think about telling him I ended things with Oliver, but really, that's not what matters. So instead, I say: *I started an internship with the radio station. I'll get to pick the bands they play. Sort of. Maybe eventually, at least.*

He says: *That sounds cool. They are lucky to have you. We all miss you.*

I say: *I miss you too. Please say hi to Jess for me. Send me some videos of your show in LA.*

He says: *So you aren't coming then.*

I say: *I don't know. Maybe not.*

And he says: *We couldn't have done this without you. Just think about it.*

I tell him I will, and to drive safe. Asher saw Jerome. That's the best news of today. And I survived ending things with Oliver. When I see him around town—if I see him—it won't devastate me. Here in this moment, I've handled everything I need to, and I'm going after something that excites me. The internship will be great, and maybe it will lead to a job, and then I can move out of my parents' house. It isn't the life I imagined, but it's one of my own making.

I can't help but wish I could tell Asher about it. If he were here, I'd want him to know how much I've grown since the first day in his grandma's house. I'd let him know that I conquered my greatest fear. Instead, I get on my bike, and head back home.

The house smells sweet when I walk inside, and I find my mother in the kitchen with flour covering her face, and some of the walls.

"What are you doing?" I shriek as if I'm the one who will have to clean this up.

"Well, hello to you too. I'm baking for the Holy Cross bake sale."

"Bake sale?" I look at her quizzically, most of all because I have no idea what the Holy Cross is.

"I ran into Mrs. Blair the other week," she proceeds, and I try not to feel hurt by the Blair name. "She let me know that her church is having a bake sale. She used to bake a bunch of pies and cupcakes for it, along with Mr. Blair, but she wasn't feeling up to it. I let her know I'd help."

"That's nice of you, Mom." I don't mean to, but it sounds like I may cry.

"My dear, what's wrong?" She rushes to set aside a tray of cookies, brushes off her hands, and then embraces me in a hug.

I can't help the rest of it from spilling out. "I ended things with Oliver." I'm sobbing loudly now.

"Oh, dear, I'm so sorry." She's rubbing my back.

I feel weak, like I can't stand anymore. "I don't even care about that, I really don't. I know that's horrible, but I'm just glad he's okay."

"Of course, that makes sense. He broke your heart, and then that accident was scary. That's a lot to handle."

"But he's okay now. And I saw him with Jocelyn and..."

"If she's the problem, don't let her be a problem. She's a horrible friend."

"She is. She is a horrible friend, but we aren't friends anymore."

"Good. I'm glad I never liked her." She pauses, waiting to understand if there's more.

"I don't think I did either. I don't think I ever liked her *or* him." I'm sobbing, but the words keep pouring out of me. "They were laughing today, so hard, when I saw them. I've never laughed that hard with either of them. That's when I realized they were just a chapter in my life and getting away from them is the best thing I can do for myself. We weren't a good match. We didn't pick each other. We fell into our relationships, and then just held on, even though we weren't good for one another."

My mother is nodding her head like what I have to say makes perfect sense. "I'm so proud of you, Reagan."

"What? You are? Why?"

"Of course I am. You're figuring it out, my love. You are figuring yourself out. That takes people decades, sometimes a whole lifetime. People waste years of their life tied up in people or things or jobs or identities that aren't right for them. Here you are, in your twenties, figuring it out."

The timer dings on the oven and she excuses herself to go take out another batch of cookies before spooning more onto another tray and popping them back in the oven. I take a minute to think about what she's said about figuring it out. I still don't know about Asher though.

"There's just one thing."

She turns around to show she's listening, then she turns back to the oven to close the door.

"Asher. I don't know how I feel about him, or the band. I don't want to think I was working with them just because of him. I don't want to keep choosing things I like because of what other people like."

"Do you think that's what you did with him?"

"No." I cry harder. "I don't. I really don't. He intrigued me at first. It felt good to be seen, and good to be listened to. Oliver never listened to me. At first, it was about making Oliver jealous, but then it was an adventure we shared. The more I did it, the more it felt like it was exactly what I was supposed to be doing. Then I saw how much I cared about Asher. And I just want to be adjacent to his life. I could be a friend, or I could be more, I just couldn't be less. Now I am. I *am* less, and I can't fix this because I know I deserve more from him. He can't treat me the way he did and expect me to be a part of his life. So we just walk away from each other now? This amazing life we could have shared is over, and that breaks my heart."

If I was sobbing before, now I am drowning. We sit on the floor together, my mother and me, until the oven buzzes again. Before she can come back to me, the phone rings and she apologizes before answering it. She disappears, and I keep crying until the tears stop. I pull my knees to my chest and steady my breathing. I'm right side up, but not ready to be standing.

***

"How are you feeling?" she asks, handing me a tissue and a cookie.

"Better, I guess." I wipe away the tears, then take a bite. The warm chocolate burns my mouth.

"I know this is hard, but you're right. You deserve the best. I'm so glad you know that."

"Why is it so hard to get the best?"

"The world will always ask you for less, but you must be determined to only accept what you deserve. That is exhausting, but a worthwhile goal.

You are learning to be secure in your own person, and that is something you must always hold on to as you walk through the world." She helps me up. "I will always be there, fighting to give you more in this world."

I believe her with everything inside of me.

"Now, I need to ask you for a favor."

I roll my eyes, not sure what could be so important right now. I don't answer, and instead, grab another cookie. "Are you for real? You're going to ask your heartbroken daughter for a favor?"

"Some would say she could do that better than a daughter with a full heart who may get distracted." I groan. "Can you please start taking some of these treats over to Mrs. Blair's?"

"You have to be kidding me."

"It's for the bake sale. Please."

"You know, this feels all too familiar."

"It does, I know. But we're talking now. That's a big difference."

"Fine. I can do it."

She reaches behind me and passes me a tray of cookies. I grab my jacket and try not to think about all the ways this time will be different from last time.

The sky is dark, but it is finally starting to release some drops of rain. I hurry straight toward Mrs. Blair's. The drizzle falls against my head, and I try to shield the cookies. When I get to the front porch, I find the front door is ajar. This time, I am certain there won't be any serial killers hiding inside, so I stroll in and holler. When she doesn't respond, I kick off my shoes and yell louder.

"Mrs. Blair? Hello, it's Reagan. I come bearing cookies this time." I chuckle to myself, hoping she'll hear me before I scare her to death.

It's quiet again, so I tiptoe inside. The room is dark, and now I'm second-guessing the serial killers. Again.

"Hello?"

Then I hear soft guitar music, and I spin around.

Lyrics start. "When no one else can understand me, when everything I do is wrong, you give me hope..."

It's Elvis. His voice is unmistakable.

"That's the wonder of you..."

Suddenly, the living room lights up. Someone hung twinkly lights in a zigzag pattern across the ceiling. They stretch across the room, strung from every corner. I slowly, cautiously, stroll over, uncertain as to what is happening. I look at the coffee table and find a bottle of whiskey, a muffin, and a card.

I know saying sorry isn't enough, but I'm hoping it's a start. I'm sorry for everything I said that hurt you, and for everything I didn't say that hurt you all the same. Please forgive me.

—Asher

The song stops, and I almost think I'm dreaming, but if I were I'd wake up before he appears.

"Hi, Reagan."

I spin around. He cut his hair. What a stupid thing to notice first, but it's what I see. Then it's his eyes. They light up as soon as he sees my face.

I open my mouth to say something, but nothing comes out.

"What do you think?" He gestures toward the haircut.

"What are you doing here?"

"I made a mistake. A lot of them." He moves closer to me, and I almost want to back away. I'm still holding the tray of cookies.

He's getting closer. I panic and set them down on the ground in front of me. He starts to laugh.

"What? I didn't know what to do with them." I gesture to the cookies, and he shakes his head, but that dumb smile stays stuck.

"I missed you."

"That's the best you can say?" I tease. It comes naturally.

"I missed you *a lot.* And I finally read your note." He's standing there. Just in front of me, with only a tray of cookies separating us. "I made so many mistakes. I should've been honest with you from the beginning. When I met you, I thought I'd help you shake yourself free from a bad breakup, but you ended up helping me become the person I wanted to be for so long. You never gave up on me, until I gave you a reason to. And I'm so sorry I gave you that reason." He bites his lower lip, looks down at the cookies, and then back at me.

"How are you here? What about the showcase?"

"That's partially why I'm here. I need my band-slash-social media manager at the show. It's a big opportunity for us"

"Partially? What's the other part?"

"How attached are you to those cookies?"

"I just met them. Not very."

"Good." He kicks aside the tray and cookies go flying.

I try not to look offended. "My mother isn't going to like that you did that."

"She knew the risks when she sent you here."

"When she did what?"

"I called her earlier today. Told her I was coming home and asked for her help. She was supposed to find a reason to send you here."

"Are you serious?"

"Deadly."

He moves closer. There's nothing to stop him now.

"Did she tell you about Oliver?"

"Just that she didn't think it was worth worrying about. Was she right?"

"Yes," I say, smiling.

"Reagan, I have something to ask you."

I take a deep breath. This time, I'm scared of what is about to happen, but I know I can't stop it. I nod.

"Can I kiss you?"

And before I respond, I surprise myself by kissing him first. The moment is electric. It stops time and lights up my whole body. This is what love is meant to feel like. When we pull away, we're both smiling so much it hurts.

"I've waited a long time for that to happen," he sings sweetly.

"Well you could've done it a little earlier if you ask me."

I push him back a little, and he leans in again for another kiss.

"I have something else to ask you," he whispers close to my ear.

"Mmhm?"

"Do you want to go confront our biggest fear?"

"What?" I chuckle, but I know exactly where this is headed.

"So, there's a plane taking off in, say, fifty-five minutes for Los Angeles, where a little-known band called My Guys is planning to play their first show as a complete band. We'll close out the week with a showcase. We've recently recruited our guitar player, Jerome Rossi. But like I said, we're missing our manager. She's the best in the business. So what do you say?"

"Really? You're playing as My Guys?" I smirk and think about suggesting they use Umbrella, but before I can suggest it, he interrupts me.

"We're not Umbrella anymore—we're different now. We're better." He throws me a wink. "So, I'll ask you again, are we going to catch this plane?"

I take his hand and settle into what it feels like to get everything you ever wanted.

"Let's go."

Acknowledgements

A huge thank you those who worked on my book with such care. This includes my editor, Jessica McKelden, who provided comprehensive feedback. Writing my first book was a vulnerable experience. You helped me get better and were kind along the way. This also includes my wonderful cover designer, Driss Chaoui who was able to design a cover I absolutely love while also illustrating the heart of the story.

Thank you to my dear friends who read this book and provided input throughout the book's evolution. Special thanks to my friend Kat Chen who was one of the first to hear about and read this story. Thank you for encouraging me to keep going. Another hearty thank you to my friend Sophie B. who embarked on the self-publishing journey with me. Doing this with a friend was a lot more fun and a lot less scary.

Thank you to the cities and songs mentioned in the book which hold a special place in my heart.

Thank you to my family. To my parents who encouraged me to go for it. And another big thank you to my wonderful husband, Ruben, who cheered me on, and kept our home together while I snuck out to work on this book more times than I can count.

About the Author

Honi Olmedo has a bachelor's and master's degree in business, which at times compliment her writing, and other times, compliment her day job. Written slowly and painstakingly over the course of many years, *The Parts We Play* is her debut novel. Olmedo resides in sunny Phoenix, Arizona with her husband and daughter. When she's not writing or working, she can be found enjoying her husband's cooking, chasing her toddler, and spending some time outside – preferably drinking wine or coffee on a patio.

www.ingramcontent.com/pod-product-compliance
Lightning Source LLC
LaVergne TN
LVHW011617220125
801765LV00021B/1133
9798991784207